I0619733

YOLO 2

Sa'id Salaam

Published by Black Ink Publications, 2020.

YOLO 2

First edition. March 20, 2020.

Written by Sa'id Salaam.

YOLO 2
Chapter 1

"Aaagh! Shit! Fuck! Shit! Fuck, shit!" Killa shouted as Yolo's cab drove away from the hospital. He had had a clean shot at her, but couldn't take it. As bad as he wanted to kill her for killing his son and kitty he just couldn't pull the trigger. He was so worked up he had to kill somebody so he scanned the streets with his scope. A group of skin heads marching up the street spread that killer smile across his face.

"White power!" Killa giggled as he lined his scope up with the confederate flag on one of their t-shirts. The large silencer at the end of the barrel muffled the shot. It was silent, but deadly when it slammed into the man lifting him off his feet.

"Shit!" his comrade shouted when he landed with a big hole though him. Killa took aim again and shot the next the skin head right in his skin head. The rest had seen enough and took off running in different directions.

Killa hummed the music from Benny Hill as he chased them with his scope. One by one he gunned them all down. It's been said that the only good racist is a dead racist, so these guys were now great.

A purse snatcher snatched an elderly white woman's purse of her shoulder. The lady fell to the sidewalk and was drug a few feet before losing her grip. No worries because Killa had him in his sights. The bullet entered the base of his skull and nearly took his head completely off his neck.

"Bitch ass," the woman spat as she pulled her purse from his dead hands. She waved her wrinkled old hand in thanks before walking off.

"Whew! I feel much, much better now," Killa sighed when he got that off his chest. Nothing relaxed him as much as killing someone who really, really needed killing. The thought sparked an idea that sent him on his way smiling and nodding.

*****

"I knew you loved me," Yolo sang smugly to herself when her cab pulled away. She had no doubt that he was there staring at her through a rifle scope. She didn't see him but she definitely felt him. They were two of a kind, soulmates, even if they couldn't be together.

She too had had plenty of opportunities to kill him over the course of the last few months. Many nights she had sat up in bed staring down at him watching him sleep. Quite a few nights she took naked pictures of him too, but he didn't need to know all that. "You love me, and I love you!"

"Huh?" the driver asked via rearview mirror. The dangerous glare she shot translated to 'I'm not talking to you so drive the car before I kill you and drive it myself'. He obviously understood and kept driving. Yolo turned back to the babies seated on each side of her.

"No one's gonna cook you guys," she vowed getting smiles out of them. They stared up at her listening intently as they rode to the airport.

Yolo guessed Killa would also be at LAX and she was right. She planned to highjack a plane, kidnap Killa, and take him to some deserted island so that they could be a family, but had no such luck. Killa was in the airport, but he was in the international part of it so their paths didn't cross. Good thing too, because high jacking a plane is a bit much; especially with a child carry in each hand.

The babies were wide awake for most of the flight back to New York. They finally conked out shortly before landing. Yolo learned from the best and already had a car parked in the long term parking section. Just like Killa taught her she a car in several cities for emergency use. All with Id, cash, and of course guns. She was pleased that the twins were still sound asleep when she reached her first destination, that way they couldn't see the tears.

"Awe man!" Yolo pouted and poked out her lip when she pulled to a stop in front of the wreckage that was once nurse Marquita's home.

All that remained was charred bricks and sad memories. The only mother she had ever known had died at the hands of the Black Mob. She and Killa had crisscrossed the country killing any and every one remotely associated with them, but the pain still remained. Tears warmed her face as her body shook from the sobs.

The tears began to dry as sorrow turned to anger. Yolo felt the urge to kill someone. Murder always made her feel better when she felt down. Killa taught her that the world was filled with really horrible people who really deserved really horrible deaths. There were rapists, child molesters, killer racist cops, book publishers, basketball wives, and those awful Atlanta housewives. A smile spread on her face from the thought.

"Hello kiddos," Yolo sang when she found her twins wide awake when she returned. She noticed they were synced up, eating, sleeping, and shitting at the same time. It made sense since they had spent first few months of their lives holding hands in an incubator.

"Let's go home," she suggested and put the car in gear. The destination was Wyandanch New York. Yolo had purchased the house she lived in with She-Ra a few years back. She had it totally renovated and updated except for the tub in the master bedroom. It was where she learned how to cut up bodies and held sentimental memories. She had also left the dead girl under the basement. It would have been a lot of work to dig up the concrete and lay more so she left it. Instead she built a playroom for the kids.

"Honies, we're home!"

Chapter 2

"Honey, I'm home!" Killa cheered when he got off the plane in South America. The smile faded away when he didn't see his grandmother and rest of the family. Sincerity was the only one standing there and she had that 'You got some 'splaining to do' look on her face.

"Well?" she demanded, crossing her arms over her chest and tapping her foot. She squinted and leaned in to spot any lies. She knew him well enough to spot his telltale signs of telling a tale. He was his own lie detector. First he would 'Huh?' as if he didn't understand. Then he'd scratch his head, shift his feet, and hit you with a totally irrelevant 'You know what I'm saying'.

"Well what? It's over, case closed. Last time I saw Yolo it was through a rifle scope," he said. The lie detector said he was telling the truth, but she wasn't finished.

"And, did you fuck her?" she wanted to know.

"Huh?" Killa asked shuffling his feet and scratching his head. "You know what I'm saying?"

"Yes, I do. You fucked her again! I can't believe you!"

"Okay, see what had happen was. Okay, um... technically it was rape. She tied me down while I was sleeping and..."

"Wait!" Sincerity shouted pausing the story. "So you and her were sleeping together, in the same bed?"

"Nah, yeah cuz... Huh? I mean I was mad tired. You know we was killing the whole Black Mob. Murdering in Memphis, killing in Cali, deadin' 'em in Dallas, offing 'em in..."

"Killa!" she shouted to get him back on point. "What I wanna know is how that little... girl, tied your big ass up and raped you!"

"Like I said, I was sleeping. I woke up with my arms and feet bound to the bed and her on top of me," he explained.

4

"I ain't heard shit about a condom! I just hope you ain't get that bitch pregnant... again!"

"Huh?"

"I can't stand you!" she snarled and marched off towards the car. Killa was treated to her ass, an ass that was shifting angrily under her skirt. He enjoyed the show knowing it would be as close to her ass as he would be getting for some time to come. The ride to the house was made in total silence, but it got loud once they arrived.

"Xavier!" Grandma Diedra shouted and threw her arms wide for a hug. A 'grandma's hug' can kill Killa took one last breath and braced himself for the violence to come.

"Ugh!" Killa grunted when his grandmother slammed into him and began to squeeze. She was just like an anaconda coiling around its prey. Cameisha winced in pain, happy it was him instead of her. He was two seconds away from passing out when she released her grip.

"How are you? Are you hungry? Have you been eating?" she fussed dragging him towards the kitchen. The rest of the family followed them to continue the welcome home.

"Unc, Look-it!" Meisha cheered holding up her new son.

"Uh oh! Dope boy and dope girl have a baby! Hope it's not dope baby cuz you know who will write a book about it!" Killa cracked up.

"If he does, it'll be dope!" Sincerity spoke up on behalf of her favorite author.

"Actually we name him Cameron Forrest," Meisha said proudly. The mention of Cam's name always paused time for a split second.

"Nice!" Killa nodded in agreement. Trigga still couldn't see so he smiled in the direction of his voice. His hearing took up the slack for his lost eyesight and he correctly extended his hand to be shook. "Cute kid."

"Thanks," the dope couple thanked in chorus.

"Sit down and tell us all about your adventures!" Diedra eagerly requested. For all of her prim and proper sophistication she absolutely loved that gangsta shit.

"Don't forget to tell you how she raped you at the end," Sincerity tossed in for good measure.

"Rape! Girl ain't nobody raped that man," Cameisha shouted and laughed. "Told you he was gon' hit that."

"Just hope you didn't get her pregnant again," Grandma huffed. "Which reminds me, where are the babies?"

"Huh? With family," Killa said in a tone that meant nothing else was coming. They all knew the tone and left it alone. He went on entertaining the family with tales of murder and mayhem.

Grandma got a real kick out of Yolo nailing a perfidious pastor to his pulpit. Killa left out the part about letting her keep all that money. They were all already set for life, but Sincerity would have still had something to say about it. After dinner Trigga led him out o the back deck to show off his new hobby.

"Nice!" Killa exclaimed at the foot long buds of colorful sticky weed. He damn near got high just from smelling it.

"Got it down to a science," he said proudly as he lit up a joint. By the end of the weed Killa was just as blind as Trigga. He felt his way inside and plopped onto his bed.

"Mm hm," Sincerity said snarling down at him. "I got you."

*****

"What the..." Killa grumbled when he awoke the next afternoon. The first thing he noticed was his hands and ankles were securely tied to the bed posts. Next he realized that he was still high from Trigga's strong ass weed. Finally, he noticed that Sincerity was wearing nothing but a sideways grin. He gave his restraints a few tugs before accepting his fate. Yup, he was about to get raped... again.

"Bet this is what a fly feels like when it's trapped in a spider's web," Sincerity mused. When she took his clothes off last night and saw that good dick she decided that she would take some. Why should she deprive herself just because he fucked up? He would get some pussy but it would be under her terms.

"Let me up!" Killa barked trying to sound tough and failing. His voice cracked revealing just how vulnerable he really felt. Still it felt good to be able to relax. Oddly enough he had felt safe with Yolo as well.

"I'm sure I will," Sincerity sighed. She came over and flipped his flaccid penis from side to side. "First, some breakfast."

If Killa wondered what was for breakfast he soon found out when she climbed on the bed and stood over him. She then slowly lowered her neatly trimmed box towards his face. Her vagina lips seemed to swell and pucker up as it got closer. It looked like it wanted a kiss so Killa gave it one. Then another and another followed by a lick.

"Sssss!" Sincerity hissed when she felt his tongue bypass both her outer and inner lips and slip inside of her.

She began rotating her hips along with his tongue movements. It would have been a good time to talk some shit but the poor girl couldn't even remember how to speak. Not a single word came to mind but he clearly understood the grunts and groans coming from her. Killa knew his woman well enough to know she was on the precipice of release. One final lick and she went over the edge.

"Argh!!!" Sincerity growled as she bust a well overdue nut. She totally lost her cool as she slobbered and shook. Finally she fell over, spent like an empty shell casing.

"Now, let me up!" he demanded once more. The pussy juice on his mouth made him look like a glazed donut.

"In a minute," she said grabbing his now rock hard erection. She gave it a few strokes that made it throb even more in her hand. Normally she would have returned the favor of oral, but not today. Today it was fuck Killa even though she was about to fuck Killa. Still she had to fuck with him.

Sincerity inched towards his dick, kissing and licking his six pack as she went. She opened wide and put her mouth so close that he could feel the heat and moisture of it. Then closed it with a shake of her head along with a, "Nah."

"Nah! Wh, wh, what you mean nah?" Killa whined. Nothing in the world says good morning like an early morning blow job. In a recent survey nine out of ten men said that they would prefer head over coffee. The tenth didn't answer, he just pulled out his dick. It's a wonder it hasn't put coffee out of business.

"Nah, as in you don't deserve no head!" Sincerity shot back. Killa didn't protest any further when she straddled his hips. She rubbed his dick in the puddle he'd left behind then squeezed him inside. Halfway down she changed her mind and changed directions.

Killa watched in awe as she slid backwards down on his dick. When she lifted up again she had left a coat of thick creamy lotion on his shaft. Suddenly she slammed back down and lifted back up again. He knew he was already in the dog house and that a premature ejaculation would only make things worse so he closed his eyes and tried to focus on something else. The problem with that was that he saw Yolo's face. He quickly snatched them back open to tough it out. Luckily for him Sincerity was backed up and didn't last long.

"I swear I can't stand you!" were her final words before reaching another room shaking orgasm. Killa let go with her and they both let out screams that cleared the birds from the nearby trees. They both then laid there for a few minutes while their breathing and heart rates returned to normal.

"Mm hm," Sincerity huffed as she stood. She really wasn't mad anymore but wasn't going to make it easy on him. She untied one wrist and walked into the bathroom to shower.

"Love you too," he told her back and sat up. Once he freed his other hand he rubbed the marks left on his wrist by the rope. A minute later he undid the knots on his ankles and joined his woman in the shower.

Killa delivered some killer back shots, which helped his cause, while in the shower. One more nut and Sincerity was Team Killa again to the fullest. They were hand in hand when they joined the family for brunch out on the patio.

"Good morning!" Sincerity sang cheerfully.

"I know, we heard!" Grandma cackled and high fived her granddaughter.

Cameisha had got some dick that morning too but had kept her face in a pillow to keep from telling on herself. Grandma accepted that she was grown with a kid but still pressed the couple to get married. Cameisha had agreed but only if her dad walked her down the aisle.

"Dig in!" Diedra announced pointing to the wonderful table full of food. The extended family ate, talked, and laughed over the meal. It was all fun and games until Sincerity popped the question.

"Now that the Black Mob is dead and Yolo is... whatever, can we go home? Please!" she pleaded.

Cameisha was wanted for a couple murders in a couple different states and knew she could never return. That meant Grandma was staying as well. Sincerity was homesick and missed her eccentric father, Karate Joe.

"To New York?" Killa asked, ready to make a million excuses why they couldn't live in New York. Numbers one and two being his sons, he didn't want them growing up in the city.

"Anywhere," she replied causing him to nod slowly.

"I guess I'll have to come back and forth," he conceded in an effort to please everyone. If Killa had a chink in his armor family was it. It could very well get him killed one day.

Chapter 3

Yolo may be a lunatic but she was also a very good mother. Her maternal instincts took over the second she gave birth. She hated that she had missed out on the opportunity to breast feed due to gallivanting around the country murdering mob members. Now her babies were her top priority.

The children didn't understand the bedtime stories she recited to them every night but they stilled smiled, giggled, and kicked their little legs happily none the less. It was probably best that they didn't understand since her favorite stories were about their famous father. She had picked Killa's brain nightly during their time together, getting all hot and bothered by his many adventures that she now relayed to their children.

Despite a few horrible memories from the house Yolo felt totally at ease. Wyandanch was a happening town with plenty of shit happening but she was tucked away in a quiet corner. Quiet except for when the school bus let the local kids out.

She often watched with a scowl as a group of mean girls taunted her young neighbor. The cute girl was a bit of a Raggedy Ann in her Goodwill clothing and large unpermed afro. She would duck her head and take the abuse until she got inside her house. Yolo only saw her mom and a man she assumed to be the girl's father once. She and the girl had never crossed paths until one Saturday Yolo was taking the kids to the car for a trip to the park.

"Ooh babies!" the neighbor shouted and came running over to Yolo as she struggled to carry both babies in carriers. She almost shot, but Yolo felt no threat. "Are they twins?"

"Um... yeah," Yolo answered with a discerning frown as she analyzed the young girl. She sniffed the air to see if she had an odor, she didn't.

10

"And what's your name little girl?" the girl asked as Shyne cooed and kicked with excitement.

"They can't talk," Yolo answered, wondering if she were a little slow.

"I know!" she giggled while wondering the same thing about her. "I'm Christi."

"Yolo, and that's Shyne and Sun. S-U-N," she spelled out, so as not to get into another inane 'who's on first' about her son's name. Quite a few times people had asked her son's name and when she replied Sun they had said, "Yes, your son. What's his name?"

"Nice to meet you guys. If you ever need a babysitter just let me know. I don't charge much," Christi said almost pleadingly.

"How old are you?" Yolo asked, guessing 14 in her head.

"I'll be 16... in a year... and a half," she replied using pre-teen mathematics.

"Well Christi, you're a bit young," Yolo said breaking the girl's heart. She poked out her lip and lowered her head sadly in defeat. "Actually, I guess... you could help out. Like be my assistant.

"I could! I could help you around the house and with the kids!" Christi cheered at the great idea.

"Let's say... for a hundred bucks a week?" Yolo asked, hoping that she wasn't low balling the girl. She had missed the babysitting age growing up. Too busy running around killing people.

"Whoa!" she swooned. A hundred bucks a week meant no more hungry nights. No more washing out her two pairs of panties. No more no eating lunch because she had no money. "When can I start?"

"You can start right now. Go ask your mom if you can go with us to the park."

"Oh, I can go. She's not home anyway but she wouldn't care if she was," Christi explained.

"Maybe you should call her," Yolo said, getting curious about the girl's living conditions. When she did see her mom she was always fly so why was her daughter looking so tacky?

"On what? We don't have a phone. My mom does, but I don't know the number."

"How 'bout your dad?" Yolo pried.

"That would take too long to find out who he is and then where he is," Christi giggled showing her sense of humor and need for braces.

"Come on," Yolo huffed. She strapped the twins in their car seats as Christi got in the front passenger seat and buckled up.

"So was that guy your mom's boyfriend?" Yolo asked as they rode to the park. She recalled being creeped out by the creepy dude who had stared her up and down while licking his lips.

"Who Cassious? One of them. I can't wait until he leaves like the rest!" Christi snarled in a tone that said there was more going on than she was saying. Yolo decided not to press the girl, but if she ever found out that he was touching her he was going in the tub.

*****

Yolo fell in love with Christi as she watched her play with Sun and Shyne. The twins squealed in delight as they frolicked on the blanket. They were having a great time but she decided to cut it short when she heard the girl's stomach growling. Either she had swallowed a mountain lion or she was starved. Yolo figured that it was the latter since there weren't any mountain lions on Long Island.

"I need to stop at the mall for a few things. I guess we can get lunch while we're there. Are you hungry?"

"A little. I guess you can take it out of my pay," Christi replied proving that the girl had dignity. Yolo planned to make sure that she kept it.

Yolo regretted only ordering two slices each at the busy food court. The hungry child smashed the first slice without even taking a breath before starting on the next. She was only two bites into her first slice and Christi was halfway done with her second.

"I shouldn't have eaten such a big breakfast," Yolo complained and slid her last slice across the table. Christi mumbled her thanks around a mouthful of food. Once she scarfed it all down she slurped on her soda.

"Uh oh! Duck!" Christi exclaimed wide eyed as if she'd seen a ghost. Yolo looked around to see what had her so shook and saw the mean girls. They spotted her too and changed directions.

"Get up! Sit up straight!" Yolo growled in a tone that made the scared child pop up straight.

Yolo quickly ascertained that the pretty light skin girl leading the charge was the leader. She wore two feet of weave on her head that cascaded over her heavily made up face. All the latest fashions and trends were present on the four girls. That's what gave them the right to pick on the less fortunate. Even though in all actuality their vanity and lack of morals made them the less fortunate. Every label on their bodies represented another mile on their vaginas form the neighborhood dope boys and sugar daddies.

"Look, if it ain't Pissy Crissy!" the leader announced upon arrival. Her cronies cracked up and launched into their favorite chant of "Pissy Crissy, Pissy Crissy."

"Pissy Crissy?" Yolo leaned in and asked as they chanted.

"They try to say that I smell like pee cause my clothes are old," she explained twisting her lips up at the ridiculous notion. She was cleaner inside and out than the four of them put together.

"Okay, okay, that's enough!" Yolo said bringing the chant to a halt. "Her name is Christi, not Pissy or anything else. The next person to call her out of her name deals with me!"

"And who are you 'posed to be?" the leader chuckled as if it were a joke. "You and your ugly babies!"

"She must want a one with you!" One of the sidekicks suggested in reply to the mask of murder spreading on Yolo's face.

"I wanna give you a two, I don't do ones," Yolo growled, referring to the 22 in her purse. Her eyes darted around at the hundreds of people who were about to witness a murder.

"Better keep yo ass I that chair," she shot back at Yolo, before turning her attention back to Christi. "See you on the block Pissy Crissy. I'ma beat that ass fo' you," she threatened, turned, and walked away.

Steam was practically coming from Yolo's ears at the insult. Not only had they tease her new friend one of them had called her babies ugly. They had to pay. They all would be dead by nightfall. Yolo watched the mean girls switch their asses into the bathroom and smiled. She recalled her baby daddy telling her about how he had dealt with some disrespectful little bad asses in his projects, and stood.

"Where are you going?" Those girls will jump you!" Christi warned as she watched Yolo stand.

"I hope so. Watch Sun and Shyne," she said, smiling as she followed the girls into the bathroom.

"Is this bitch crazy?" the leader asked her friends when Yolo walked in and locked the door behind her.

"Gotta be!" her friends assumed correctly. They had no idea just how crazy this chic was. She was a real lunatic.

"Shoot a one with her!" Another said, as if they weren't going to jump in. Yolo knew they would and actually looked forward to it.

"I told you, I don't do ones. However, I'll take a four," Yolo said just as the girls moved in.

The poor girls tried to jump Yolo, but got jumped instead. She dodged the leader's wild blow, causing it to strike her friend instead.

When Yolo came up she brought a nasty uppercut along with her knocking mean girl number one out cold. She was the lucky one because the rest of them got beat badly. Yolo punched, kicked, elbowed, and kneed them until they had had enough.

"Stop! Please stop! We had enough!" One pleaded and spit out a bottom tooth. The rest of the crew also held up their hands in surrender and huddled closely together.

"Okay, but no more Pissy Crissy," she warned wagging a finger at them.

"Pissy who? Christi's our girl!" The leader exclaimed now that she was awake again.

"Okay. Now get cleaned up," Yolo ordered, but stopped them before they reached the sinks. "Not there. In there."

"There?" One of the mean girls whined and pointed at the stall Yolo pointed at.

"Yep, and don't flush it. That is unless you girls want another 'one.'"

The mean girls rushed into the stall and washed off their lipstick and eyeliner with some stranger's left behind urine. They winced in disgust from the smell and feel of the cold urine.

"Weaves too," Yolo directed when they were done removing their makeup. They girls complied, and helped each other out of their weaves. "Now, I believe that you all owe someone an apology."

"We're sorry!" they sang, like a girls R&B group.

"No, not me," Yolo said, as she departed from the bathroom.

"Are you okay?" Christi asked while checking Yolo up and down for injuries. She should have checked her knuckles, feet, knees, and elbows.

"Mm hm," Yolo hummed and checked on her babies.

"What the...," the girl asked as the lumped of mean girls made their way over. They now looked like a group of little boys who had fallen off their bikes as they limped and hobbled all bruised and lumped up.

"We sorry," they all said as one which was fitting since they had all got their asses whooped as one.

"Okay?" Christi questioned looking to Yolo for confirmation. Yolo just shrugged as if she had no clue as to what was going on. The mean girls offered a royal curtsey to Yolo and the twins and then limped away.

"Come on, let's go do a little shopping," Yolo suggested. She practically had to force the girl to accept some clothes. It wasn't until she agreed to deduct it from her pay that she conceded.

Yolo was impressed when she shunned all things tight, short or trendy in favor of classy and comfortable. A bond was formed that day. From that day on anyone who fucked with Christi was getting fucked up. Yolo said that!

Chapter 4

"I still don't think this is a good idea," Killa groaned for the hundredth time as they boarded a plane.

"I know. You've said it a hundred times already," Sincerity replied. She then launched into her top one hundred reasons why they should return to the states. The first being her father and the last being the usual, "Besides, you said Yolo was gone and no longer a threat. That there was nothing to worry about."

"Nothing but me being wanted in almost all fifty states!" he shot back. The back and forth debate ended once they landed in Miami. After a brief layover the family caught a connecting flight to New York.

Killa grew deadly silent once the plane landed at J.F.K. He was on his killer shit as his mind transformed into a super computer and began processing their surroundings. In a split second he processed each sight and sound all while answering his curious son's questions. They had packed lightly for their travels, doing so allowed them to be able to take the subway over to Manhattan. Once there they caught a gypsy cab over to the Bronx.

The new generation goons were on some new shit ever since Killa had taken off his belt and literally whipped their little asses. Now instead of terrorizing the projects they protected them. A goon with a submachine gun whistled loudly at the arrival of the taxi. All intruders were announced and screened upon arrival. A second double whistle meant that the intruder was a friend, not foe.

"Killa!" the teen cheered, much the way kids do when they see their favorite super hero. This was Killa's territory, Batman and Spiderman weren't shit around here.

"'Sup yo," Kill replied coolly, while Sincerity shook her head. It always tickled her to see the way people looked up to him. After graciously shaking the kid's hand Killa led the way into the project's courtyard.

"My favorite villain," Killa said and smiled at the new leader of the goons. The six foot two teen smiled back and stood to shake his hand. The kid earned the name Villain by doing a bunch of villainous shit during the course of his short young life.

"What's poppin' Unc? Been waiting on you," Villain said as he handed him a hand gun.

"I heard you got a new operation going on?" Killa said, tucking the pistol into his waistband.

"Yeah, but noting in the projects. Niggas wanna get high they gotta go over to Ogden," he said proudly. He made his block safer, at the expense of someone else's but it was a start.

"Where's my pops?" Sincerity cut in as she looked around. Villain pointed up and shrugged as if to say where else.

Killa, Sincerity, and little Xavier all lifted their heads towards the sky. There they saw Karate Joe running around the edge of the roof. Sincerity shook her head because she knew that he was wearing a blindfold.

"Man, I use to hate when he made me do that," she huffed at the memories. She had been his number one student back in the day.

Leading the way into the building Killa held his breath.

"I see niggas still peeing in the lobby!" Sincerity fussed as the tart smell invaded her nostrils.

It was obviously an unwritten rule that the elevators, stairwells, and lobbies in the projects must smell like urine. The elevator reached the top floor, they got off and walked up an additional flight and stopped out onto the roof. The karate man immediately stopped in his tracks and smiled sensing his daughter's presence. He then pulled off his blindfold and rushed over to greet her.

"Daddy!" Sincerity squealed as she met him halfway. Killa twisted his lips up at her calling him daddy, but held his tongue. Karate Joe was after all her father.

Karate Joe hugged his daughter, twirling her around before setting her down. He then shook Killa's hand before hugging his grandsons and turning back to his daughter.

"Ha-ya!" he shouted as he threw a karate chop towards Sincerity, that she narrowly ducked. She dipped under it and came up with a flurry of chops and kicks of her own.

"Damn!" Killa laughed as the aging man put his arms behind his back and evaded everything that was thrown at him. "That's why I have a gun."

"I still can't hit you!" Sincerity pouted out of breath form the attack.

"Sure you can. Love, honor, and respect causes you to hesitate preventing you from doing so," he assured her because fact was that she was damn good. "Are you back for good"

"America, yes. The Bronx, no" she replied wistfully since she still didn't know their destination.

"But, you guys can talk, text, and video chat," Killa said as he headed him a satellite phone. Karate Joe took it and bowed. "Um... okay."

Karate Joe and his daughter bowed towards one another like teacher and student and then hugged like father and daughter. As he was putting on his blindfold back on his family was once again hitting the pissy stairwell.

The couple made their rounds to visit their few closest friends before heading back out. This time they flew out of Newark, New Jersey to be sure no one could spot a routine in their movements. Routines got peopled killed.

"Atlanta!" Sincerity cheered when they reached the gate. She had always wanted to move there and was finally getting her chance. Only Killa's hide out wouldn't be quite what she expected.

Once they landed in the A they took a train to where Killa had a car parked. They drove around the perimeter and headed east of Atlanta. A few dirt roads later they had arrived.

"To the Bat cave!" Sincerity quipped as they navigated the long winding driveway. It appeared as if they were driving in the woods that is until they reached a clearing with where a modest two story home set.

"Don't worry, we'll find something closer to civilization," he advised. "I just gotta get a few things set up."

"Mm hm," she replied twisting her lips dubiously. She knew her man and knew he was up to something.

She was right to because he was. He was up to something clever, ambitious, and oh so very violent. Kill wasn't a murderer, but he was a killer and the world was just full of wicked people who needed to be killed. His plan was to make the world a better place by getting rid of one unwanted presence at a time. Or two or three, or a hundred; if necessary.

"A necessary evil..." Killa mused, as he tried to come up with a name for his new website. It would take him a couple of weeks to get it up and running, therefore he had time.

The site was a place where oppressed people could come vent about people in need of death. There was no fee, no contact information, and no feedback given. Discreet servers routed the sites signals all over the globe making tracking it impossible. Killa would independently verify the information shared and decide on a case by case basis on how to proceed.

"Ooh! 1-800-Killa!" he typed proudly once he settled on a name. Branding is everything you know.

"Killa! KILL-AH!" Sincerity shouted from upstairs for the hundredth time before he finally heard her. The finished basement had become his man cave, the place where he pursued his passion.

"Yeah!" he shouted, matching her perturbed tone. He knew she hated being ignored, but he hated being interrupted.

"Come eat!" she yelled back minus the attitude.

"Eat? I just ate," he said to himself and looked down at his empty plate. He grabbed it and took it with him for proof. "I already... Oh my!"

"Oh my, is right," Sincerity giggled at his reaction. His reaction was definitely an appropriate reaction since she was butt naked on the sofa with her luscious legs spread wide open. The position was known as 'Dinner is served'.

Killa closed the distance between them in three large steps. He then planted both feet and executed a perfect swan dive into her vagina. Sincerity thought that it would be cute to grab the back of his head kike he did her when she gave him head. Killa just shook his head, which only helped her cause. He damn couldn't say anything with his tongue deep inside of her. Sincerity bust a slobbering body shaking and shivering nut. Her plan was to return the favor once her breathing returned to normal but Killa had other plans.

"You good? Good!" he asked and answered before he jumped up and rushed back down into the basement, as she watched curiously. A resent request had caught his eye, before going upstairs, and he was anxious to get back to it. Killa was about to do some killing.

Chapter 5

"And your daddy killed all the bad guys!" Yolo sang as if her bedtime stories were Mother Goose in nature instead of Father Killa. None the less the twins seemed to love it. They smiled their gummy little smiles and kicked their fat little baby legs with happiness.

"Dada, Dada," they repeated every time she said the word. A lot of single baby mamas never speak of their baby daddy, at least not in a positive light, but Yolo was different. She told her babies about their father every chance she got. She even went as far as to promise them that they would all be together one day, or she would die trying to make it happen.

Once her babies drifted off to sleep Yolo settled in the den to partake in her favorite pastime. Searching the internet provided fodder on all the latest about the murder and mayhem going on across the globe. The situation in Syria spread a nasty scowl across her face. ISIS and other groups who gave Muslims a bad name pissed her off. Even she was smart enough to realize that their atrocities had nothing to do with Islam. Those people were just plain evil and evilness was from the devil.

"Wish I could come cut your head off," she growled at a deviant holding the head of an innocent civilian. She clicked away and ended up a t a story of Americans going to Africa to kill protected animals. It was really sad lions and tigers ambushed and murdered for sport. Yolo had just made up her mind to go hunt one of the perpetrators down when a local news story caught her attention.

"In local news a body found in Amityville has been positively linked to a series of brutal rapes and murders in the area. Sixteen year old Sa-na-tor... wait Sa-nor-ma... The sixteen year old girl was walking home from a party at one in the morning when she was abducted..."

"And just what was a sixteen year old doing at a party at one o'clock in the morning?" Yolo asked the T.V. On cue the girl's ratchet ass mother popped on screen to explain. Actually her appearance alone was enough to explain.

"They done kilt my Sanadorishia Monay!" she wailed even though not a single tear fell. She flailed her bright orange nails that matched her long orange wig. Orange eye liner and lipstick kept her shiny gold teeth company. The gaudy outfit she wore was more clown wear than couture. A look behind her revealed either the circus had come to town or Amityville was having a clown contest.

"This brings the total to six confirmed deaths. Police say it's the work of a serial killer..."

"More like a cereal killer," Yolo huffed indignantly. "Some cocoa puff preying on little girls. I should go kill him. I am going to kill him!"

*****

The very next night Yolo decided to take a little drive over to Amityville to see if she couldn't make murder something. That meant that Christi would have to watch the kids. It wasn't a problem since she spent most of her time at Yolo's anyway.

Yolo was actually quite the perfect big sister. She was smart enough to help with homework and she listened to her problems. The girl's main problems were her mother and her slew of boyfriends. The woman stole almost every article of clothing Yolo had brought the girl. That included the panties and socks. Christi had to keep her clothes next door at Yolo's to keep them. She was always over there so it was no problem to shower and change her clothes while there.

"Ooh where you going?" Christi asked excitedly when Yolo emerged dressed like the fast ass teen girls whose parents allowed them to dress like miniature prostitutes.

"Out," she replied since saying I'm going to hunt down and kill the Amityville Rapist would have been TMI at the time.

"Is he cute?" Christi giggled. She had only recently realized that boys were cute and that was something to giggle about

"Doesn't matter," Yolo chuckled. It really didn't since he was going to die anyway. She planned to make it a closed casket affair when she found him.

Yolo kissed her babies and playfully punched Christi in her arm before leaving the house. She had to pull her panties out of her ass twice before even reaching her car. The tiny shorts kept riding up in her ass causing her cheeks to jiggle in the night air. The half shirt showed it was possible to regain a six pack after giving birth. To make a long story short Yolo was looking good. Rape bait as she called it.

The brand new Audi Yolo drove contradicted her get up so she parked it a few blocks away and walked the rest of the way to reach 'The Block'. 'The Block' as it was dubbed was where most of the weed and coke was sold. All the dope boys milling around meant the girls would be both and forth looking for attention. It was the perfect hunting ground for a rapist.

Yolo fell in step behind a couple of teen girls and walked over to The Block. She smiled at their banal talk about stuff that seemed so important at that age. None of the sneakers or purses they coveted would get them into college or a job and they definitely wouldn't get them into heaven.

"Sheesh," Yolo said to herself at the legions of crackheads roaming the streets. The ones with money to spend moved briskly with a purpose. The broke ones staggered around like the living dead. Soulless eyes searched the night for something to steal or suck in exchange for a few bucks. Even some of the men gave head for a blast. And plenty of the dope boys settled for one of them on a late night.

Yolo clutched her clutch purse tightly as she walked amongst the living dead. Not because she was afraid someone would steal it, but because it contained a small but large caliber semi-automatic pistol. The compact 40 cal would make a nigga do a back flip if she hit them with it. She stuck her finger into the specially designed purse that allowed her to fire right through the bag.

"Who got the fattest sacks?" Ratchet girl one asked her partner. She could only get ten dollars out of her selfish baby daddy and wanted to make the most of it.

"Slick's slick ass got some nice bags," Ratchet girl two replied. "With his raping ass."

"He got you too? Nigga took me to the park and just took the pussy," the first one shot back. They now had Yolo's full attention.

Slick was one of those dudes who believed that if he spent a few bucks he was entitled to fuck. In his mind taking pussy wasn't rape. He'd been doing it for years and no one had ever called the police on him. Some girls hung even hung out with him again afterwards giving him the opportunity to take it again.

"Which one is Slick?" Yolo called out from behind the girls. They both turned with that 'Bitch, who the fuck is you?' look upon their faces. Good thing that they didn't say it because they would've gotten their cute asses kicked.

"The tall slim one, who think he cute," Ratchet two replied and pointed to the group of weed peddlers standing in front of a Chinese restaurant.

"I see," Yolo said since slick stood out by being tall, slim, and cute.

"Ooh girl! Where you get them sneakers?" the first one demanded.

"Those are to die for!" the second one gushed.

"No, no they're really not. They were made in some third world country by a child worker for half a penny an hour then shipped here and sold for two hundred bucks each to dumb ass black folk," Yolo ranted.

"So! At the mall?" they asked totally missing the point. Most do.

Up close Yolo noticed that Yolo was a real pretty boy who liked pretty girls who were pretty young. He preferred the newly pubescent because they didn't expect much. He figured why spring for dinner, movies, and hotel rooms when a blunt and some cheap wine could yield the some results.

'TURN UP 2000' was the latest fad in cheap liquor. The good ol' boys at the liquor companies always had a super strong product just for the ghetto. They knew that keeping them drunk would keep them fucking and fighting. That's why they also owned the abortion clinics and the funeral homes as well.

It was quite amusing to them to hire a black spokesperson to help push poison on his own people. There was usually always some dumb ass rapper willing to rap about getting laid, getting drunk, and killin' a nigga.

"'Sup Fredrika, Yvonne," Slick said smiling at the two young girls when they came to cop a sack from him.

"Nuffin," Fredrika, known to Yolo as Ratchet one, shot back with her hand on her hip. "You know I don't fuck with you!"

"I know you ain't mad! Girl, you know you wanted me to hit that!" he shot back grabbing his dick through his pants.

"Whatever!" she frowned and snatched her weed. She made sure to toss her weave when she spun on her heels and stormed off.

"Call me," Yvonne whispered before rushing off to catch up with her friend. He turned and smiled down at his new customer.

"What's good ma? Who you?" Slick demanded. He frowned up his face to show how fine he though she was. Yolo always wondered why men did that but now wasn't the time to think or ask about it.

"Yolo. I heard you got them fat sacks of that good," Yolo said putting on a good performance.

"It's all... good," Slick said grabbing his dick once more and licking his lips likek he was LL Cool J. In his case the LL was about to mean no Longer Living.'

"Ki-ki-ki," Yolo giggled like the young girl she portraying. She did take a gander at the handful of dick though. Slick saw her and thought he had her.

"A-yo, let's go get us a bottle of 'Turn-Up' and turn up!" He offered like it was just the greatest idea in history.

"Me! For real?" she asked wide eyed as if honored. She stifled a giggle at knowing he was the one who was going to turn up. Dead that is.

"Hell yeah with yo' fine ass," Slick said turning her to the side so he could peep her backside.

"Well, okay," Yolo conceded. She followed him into the corner store to get corner store stuff. She got a cigar, lighter, and an ice cold bottle of Turn Up. He didn't bother buying condoms since he planned to use her vagina as one; bust a nut in it and then toss her aside.

"Shit we may as well go park at the park," Slick suggested when they reached his car. Good thing Yolo knew how to open a car door because chivalry was dead to dude.

"Is it far?" Yolo asked wondering about how long it would take her to get back to her car since he'd be staying in the park since dead people don't drive well.

"Nah," he lied and set off on the drive across town. The fifteen minute ride would take an hour on foot. That would mean a change in plans. A slight change to the where while the who and when stayed the same.

"Can we go under the pavilion?" Yolo asked, in the whiny voice of a teenage girl, when he parked the car.

"Nah yo, let's stay here," he said smoothly and rubbed her smooth legs. Yolo was totally shocked when her vagina jumped from his touch. She was also surprised when her juices began seeping into her panties.

"I can't get my legs all the way open in a car," Yolo pouted.

"Come on!" Slick shouted and snatched her out of the car. She had to run to keep up with him to the pavilion.

"I really don't want to drink," Yolo proclaimed when he cracked open the bottle. "Can you just eat my pussy first?"

"I don't eat no pussy, I beat the pussy," Slick laughed like it was the funniest shit. At least he died with a smile on his face.

"Oh okay, bye then," she said twisting her lips ruefully. A tug on the trigger caused the 40 cal to back then bite. The heavy slug made him do a somersault when it hit him. Yolo was so impressed she held up an imaginary scorecard to judge the flip. "Ten!"

Yolo was pretty sure he wouldn't mind if she kept the weed so she took it. She poured out a little liquor careful not to leave any prints and left him the bottle. Took his car too and drove back to her own. Fire works better than wiping for prints so she stuck a rag in the gas tank and hit it. She waited until it caught on fire before pulling off.

Yolo was still hot and bothered from the touch of a man so she sped home to get some dick from Killa. Christi was balled up slobbering and snoring on the sofa when she made it home so she let her be. She took the steps two at a time and rushed into her bedroom.

Up in her room she peeled off her shorts along with her moist panties with one hand and navigated her phone with the other. Her gallery contained over a thousand pictures of Killa's dick. He hadn't sent a single one of them. She had snapped most of them while he slept during the time they had spent together, but there were also a couple that she had snuck in while he was in the shower or changing. She even had a clip of her riding him while she was raping him. She looped the clip so that it would play over and over while she played in her pussy. It didn't make it through once before she came. It kept going and so did she. She had lost count of her many orgasms when she finally gave up.

"This is your pussy boo," she told the picture of Killa she used as her screen saver before giving it and kiss and drifting off in a deep sleep.

Chapter 6

"Hey Mama! How was your date?" Trey asked when his mother returned to their St. Louis apartment. He sounded so sincere that a casual observer would have thought that he really was.

"The usual," she shrugged hoping that would be the end of it. So much had changed so quickly it was hard for her to believe that what was going on was actually going on.

"Well, don't you usually break me off?" he asked in that 'bitch betta have my money' tone of voice that pimps used on their whores.

Trey was already probably mentally retarded and all the weed, liquor, and rap music he consumed all made him worse. The latest rap sensation named 'Pimp Daddy Pimp' convinced him that he was a real pimp. Trey was too lazy to go out and find him some whores so he forced the women around him to turn tricks.

"Son I..."

"Bitch, my name is Pimpin' Trey! Call me out my name one mo' 'gain and I'ma put my pimpin' foot up yo' hoe ass!" He growled like a pimp.

No one wants a foot up the ass so his mama reached into her bra and broke bread. The hundred bucks indicated that she had rented out her vagina instead of her throat. They had the same results but different prices.

"Good girl," Trey said, patting his mother on the head like a puppy who had performed a trick. Well, she had just performed a trick, but she was no puppy. She was his mother and paradise lays at the feet of our mothers. That means he had earned himself the hellfire in the future.

"Now clean that box out and get it ready for your next date," he said now sounding like a coach. Even gave her a pat on the ass to get her started.

The front door opened and in walked his younger sister Bria. She loudly popped her gum and wore a truculent look on her face. The weed smokin', liquor drankin', pill poppin' teen didn't mind fuckin' for money since she had already been fuckin' for free. It was the turning the money over part that she wasn't feeling. The local dope boys paid well to spend sometime in the cute girl's insides.

"Come on with it," Trey warned with violence in his voice. He had taken all he was going to take from the insolent girl. Pimp Daddy Pimp's latest single 'Gorilla Pimp' told how to solve this problem. Bria was about to be in trouble.

"Make me sick!" Bria protested and produced a twenty and a fifty. That was the wrong answer.

"Bone told me he gave a hunned dollar bill. Now come on with it," Trey warned. Pimped actually.

"So I don't get shit, huh? Fuck that!" she said crossing her arms to show that she was dead serious.

"Aight now, you fuckin' with a pimp's money! Oh and he also told me that you were holdin' out on that throat! Quit trying a pimp's nerves and suck some dick! Let a nigga put his money where your mouth is."

"First of all, you ain't no pimp. You Trey Jenkins, a nigga who bullies his own mother and sister. Secondly, if you want Bone's dick sucked so bad then you go suck it!"

Trey moved across the room so fast that Bria didn't get a chance to blink let alone duck. He snatched her by her throat and lifted her up in the air. Her feet kicked wildly as she pulled at his fingers.

"Un uh! Don't do her like that!" Mama protested from a safe distance. She wanted to help her daughter, but didn't want to get choked too.

"Get out a pimp's bidness!" he shouted back. He let his sister down and snatched his pants open.

Bria gasped for breathe as Trey shoved his flaccid penis in her mouth. The purpose was to humiliate her but he ended up with an erection. Since he was hard and already in her mouth he decided to go on and get off.

"Argh, ugh," Bria gagged as he slammed in and out of her larynx.

She had been saving her mouth in case she ever got a boyfriend, but he'd just ruined it. Unfortunately he was sick enough to be excited by the incestuous rape.

"Shit!" he exclaimed as he exploded. Tears streamed down her face as his semen seeped from the corners of her mouth. He continued to hump her face until he was as soft as he was when he first put his penis in her mouth. With his actions he confirmed his reservation in the hellfire.

"I HATE YOUR ASS! I HOPE YOU DIE!" Bria shouted as she wiped saliva and cum from her mouth and chin.

"Yeah, yeah, yeah. You just make sure you get my money," Trey laughed, thinking it was all a joke. "Now y'all hoes get ready to get my damn money!"

"Come on," Mama comforted as she helped her daughter from the floor.

"Get off me," Bria growled and pulled away. The lady hadn't helped her when her son face fucked her so she didn't want her help now. What she wanted was a hitman to come and kill her brother.

Bria's internet search for a hitman yielded a nothing but a bunch of movies, rap songs, and a few books, no killers. She searched killers and fared about the same. She continued to click page after page until finally she came across 1-800-Killa.com. It felt good to vent as she laid out today's events. She thought it was a novelty site, but uploaded her brother's picture none the less. She also filled in his name, hang out spots, and the make and model of his car as well. Last but not least, she got to recommend a choice of death.

"Hot!" Bria cheered as she made her selection form the choices of mild, medium, or hot. Visitors of the site could also choose between stabbing, shooting, or the culprit being beaten to death. "Beaten, please and thank you."

"Quit playing and come on," her mama pleaded. Her brother was in the mirror fixing his pimp daddy pimp curls and getting agitated. The women left their home to trick as Bria's request reached its destination.

"Sho-nuff?" Killa grimaced at the disgusting details of this latest request. He didn't think the site would take off quite as quickly as it had, but it did. Every day tons of people reported husbands, wives, bullies, and other assorted bad people in need of a violent death. This one in particular had caught his eye as he prepared to catch a flight. Once he reached his destination then he'd catch a cab, catch a body, and maybe get a drink.

"Where to now?" Sincerity asked as Killa packed a tote bag. She knew the population of somewhere was about to go down.

"Midwest to holla at a real life piece of shit" he replied hotly. As usual Killa wouldn't announce his presence. He would come and observe to make sure it was as bad as they say it was. If it was he would make it better.

"Got time for some back shots before you go?" Sincerity wondered. She wasn't sure how long he would be gone so she wanted to get some before he left.

"There's always time for back shots!" he replied frowning at the silly question. Even if there isn't time, you make time for back shots.

"Yay!" she clapped and flipped over onto her hands and knees.

Killa slid into her like a runner sliding into home plate. They quickly found their rhythm and filled the room with the wonderful symphony of sex. Her juicy vagina splashed with each stroke. The sound of skin slapping blended nicely with their moans and groans. Sincerity's orgasm caused her to clinch her vaginal muscles tight, as a result Killa only lasted two more strokes before giving her a big going away present.

"Y'all come back now, ya hear!" Sincerity called out as he pulled out and slipped into the bathroom. Poor girl was worked so good that she fell asleep right there with her ass still in the air.

Killa chuckled at the sight when he came out of the bathroom. He gave her a peck on her ass check, because ain't nothing wrong with that, and left the house.

*****

The last time Killa visited St. Louis he and Yolo were too busy murdering mob members to enjoy the beautiful city. Now that he had a couple of days to spare he decided he'd check out the city's sights, sounds, and people. The first thing he noticed was that there was some country ass folks in St. Louis.

"A-yo, where's the baggage claim?" Killa asked a man in skin tight jeans and snake skin boots. The big ass single gold tooth in his mouth fit his Jheri curl to a T.

"Over thur," the man said sounding just like the rapper Nelly. Killa nodded his thanks and squeezed his lips tight to keep the laughter in check.

The man reminded him of the flamboyant pimp he and Yolo cut into itty bitty pieces. The man called himself Cock-a-do and dressed in clothes made from or accented with rooster feathers. Yolo had easily infiltrated his stable and got him alone. Killa had been in his feelings when she killed him before he arrived but at least she had taught him the proper way to cut up a body.

"Just like chicken," Killa laughed at the memory. His stroll down memory lane was cut short when he accidently bumped into a man at the baggage claim. "Excuse me, my bad."

"Damn right it's yo' bad, country ass nigga! I should slap yo' bitch ass!" the man snapped. His pants were even tighter than the first man's and had a large lump in the middle. Instead of a Jheri curl he had big bouncy Shirley Temple curls. He also had two large body guards who moved in to guard his body.

"Bitch ass?" Killa asked as he looked around at all the cameras and potential witnesses to the pending murder. Even unarmed he could have easily sent the three of them to the 'upper room'.

"Yeah, bitch ass, fuck ass, hoe ass nigga!" he shouted as his body-guards restrained him. "Let me go! Let me get him!"

"Catch you later," Killa nodded as he retreated. There were people present and dude was causing a scene. He took mental snap shots of the man to save for a later date.

Killa had reserved a car and a room for his week-long stay. He figured it shouldn't take longer than that to see what he needed to see. If the claims against Trey were true he had an extremely violent death in his near future.

"Oh, we have a package for you Mr. Bush!" the pretty hotel clerk advised as she checked him in.

"Call me George, and thank you," he said leaning over the counter to get a peek at her ass when she turned to get his package.

"It's heavy!" she said as she placed it on the counter.

"It's a bomb," Killa joked and they both laughed. Actually it was a bomb and a couple of guns but he made it sound like a joke.

"Well, if you need... anything..." the clerk said with a pause that included her into the anything. The handsome stranger was a re-freshing change from all the cowboys in town.

"That's what's up," he agreed. Had it not been for Sincerity's part-ing back shots he may have just taken her up on her offer. Which is exactly why Sincerity had did it.

Chapter 7

"Mmmm" Yolo moaned as she awoke the next morning. Murder always made her sleep like a baby. As usual her babies were the first thing on her mind when her eyes opened. The multiple orgasms had caused her to oversleep. She blinked at the clock to see if it would change but it was still almost noon.

"Shit!" she shouted and leapt to her feet. She rushed into the next room and frowned at the empty cribs. The violent woman kept at least one gun in every room of the house, besides the armory of weapons the basement. Her room contained twin nine millimeter pistols on the nightstands and an AK-47 behind the door. Each bathroom held a Mac 10 submachine gun. There was even a 40 cal in the fridge and a 22 in the cookie jar. Even the nursery held a 12 gauge shotgun under one of the cribs. Yolo pulled it out and crept down the stairs.

"What the heck!" Christi screamed when she saw Yolo with the large weapon in her hands. The babies who were already laughing and playing turned it up a notch when they saw their mother.

"I um..." Yolo said feeling slightly embarrassed. She rushed from the room and back up the stairs to put the gun up before joining her little family.

"Mm hm," Christi teased. "I see someone must have been tired."

"Well, I was, but not like that with your fresh self. I was out making the world a better place" Yolo said proudly. She grabbed the remote to catch the news in hopes of hearing about The Amityville Rapist. He happened to be the top story but not exactly how she expected.

'The serial rapist and killer dubbed The Amityville Rapist has struck again. The body of 17 year old Fredrika Jackson was found early this morning...'

"Oh no! How could..." Yolo shouted before covering her mouth upon recognizing the victim as one of the girls she spoke with the night before. No way could Slick have killed her because he was dead himself.

"You know her?" Christi wondered from her reaction to the girl's picture on the screen.

"Yes, no, kinda," she said in confusion as the reporter reported. Once she wrapped up her spiel she handed the microphone over to the detective handling the case. He quickly had Yolo's full attention.

"Hubba-hubba," Yolo said cracking her little friend up which in turn caused the twins to laugh. All jokes aside she was quite taken by the handsome man on the television. The smooth chocolate man had a clean shaven head and a slight moustache. His tall, lean frame was the perfect hanger for the Brooks Brother suit he wore. "If I didn't have a man already..."

'We need the public's help! So far we have no witnesses nor leads. All we know is that the offender is short with a light complexion, and has brown eyes...'

"He just said that there were no witnesses so how he know what the killer looks like?" the observant girl wanted to know.

"Shh!" Yolo shushed since the pretty black man was still speaking. She had also heard the contradiction, but didn't contradict his pearly white smile.

'His DNA is not in any of the police data bases which means that he's probably in his teens. We're assuming that the victims are either familiar with or at least comfortable with the predator due to the lack of signs of a struggle that usually accompanies a stranger's abduction. If you have any leads or possible information please call 800-555-1234.'

Christi laughed as Yolo scribbled down the number. She assumed correctly when she figured it was for her own personal use and not to report any crime.

"Whatever!" Yolo huffed. "Now get ready and let's go get some lunch."

Yolo dressed Sun while Christi dressed Shyne. She then took a twirl in the shower before dressing in a casual pair of capri pants and shirt. Once they were all dressed they stepped out for a day on the town.

"Ooh, there go Christi," Yolo laughed when they drove past her mother wearing one of her outfits. The grown woman was a lot thicker than her daughter so the loose jeans fit tight.

"Ha-ha, very funny," Christi chuckled as she watched her mother walk to the weed spot. That's why there was never any food in the house. Some man would always come by to feed her dick and fast food while her daughter was left to fend for herself.

*****

Killa scrunched his face and shook his head at the room service menu. He decided to pass on the bland food and sample some of the local favor instead. A pretty blonde clerk was now on duty and she too smiled flirtatiously at Killa as he crossed the lobby. He tipped the valet when he arrived from the underground parking garage with his rental car.

The scenery changed drastically when he left the downtown area and entered the hood. A pack of young girls ambling by dressed like mini prostitutes smiled and waved as he paused for a red light. Killa's heart was too cold to break, but he sight saddened him none the less. If everyone became pimps, hoes, hustlers, and players then who would be left to raise the children.

Killa turned on the radio to ease his mind but that only made matters worse. A foulmouthed rapper with the cadence of a Mother Goose fairytale made him writhe in his seat.

'I put my mama on the rock, then put her on the block. Put my sister on the track and told the bitch to brang it back. Even granny selling love cuz' pimpin' is as pimpin' does'

'And that was last single was *'Pimpin' Is'* the latest single by our very own Pimp Daddy Pimp. Be sure to come out to the arena tomorrow night and catch the show' the announcer announced before throwing on another profanity laced tirade against women. Men are supposed to be the protectors and maintainers of women but obviously this dickhead hadn't gotten the memo.

The homegrown hometown favorite had single handily fucked up his community. Thanks to the deficiencies of daddies in the hood the kids were forced to find role models somewhere else. Too often they turned on the television or the radio and found one in an athlete, actor, or rapper.

Pimp Daddy Pimp had all the kids thinking it was cool to be pimps and hoes. The boys all emulated him while the girls allowed themselves to be degraded by allowing themselves to be pimped. In his latest song he said if you couldn't find a whore then pimp the women in your house. That's why Trey was on the plate.

"I'm definitely catching the show," the Killa snarled. That meant Pimp Daddy Pimp would be giving his final performance because he was about to get fucked up.

Killa pulled up to the diner Bria said that her brother hung out in. He spotted his target sitting in a back booth with a few more beginner pimps. They were taking turns trying to turn out the pretty waitress, but were getting nowhere. However, what they were getting was spit in their food every chance she got to.

"You're not from 'round hurr are you?" the waitress asked when she stopped at Killa's table.

"Nah, here on business. Or should I say hurr?" he asked so she would show that pretty smile once more. It worked.

"Not unless you from hurr!" she cracked up. "What can I get you? From the menu that is."

"Of course," he said taking note of the nasty glance she shot the nasty niggas in the booth. "I'll just eat whatever you suggest."

"See! Now you almost made me say something nasty to you!" she cracked up showing that smile once again. Killa took a closer look at the pretty brown girl and nodded in approval. In an instant he could tell that she was clean and down to earth.

"You doing an awful lot of smiling down thurr Darlene. I hope he paying for that!" Trey yelled over like he was her pimp.

"I hate that bastard! All them bastards, but 'specially him!" she growled in a whisper with a now fake smile pasted on her face.

"Why?" Killa pried looking for confirmation.

"First of all he keep trying to get me to prostitute for him. I don't even be fucking like that and he trying to pimp me! Then because that nigga pimpin' his own sister! And his mama!"

"So why you not fuckin'?" Killa asked as if that was all he heard. She frowned at him until the joke processed then she laughed out loud.

"Well, anyway. You a Yankee so I know you don't eat pork, so I'll order you a double cheese double meat and fries."

"Sounds good," Killa agreed and watched her ass as she walked away. Her panty lines suggested that they were French cut which were his favorite. He then concentrated on eavesdropping on the dead man's plans for the night. Plans that he intended to cancel.

"Got this new bitch I pulled over in Ferguson. I'ma put the dick on her and then put her on the track next to my mama and sister," Trey said cracking his friends up. At least they got to enjoy his company one last time.

*****

As soon as dusk fell over St. Louis Killa crept out on the prowl. He slipped back into the ghetto and staked out his victim's rundown house. The sheer curtains allowed him to watch the occupants of the house. The two woman of the house got dressed to be ladies of the night and then departed.

"Last time," he said to himself on their behalf. His first mind was to kick in the door and put a bullet through Trey's mind, but he didn't. The girl had specifically requested that he be beaten to death and like Burger King he wanted the customer to have it her way.

Still Killa tucked his pistol just in case he encountered any intangibles. 511 Beacher Street was about to be a murder scene. Killa's eyes darted in each direction as he approached the front door. At the same tiem he slid a pair of brass knuckles on each hand.

"My new bitch!" Trey cheered at the soft tapping upon the door. He rushed over, snatched the door open, and got the surprise of his life. It would also be his last.

"Ugh!" Killa grunted and socked Trey with everything he had. It was plenty too and removed all his front teeth. Trey stumbled backwards and fell over the coffee table.

"Who are you?" What do you want?" he asked hoping to give it to him to prevent getting hit again. It didn't work because what Killa wanted was his life so he slugged him again this time breaking his jaw.

"I'll ask the question. I actually have just one. Why in the hell would you pimp your own mother and sister?" Killa growled and threw another punch. Trey put an arm up to deflect the blow and got that broken too.

"Oweee!" Trey managed to squeal through his clenched mouth since his jaws wouldn't open. "It's the music sir. The rap music, it fucked me up! It's Pimp Daddy Pimp..."

"Got you killed!" Killa interjected and finished Trey's statement at the same time. He then finished his life. Each blow landed with a satisfying crunch of bone and cartilage.

Trey tried to crawl away but didn't make it very far. A savage blow to the back of his head crushed his skull in. Even that didn't stop the beating. Killa was in a murderous zone and beat the back of his head in.

Killa slipped out of his now bloody coveralls, revealing his One Ummah sweat suit underneath. He then shoved it and ruined boots he wore in a bag. After a quick look to the left and then right out the front door he slipped out and walked briskly to his car. Not a moment too soon either because a car pulled up as he was putting the bag of clothes in his trunk and prepared to change his shoes.

He correctly assumed that it was Trey's date from nearby Ferguson. He watched the cute girl shake her cute ass as she approached the house. He watched in amusement as she tried to be cute when she knocked on the door. No way was Trey answering that knock.

"Uh-oh," Killa chuckled when she tried the door and it opened. "Wait for it... wait... wait... for... it...huh?"

Much to Killa's surprise the woman didn't come out screaming as she should have. The room was covered in blood from the dirty floor to the water stained ceiling, yet she still ventured inside. He got behind the wheel and started the car, but instead of pulling off he waited and watched curiously.

"Well, I'll be damn!" Killa laughed when the girl came out with a flat screen under her arm and her pockets stuffed.

*****

Killa had all but made up his mind to return home to Atlanta but a chance encounter changed his plans. He was stopped at a red light when his whole car vibrated from the heavy bass of from the SUV coming up behind him.

'Pimpin' ain't dead, des' hoes just scared. I'm pimpin' nigga's daughters so daddies beware. Pimpin' ain't dead...'

Killa almost ran the red light to get away from the disgusting lyrics until he looked over at the completely wrapped truck. Yup, it was Pimp Daddy Pimp's vehicle. It got even better when he got a look at the rapper sitting in the backseat.

"Sho-nuff!" he said happily to himself seeing that it was the same smartass from the airport. Thoughts of BIG and Tupac getting killed in stopped cars flooded his mind. He grabbed the gun and reached for the handle. A girl popped up from his lap with the wet mouth of a blow job in process and saved his life. Well, not actually saved, but extended it for a while longer.

Killa lagged back and fell behind the truck. A few blocks later the SUV came to an abrupt stop that made him think he'd been spotted. Again he grabbed the gun ready for war. The back door flew open and the girl was shoved out onto the street.

"Fuck you!" she spat after spitting out a mouthful of semen.

Killa was delighted to get to use the device he had shipped. He reached into the bag and armed it as he sped up to catch the vehicle. When the vehicle stopped at the light Killa made his move. He whipped up alongside it and shot the driver and bodyguard, who was riding shot gun with a shot gun. Pimp Daddy Pimp locked eyes with his killer just long enough to place his face.

"You!" he said remembering their encounter at the airport.

"Yup!" Killa replied and tossed in the bomb. He mashed the gas and quickly pulled away out of the blast's zone.

Pimp Daddy Pimp made a move for the door but didn't quite make it. The low explosive charge went off with enough force to stun and maim. That allowed the white phosphorus to burn him alive until he was dead. The irony didn't escape the comical killer either.

"Turns out Pimpin' is dead," Killa chuckled and headed back to his hotel.

Chapter 8

'In breaking news out of St. Louis Missouri, controversial rapper Pimp Daddy Pimp was killed along with two of his bodyguards. The foulmouthed lyricist who was known for the song *'Pimp yo mama'* died in an explosion. Police say that military grade munitions were used in the assassination of the rapper.'

"Assassination? That's for important people. Them niggas got kilt!" Yolo joked to the twins who laughed accordingly. "That reminds me of a story your daddy told me."

"Dada! Dada!" Sun and Shyne repeated excitedly. Anytime their mother mentoned his name or showed them his picture they broke into their little cheer. "Dada, Dada!"

"That's right your daddy fed a rapper to the lions at the zoo. See me, I would have cut him up while he was still alive and made him watch them eat his body parts. But, that's just me."

As Yolo spoke she pulled up more information on the recent bombing. The crime scene photos and reports told her exactly what she had suspected. Killa was back.

'In local news The Amityville Rapist struck again last night. Fourteen year old Yashika Monae Lewis was raped and strangled in her bedroom while her mother was competing in a Tonk contest at a local bar.

Police say the perpetrator cut off both of the victim's hand which indicates that he's increasing in violence. Here now is detective Warren, head of the taskforce in charge of catching this monster.'

'Thank you. The perpetrator has become more brazen by attacking the latest child in her own home...'

Yolo felt moisture seeping into her panties as she watched his thick lips move as he spoke, she imagined them moving against her vagina and smiled. The smile was quickly replaced by a frown when she noticed a deep scratch across the cops face. The pink groove made a stark contrast against his dark brown skin. There was another smaller scratch on his neck as well.

The frown on her face deepened as she processed all of the information. She added it all together, took it back apart, multiplied it, and divided it, and then finally came up with her answer.

"You son of a bitch!" Yolo growled at the cop on the screen. "No wonder his DNA isn't on file! No wonder her hands were cut off! You dirty ass did this shit! You wanna cut off body parts? Well, I'm going to show you how it's really done."

With that Yolo decided to catch a predator.

*****

"Just what are you up to?" Christi asked once more as Yolo snapped pictures of her. The excuse of wanting to see her in the new outfits they picked up wasn't flying.

"You can't talk and smile at the same time!" Yolo snapped sarcastically as she snapped more pictures of the cute teen. Nothing sexy unless you're a child molester or perverted cop who preys on young girls, and whose days are numbered because he's going to be brutally murdered.

Yolo had gone to great lengths to set her trap. She had a slight setback when she couldn't find any lions to feed the man to. She couldn't find any pigs either, so she came up with something far worse. It was something fucked up actually, but it can't be said that he didn't deserve it though.

It took some doing but she finally was able to get it all together. She rented a small house at the end of a cul-de-sac. She purchased a couple prepaid cell phones, some scalpels, saws, a morgue table, and a set of non-stick cookware.

Another girl was murdered before Yolo could execute her plans to kill the killer cop, and she took the girl's death personal. She planned to make her killer suffer for not only her death but for each and every victim's life he had claimed. A bullet in his brain was too quick. No way was he getting off that easy. The trap was set and now it was time to add the bait.

*****

"Mmm," Detective Warren moaned at the young girl who came across his screen. It was a wrong number since the test was for Keith, but that didn't matter.

Yolo had stalked the cop for a few days which only made her angrier. Not only did the cop have a beautiful professional wife, he also had a pretty teenaged daughter of his own. He considered the less fortunate ghetto girls as disposable and preyed upon them. Once he had his way he disposed of them. Leaving their dead bodies around town like garbage. What goes around comes back around.

"Wrong number, but you're cute," Warren texted back.

"LOL, OMG, IKR" Yolo texted back, trying to sound like a teen. 'LOL'

"Got any more pics?" the cop asked, feeling a stiffy coming on from Christi's cute face.

"LOL, OMG" she replied and sent off a few more of the pictures she took of Christi. The pedophile police responded with a shot of his penis.

"Nice!" Yolo said to herself as she admired his dick. "Too bad you're a married sexual predator. Not to mention, I got a man."

"Let me see yours," Warren texted with one hand while stroking his erection with the other.

"I'm only 14," came the reply that made him cum instantly.

"Even better!" he replied like a true child molester.

Yolo sighed and pulled one of her pants legs off, pulled her panties to the side, and snapped a few pictures of her vagina. She got mad at herself for becoming aroused.

"Looks tasty. Can I taste it?" the cop wanted to know.

"LOL, OMG. I guess so. My mom works nights so you can come over."

"What's the address?"

*****

"Oh, this is just perfect!" Detective Warren cheered aloud when his GPS told him he'd arrived at his destination. He couldn't believe his luck. First a precious young thing just falls into his lap, now she lives at the end of a dark block. The distance between the houses meant no one would hear her scream.

Only problem is there is really no such thing as luck. Devine decree determined matters, and it decreed that today would be his last day. He would be the one screaming to death. The how, however, was up to Yolo and unluckily for him that chic is a lunatic. This was going to be brutal.

The cop was rock hard at the prospect of another young victim. He needed to either jack off again or wait for his for it to go down since he didn't want to ring her bell like that. If anyone else happened to be home he could always pull out his badge and play things off.

"I'm here" he texted once his erection went down.

"Come on in," the reply said.

"I'm gonna cum in alright," the cop laughed to himself. "In your mouth, your ass, and your tight little young pussy."

"Come in," Yolo called out through the darkness when he rang the bell. The cop turned the knob and rushed inside.

"Ouch!" he exclaimed when the dart entered his neck. "What the hell was that?"

There wasn't time to explain the sedative since he quickly hit the floor with a heavy thud. It took a lot longer to work on Animal Planet, making Yolo wonder if she hadn't used too much. He was breathing deeply when she began cutting his clothes off. Once he was naked she drug him into the dining room to get started. She did play with his dick a little first before getting down to business.

*****

"Huh? What the..." Detective Warren said when he awoke several hours later. He tugged at the restraints holding him to the morgue table until he was satisfied that he wouldn't be able to break himself free.

"Hey, sleepyhead," Yolo sang as she breezed back into the room. "Ready for dinner?"

"I'm Detective First Class Glen Warren. You are committing several felonies by holding me against my will," he barked trying to sound like he was in control. Yolo cracked up proving that he wasn't. "What do you want?"

"Get back! But we'll get to that after you eat."

"Fine. Now, let me loose so I can eat," he sighed as if he wasn't going to try to subdue her the second she did. Yolo was a bit old for his taste, but he would still rape and murder her so his time wouldn't be wasted.

"I'll feed you," she said and retreated into the kitchen. The cop took the opportunity to try his restraints once more. It was only then that he realized that he couldn't feel his legs.

"I can't feel my legs," the cop moaned when she returned. To make matters worse he couldn't look down because his head was strapped down.

"Yesss! It worked!" Yolo cheered and pumped her fist triumphantly at her first successful epidural. Last time she tried to give one she failed miserably and had to listen to the girl's screams the whole time she cut her up.

"I'll let you feel them in a few minutes," Yolo offered. She left out the part about them being in the other room. He had already had a lot on his plate at the moment. She cut a piece of the meat and added a few vegetables with it on the fork. "Open up."

"Mm," the cop hummed as he chewed. He would have pretended it was good, even if it wasn't, but it was actually was. He nodded and smiled as he chewed then swallowed. "Delicious! What is it?"

"Deez saute with wild mushrooms and chipotle," she replied with a self-satisfied simpering smile from the compliment.

"Deez? I'm not familiar with that. Deez what?" he asked accepting another mouthful.

"Deez nuts! Got eeem!" the silly killer shouted and cracked the fuck up. The joke was wasted on the un-hip cop who didn't get it. "Actually there your nuts not deez."

"I don't understand," the cop said and opened up for another bite. Yolo shrugged her shoulders and kept on feeding him. He cleaned his plate like a good boy.

"Can I play with your dick?" she asked, batting hers eyes coyly.

"But of course! Let me up and we can really..." he said but was cut off by her leaving the room. She was back in a flash and started playing with his dick.

Generally men love to watch a woman play with their dicks, but only when it was still attached to their body. His eyes grew wide when he recognized what was happening.

"YOU CUT MY DICK OFF!" he shouted and tried again, in vain, to free himself.

"Well, you ate your balls, so I don't see why you're so upset. If anyone has the right to be upset it's the families of those ten girls that you killed! Yea, they're upset!" Yolo fumed in a tone that no one has ever lived past.

"Is that what this is about? Some street girls who refer to themselves as bitches! Who can roll blunts better than they can read. Who..."

"Who still had a right to live! Who only acted upon what mainstream media told them to be! Now not only are you going to confess you're going to apologize!"

"I'm sorry!" the cop blurted out ready for this ordeal to be over. It was almost over, he along with it.

"Not me!" she shot back and tilted the table. Horror set in when he saw he was missing from the waist down. Yolo learned to make a tourniquet on YouTube and it wouldn't hold much longer. She started the recorder and he started confessing.

Turns out ole Warren was responsible for way more bodies than Yolo thought. He'd been killing people since he was a teen. A local girl, the elderly neighbor, prostitutes, even a woman in Jamaica on his honeymoon.

He was steady confessing while she poured the gas. Why he thought telling all his sins would help was a mystery he would take to his grave.

"What are you doing?" he asked when he smelled the gas. "I told you everything! I've apologized, repented!"

I know, but God is so merciful he might forgive you. That's why I'm making hell here on earth," she explained and tossed the match. "Okay, bye-bye."

The roar of the fire was actually louder than the howl the cop let out. Yolo watched from the next room as the fire devoured the man. When the heat got too hot she got out the kitchen and left the house to born.

*****

'In breaking news a stunning confession from Detective Glen Warren that he was the Amityville Rapist. We received his taped confession last night. His badly burned body was found today. With us is Chief of Police Hatcher...

"Thank you," the top cop said directly into the camera and walked off.

"You're welcome," Yolo replied proudly. He wasn't the only one watching.

"Good job, girl!" Killa offered with a knowing laugh. Sincerity shot him a 'what you talkin' 'bout Willis' from his side. "I mean whoever. Good job!"

Chapter 9

"Look honey. You like?" Marge asked hopefully when her husband came into the bedroom. She had purchased a sexy new nightgown to entice him back into her 40 year old vagina. He hadn't had much use for it once he discovered a much younger one.

"Nice," Harold replied without even looking at it. The black lace made a nice contrast against her pasty white skin.

"Even better when you peel it off. Grrr" she growled pulling one of her big titties out of the garment. The pink nipple caught his attention for a second. His new lust interest wasn't much up top.

"Nice Marge," he repeated. The compliment covered the titty, the pot roast, and the potatoes she had cooked for dinner.

"Got another just like it," she laughed and pulled that one out too. "Stay with me tonight. I'll do anything you want. Up the ass, anything!"

Harold paused at the thought of anal sex. Another thing his young girl wasn't yet ready for. She made up for all short comings with her looks. Funny thing was that Marge once looked just like that. Now she looked like one of those cans of biscuits that you pop open with doughy white flesh seeping from the seams of the garment.

"Night Marge," he declined and walked out of their bedroom.

Harold knew his new relationship with that young girl was wrong on so many levels. That's why he had to get good and liquored up before paying her a visit. A good strong buzz to numb his conscience and keep his dick hard. Three double whiskeys and two Marlboros later he was ready for his date.

Marge heard the creaking of the stairs as her husband ascended. She crossed her fingers and spread her thighs wide in hopes that he was coming back to bed. Her hopes were dashed when his footsteps stopped halfway down the hall. He took a deep breath and entered their teenaged daughter's bedroom.

"Jenny, are you awake?" He whispered as if it mattered. As if had she been sleep he would've taken his sick ass back down the hall and put his dick in his wife where it belongs.

Jenny froze in place, consumed with fear, guilt, and shame. She blamed herself for the abuse as much as her mother did. Marge accused her of enticing him with her cheerleader skirts and tiny shorts. Marge went so far as to threaten her if she told anyone. Poor Jenny was getting fucked by both parents. One literally and the other one figuratively.

"Wake up honey," Harold slurred from the whiskey and lust. He pulled her girly blanket away and frowned down at the fully dressed girl. Not that it mattered, he had all the time in the world.

Harold peeled the jeans, sweat pants, and long johns off his daughter's body. The fact that the kid had cartoon characters on her panties didn't stop him from removing them. He felt his little erection grew and removed his clothing. He ignored the girl's tears and climbed on top of her.

"This has to stop," Marge muttered to herself when she heard the bed creaking in the next room. The child's bed obviously wasn't designed for fucking. "Hate that bitch!"

Marge was in a rage hearing sex that lasted longer than it did with her. She used the anger to fuel her internet search for a solution. It took some doing but she eventually stumbled across a killa.

'1-800-Killa, my daughter is screwing my husband. She enticed him with her tight little body and girly giggles. Harold is a good man and didn't stand a chance. Now I'm afraid she'll tell on him and he'll go to jail. Please kill her. Kill my daughter!

*****

"Is this bitch serious? This must be a joke. I'm being 'punked'" Killa said as he read the intake report. When he saw it came from Deer Park, New York he decide to pay the Dodd family a visit. He had to go to Long Island anyway so he would make time to kick Marge ass while he was there. That would be the least, if the claim was true Mr. and Mrs. Dodd would be Mr. and Mrs. Dead.

Killa bookmarked the claim and moved on to read some more. The site had really taken off and had visitors from all over the globe. Most were people venting about husbands, wives, loud neighbors, and Donald Trump. There quite a few of legitimate claims of people who seriously needed to be murdered.

"I'm gonna need a helper," Killa mused as he flagged more and more claims. The memory of all the fun he and Yolo had when they crisscrossed the country killing people put a smile on his face. He shook his head tersely to wipe it off. "Nah."

Sincerity would make a good helper herself. She was trained to go by both Karate Joe and the South Bronx. Not to mention the sex was great. The thought of sex made Yolo pop back in his head once more. He had to see her soon and didn't know how to feel about it. Just when he decided to go fuck his girl to get her out her head another intake popped on the screen. It would have gotten ignored but the location caught his attention.

"Deer Park," he said pursing his lips. He read on getting angrier with every letter.

'1-800-Killa please help me. My dad comes in my room and does stuff to me. It started a few months ago and it won't stop. Now... Now, I um, I use to have my cycle, but this month it didn't come. I'm only 14. I um... My mom blames me. She said if I tell my dad will go to jail and she'll have to get a job. I don't want him to go to jail or her to get a job. I want them dead! Please kill them.'

"My pleasure," Killa snarled. Her parents desperately needed to die and he was going to deliver it.

*****

"Aren't they just the cutest little things!" Christi cheered at the twins in their birthday suits. Not the ones they were born in, but the ones Mama Yolo dressed them in for their first birthday.

"Yes they are! Him so handsome, and her so pretty!" Yolo said proudly. The twins smiled back with their combined five teeth. "Too bad their father isn't here to see them."

"See, that's why I don't have no man," Christi said like she was a woman.

"Girl, stop! That's not why. You're 15, that's why," Yolo laughed putting her back in her place.

Sun and Shyne were growing like weeds, and into everything. They would escape their cribs at night to roam and play throughout the house. Yolo was amused at their little language. It consisted of the few English words they knew and the rest were of their own design. Whatever it was they seemed to understand it. She felt that most times they communicated through telepathy. The toddlers toddled out of the room so Yolo turned back to finish chewing Christi out.

"No boyfriend, no baby daddy! If a man ain't tryna marry you then don't deal with him. Men are the protectors and maintainers of women! Accept less and you'll get less. Way less!"

"Okay, okay" the teen surrendered. Her own mother was a proof of Yolo's advice. The woman had men in and out of her like a police car. "I hope your baby daddy marry you one day."

"He will! Our situation is complicated. We have a distraction," she said meaning Sincerity. The way she figured it she was in the way. "Let's go!"

Yolo was rich but practical. Instead of splurging on a party that the kids were too young to appreciate it so she took them to Chuck-E-Cheese. They played games and watched the giant rat prance and dance.

"Dada-Dada, Daddy," the twins said excitedly looking behind and beyond their mother. Yolo whipped her head around to see what had them so excited but saw nothing. In an instant she was suddenly sad.

"What's the matter?" Christi asked full of concern at the change in her demeanor.

"Nothing. I gotta pee," Yolo pouted and rushed off towards the bathroom. Once inside she entered a stall, broke down, and had a good cry. "I want my baby daddy!"

"Me too!" A strained reply came from the next stall where a pretty Latino girl came to lament her similar situation.

"I know that's right!" A woman at the sink confessed. "I'm tired of playing tough, I need my kid's father!

Yolo and her next stall neighbor both emerged teary eyed. They joined the woman at the sink and two more that came in. The B.M's and side chicks comforted each other until all eyes were dried.

"Group hug!" Yolo called and they all hugged. Faces were washed, heads held high, and the women all went on to continue raising their children alone. Salute!

"You ok?" Christi asked when Yolo returned to the booth. It was a good question but she had a better one.

"Where did that come from?" Yolo asked frowning curiously at the wrapped box with a pretty bow. It reminded her of a bomb she sent to a grieving family at a funeral. She leaned into listen for a tick but none was present. Christi cracked up at what she thought was a joke.

"Some man. They sure acted like they knew him,' she replied cocking her dubiously as if Yolo were holding out on her.

"Really?" Yolo said scanning the game room once more. Finally she lifted the box lid and peered inside. When she saw the content she cracked up.

"What is it? What are they?" Christi asked of the odd looking toys. The two plastic hoops were pink and blue for the twin's respective genders. A little latch on the side allowed the loop to snap harmlessly shut.

"His and her D.C 2000's They daddy is a real clown!" Yolo wore a Joker smile for the rest of the day. After the party they hit the mall. Yolo bought everything her children showed any interest in at the toy store. Once back at home they ate cake and played games until it was time for bed.

Chapter 10

Poor Jenny Dodd prayed the whole day that night would not fall, but it fell anyway. The looks her parents gave her at the dinner table terrified her. Her father licked his lips lustfully while her mom glared in disdain.

"What do you find so amusing?" Marge demanded when a satisfied smirk appeared on the corner of her daughter's mouth. How dare she be happy while she was miserable. She was the only one in the house not getting any sex.

"Nothing Mom," she said since she wasn't particularly happy. She did find solace in the decision to kill herself. If daddy came to screw her again she planned to hang herself on the front lawn for all to see.

"Well, let's all wind down and call it a night," Daddy Dodd suggested. He retired into the den to drink until it was time to go call on his child.

After cleaning her kitchen Marge went up to her bedroom. She tried a yellow crotchless number tonight hoping to entice her husband once more. The matching bra was cut out in the front showing her big pink nipples.

"Come to bed Harold," Marge purred and spread her legs to show that she had shaved her plump vagina. There was a time when he would have dived face first and tried to suck an ovary out. Now it only got a brief pause as he nodded at it like one does an acquaintance on the street.

"Go on to sleep. I'm going to get a drink," he said as he splashed on some old man cologne.

"Fuck me, Harold! Please, it's been months! Please fuck me!" she pleaded.

"Not tonight, Marge," he chuckled and walked out of their room.

"Want something done..." Marge huffed and dug into her nightstand. She pulled out a huge dildo and dug in. "Do... it... your... damn... self!"

Meanwhile Harold engaged in foreplay with glasses of whiskey and tobacco. Once he was good and liquored up he stood and made his way up to his daughter's room. He wasn't the only one creeping through the house.

Jenny froze when she heard her door ease open. She skipped the futile ritual of being overdressed for rape and slept in her pre-molestation bed wear of shorts and a t-shirt. Still, she braced herself for the disgusting feel of her father's touch. When no touch came she flashed back to when this awful phase of her life began. Her drunk father would stand over her staring and breathing heavy. Once he got good and hard he would rush into the next room and fuck the daylights out of his wife.

The next step was touching, feeling, and kissing until he finally got into her bed. It escalated each and every visit. Last night he went down on her, tonight he expected her to return the favor. Jenny almost opened her eyes hen no touch came, but the door opened once more.

"Jenny, you awake?" Harold said trying to sound sexy. He dropped his robe revealing his erection. That's exactly how he died.

'Pst' Killa's silenced pistol whispered. The slug entered his ear like a secret. A secret he would take to his grave. The liquor caused him to stand for a second but the laws of gravity are written in stone. He fell face first onto his daughter's bed.

"Are you from 1-800-Killa?" Jenny asked. It was a reasonable guess since Santa doesn't carry a nine and shoot perverts dads in their heads. He probably should though.

"I am," he replied and stepped forward. It was too dark in the room to make out his features but she saw the small pill in his extended palm. "For your problem."

"Jenny plucked the abortion pill from his hand and tossed it into her mouth. She swallowed it without water, and then took a sip from the glass on her nightstand.

"Thank you. Have you seen my mom too?" she asked hopefully.

"She's next. Who was here?" Killa asked in a low tone.

"A black guy who..." Jenny started and then stopped when Killa shook his head no. "Two white guys with tattoos. They demanded money and..."

"Very good," he nodded in agreement with her official story. The officials would have no choice but to accept it from the only survivor. They said their goodbyes with a nod and Killa crept down the hall to finish what he came for.

Marge perked up when she heard the door ease open. She hadn't heard the bed creaking so maybe she could get laid. She snatched the dildo from her guts and tossed it aside. The large plastic dick landed with a thud.

"Who are you?" Marge asked sounding more curious than afraid. "1-800-Killa?"

"That's me," Killa said with a bow.

"You killed my husband?" she asked when she saw the gun in his hand.

"I did. Time for you to join him," he replied and raised the gun.

"Okay, but fuck me first! I want something black, long, and hard inside of me before I go!"

"Huh?" Killa asked scratching his head with the long silencer attached to the gun.

To make matters even more confusing Marge grabbed the back of her knees and pulled her legs open. The curious Killa leaned in to have a look at the 40 year old vagina.

"Put it in! Ram it in!" Marge demanded tossing her hips upward.

"Okay," Killa shrugged and rammed the long silencer into her. It was so wet and loose form the dildo Killa almost lost his gun. That would have been extremely unprofessional and embarrassing.

"Aa..." Marge let out the beginning of a scream but a tug on the pistol sent a silent bullet that silenced the slut.

"My work here is done" Killa nodded in satisfaction. He crept out of the house as quietly as he had crept in and set off on his next mission.

*****

"Sun and Shyne," Yolo sighed shaking her head when she heard the pitter patter of their little feet. The twins had a knack for escaping their cribs at night so they could run around the house. She intended to install a camera in their room so she could see just how they got out.

She couldn't help but smile at the sound of their strange language and delighted laughs. Then she heard the low rumble of a man's voice and popped straight up in her bed. Anger doesn't come close to describing the emotion she felt at the intrusion. She reached under the pillow and pulled out the huge revolver that lived there.

Yolo crept down the hall until she reached the nursery. An ear to the door confirmed that there was indeed a man inside. She burst through the door and did a roll like the ones done in a cop show. Luckily for all she stopped short of firing.

"What are you doing here?" she asked, sounding baby mama-ish.

"You didn't think that I would miss their birthday did you?" Killa asked and flashed that killer smile of his.

"Dada, Daddy!" the twins told to their mother as if she didn't know who he was. She had shown them his picture and spoke to them about him every day of their lives.

"I know who that is," she said screwing her face up. "Anyway, you let yourself in so you can let yourself out once you're done.

"Huh?" Killa asked her back as she left the room. He wasn't expecting that at all. Where was the love struck girl he'd grown to at least like; just a little bit, have him tell it. He shrugged it off and turned back to his children.

Yolo may have sounded cool and unimpressed but she was fronting. She ran her ass back into the room and got right. She shaved her box, changed her panties for a pair of French cut to show some ass cleavage, brushed her teeth, combed her hair, and struck a sexy pose on her bed.

Killa played with his babies until they conked out on him. He placed each back in their crib and planted parting kisses on their foreheads. Ego forced him down the hall to at least say goodnight to his baby mama.

"Who?" Yolo called out to the tap on her bedroom door. She shook her head at the silly question and invited him in. "Come in."

"I just wanted to say..." Killa began than stopped at the sight of them sweet caramel ass cheeks. They reminded him of a candy apple so he came over and bit one.

"Oh!" Yolo exclaimed with her fronting ass. She was truly surprised when he flipped her over and kissed between her thighs.

Next it was Killa's turn to be shocked when he pulled her panties aside and tasted her bald vagina. She lifted her hips to help him remove them completely. Not even a full minute later she filled his mouth with the juices from an intense orgasm.

Killa had stripped while he ate then plunged deep inside of her. Yolo sucked and licked the pussy juice from his lips and chin. Killa filled her completely and tapped on her cervix. He attempted to pull out enough to get a good stroke going but couldn't. Yolo wrapped her strong arms and legs around him and pulled him close. She grinded and wiggled against him until she came once more.

"Shit," Killa exclaimed at how good she felt. The orgasm caused her to fall limp like a rag doll. It didn't get her off the hook though.

Killa lifted her legs far and wide and dug her out. He flipped her on her side and fucked her savagely. Yolo came again when he flipped her over and hit her from the back. He flipped her once more and fucked her face to face.

"Cum in me," Yolo pleaded when his body told her he was close. His stroke became choppy and his moans got deeper.

"Okay," Killa replied and pulled out to cum on her stomach instead of in it.

"Make me sick!" Yolo laughed and grabbed his dick. She used her wetness and milked him dry.

Killa finally rolled off and onto his back as an awkward silence filled the room. They both searched for appropriate words to fill the gap between round two because they both planned on more sex.

"So... been killing?" Yolo asked off handedly.

"Have I! The world is full of fucked up people who need to get fucked up." He replied enthusiastically.

"Tell me about it! I've been taking out a couple here and there. Thinking about setting up a website so people can report people who need dead. Child molesters and stuff," she said making love struck circles on his chest with a finger.

Killa put the dick on her so well she back in love again.

"Great minds think alike," Killa said reaching for his phone. Yolo felt a slight panic thinking he was leaving. She would kill a continent to keep him by her side. "Look it."

"Cool!" Yolo exclaimed when he showed her the 1-800-Killa website.

"It is! I get so many request I can't keep up with them all!"

"Put me down! Let me get down!" Yolo begged as she stood straight up on the bed.

"Nah, I don't know?" he replied twisting his lips in thought. He scanned her fine frame as he thought. "I could use a hand... I guess."

"Thank you! Thank you!" Yolo sang and bounce up and down. All that movement caused Killa's dick to stretch out stand straight up in the air.

"Thank me then," he suggested. She fell back on the bed thanked him orally.

Killa enjoyed her lips, throat and tonsils for a few minutes and pulled her on top of him. He rushed to get back inside of her then grabbed her ass cheeks to guide her up and down on his dick. He had it all under control so all that was left for her was to squeeze.

"Will you stay? With me, with us? Please." Yolo heard herself ask. She had so much dick in her it pushed the words out of her mouth.

"I can't. I have a woman" Killa said sounding almost regretful.

"Well, now you have two," Yolo insisted. With that she became a side chic. She planned to start a side chic support group on Facebook first thing in the morning.

"Get up!" Killa said urgently and tapped her ass.

Yolo obediently compiled and lifted up a millisecond before Killa exploded. That was round two of what would be five. They fucked one last time in the shower before taking the kids to breakfast. Killa ate light but still bit off more than he could chew. Picture Yolo being content as a side chic.

Chapter 11

Yolo wasted no time using her log-in information to log on the 1-800-Killa website. She quickly saw that Killa was right, there were hundreds of people just dying to be dead. There were child molesters, rapists, thieves, and the whole cast of Love and Hip Hop. She agreed to handle the tristate of New York, New Jersey, Connecticut. That would prevent her from having to drag the twins all over the country.

"Wyandach?" Yolo frowned as she read a local case. If this one panned out she could go murder whoever while the kids took a nap.

'Dear Killa, I'm 15 years old. My mom is 30 and so is her boyfriend. Or should I say our boyfriend because he keeps touching me. My mother knows and thinks it's cute. Says I'm going to be just like her but I'm not. I go to school and get good grades. I babysit for my neighbors twins, and she's like my sister. They are the only family I have. If something ever happened to my mom I would live with them...'

"It better not be!" Yolo growled as it began to sound more and more like Christi. "It is!"

Yolo popped up from the bed letting the laptop fall from her lap. She marched downstairs and found Christi watching a Science show. Christi pretended to be sleeping so Yolo wouldn't send her home.

"Yeah right," Yolo said not buying the sleep disguise. It suddenly dawn on her why the girl never wanted to go home. "Anything you wanna tell me?"

"Um... I love you?" Christi guessed. It was the right answer and Yolo walked away nodding her head. Christi mom and boyfriend had a brutal death coming. And soon.

Soon ended up taking a lot longer than expected. First, April had so many men in and out of her it was hard to catch her and Tremayne together. The truck driver popped in and out of town on no particular schedule. In between her vagina hosted whoever had the weed.

"She can't have any elasticity in her pussy," Yolo said in disgust as a second man of the day left the house. She was right too because her beat up box was worn out like an old slipper. Had she went to an obgyn they wouldn't even need (that metal thing that opens it up). Just shine a flash shine a flash like and have a look around. Like exploring a cave.

Most days while Christi was at school Yolo would stake out her neighbor. Tremayne showed up a few times but she had been too busy with her babies to murder them properly. Today he pulled up just as the twins blinked themselves to sleep. She rushed upstairs to get dressed to kill. Not little black dress, hose and heels dressed to kill. Black sweats, boots, brass knuckles, and fangs dressed to kill.

"Too easy," she explained to the pistol on her dresser and left the house.

Yolo used the back door and hopped over the wooden privacy fence. The couple was busy on the sofa as she eased in the backdoor.

"Mmm... this shit good and wet!" Tremayne cheered as he played in April floppy vagina. The outer lips fell open like elephant ears.

"You made it wet daddy," she lied. That was the semen left behind from 30 minutes ago. The poor fellow believed it and slid downtown. He slurped and slobbered in the next man's cum until Yolo came to send him away.

"Um, excuse me. I have to hurry up and kill you guys before the kids get up. That Shyne gets into everything!" Yolo explained politely.

"Who is this?" Tremayne asked with semen around his mouth and chin. He stood straight up to check her out lustfully.

"That bitch from next door," April hissed. Those were the last words she uttered with all of her teeth in her mouth. Yolo swung a right that cleared the front of her mouth.

"What the?" Tremayne asked before catching a barrage of blows that left him bloody. He tried to run but Yolo tripped him onto his face.

April tried to run but Yolo grabbed her by her ponytail. That only slowed her for a second. She shook her head and came out of the clip on hair and headed for the door. She didn't make it.

"Un uh," Yolo laughed and clipped her too. She fell face first and broke her neck against the front door.

"Bitch, you know who I am?" Tremayne demanded and threw up his hands. He use to knock dudes out with one punch back in the days. Only today wasn't back in the day. He threw one haymaker that Yolo easily slipped under.

She threw an uppercut to his nuts that lifted him up in the air. Yolo was all over him when he came down. She beat that man so badly he was relieved when his soul abandoned his body.

"I'll let myself out, okay?" she asked politely. No one protested so she left the same way she came. After a shower and change of clothes she used a disposable phone to call and report the murder. The last thing she wanted was for Christi to come home and find her mother like that. She did have a heart you know.

Chapter 12

The twins second birthday was spent just like their first. They seemed to enjoy Chuck-E-Cheese more since they were able to play more of the games. Sun even got up and danced with the giant rat. Just like last time pops showed up with gifts but this time he stayed.

The night ended just like last year with Killa deep inside of Yolo. They had seen each other over the course of the last year but mainly to get together and kill people. That was business, this was personal.

Killa frowned in delight as he looked down watching his dick slide in and out of Yolo from behind. She moaned and coated his dick with her juices. At the last possible second he pulled out. And skeeted on her back.

"I'm on the pill you know," Yolo reminded giving him permission to cum in her.

"I know, I just like doing that," he laughed milking himself dry with his hand.

"Round two in the shower," she suggested and got up to lead the way. Killa was right behind her and joined her under the hot water. As soon as they got in he scooped her up by her ass. She put her arms around his neck and bucked wildly. It was all he could do to hold on as she came again and again and again. Yolo held him so tightly he had no choice but to cum inside of her. His knees buckled from the explosion sending them both to the bottom of the tub.

"You sir, are a beast!" Yolo panted out of breath.

"Me? You!" Killa shot back as he too struggled for air. That was the basis of their relationship, great sex and mo' murder.

*****

"Oh! Did I tell you I wrote a book?" Yolo sang proudly once they made it back to the bed and cuddled.

"Is that right? What, and autobiography? *Yolo, the Lovely Little Lunatic!*" he cracked and cracked up.

"What, and I'm running around killing people? What kind of book is that! Mine's a love story. *Lady and The Beast*," she sang smugly.

"I hear you. Just don't use that publisher down in Atlanta. I forget the name, but we got a request about them on the site," Killa warned. Nosey Yolo leaned over to reach for her laptop. The site of her bare ass almost set off round three.

"Stop!" Yolo giggled as Killa palmed her ass. She quickly logged in and checked the recent request. "Here it is..."

'Hello 1-800-Killa. My name is Tasha Boykins. I'm a single mom of two young boys. I use to write as a hobby but decided to pursue it full-time. I did pretty well on my own and made a nice living. I guess it's my own fault for being greedy but a publisher approached me saying he could help me make a lot more money. He promised to put my book in libraries and book stores so I went with it. Sure enough he did what he said. My books are everywhere and even made it to number six on the best sellers list. Then it came time to get paid and I got a check for $57.00. The royalty report didn't make any sense at all.

I knew it wasn't right but needed the money so bad I went to cash the check. I got my kid's dressed, took a bus to the train then another bus to the bank. When I got there they said he put a stop payment on the check!

I called him and he hung up on me. Then he was all over social media flaunting his money. I called a bunch of lawyers, but I couldn't afford to pay them. At this point I don't want the money. I want him dead! Please, please kill him!'

"Okay!" Yolo cheerfully agreed. "The owner of Double R Publishing is Robert Redmond."

"What are you doing?" Killa asked when she pulled up the website.

"Sending in my submission!" she said and did just that.

"Guess you're coming to Atlanta, huh?" he sighed.

"You know it!"

*****

"Ooh Double R!" Yolo smiled when she checked her email. Killer or no killer she wanted some feedback on her book.

"We loved the first 3 Chapters you sent but in order to make a decision we need to read the full manuscript," Robert explained. Yolo started to type a reply but decided to call the number at the bottom of the email instead.

"Mm?" Robert asked answering his phone in the middle of his favorite game. He loved playing squirrel and holding nuts in his mouth.

"I wanted to speak to someone about getting published," she said trying to sound as naïve as possible.

"Mmmhp!" Robert sighed in defeat and swallowed the mouthful of semen he'd been holding.

"I win! I win!" his bodyguard cheered. He recently hired the large man when he started getting death threats. The man figured the large man when he started getting death threats. The man figured since he was protecting the man he should be giving him some head too, and he was right. The irony was that he was paying the same amount he was stealing. Had he paid the authors for their hard work he wouldn't be having these problems.

But wait, problem isn't the right word. Rain at a picnic is a problem. Rush hour traffic is a problem. Yolo on your ass is so much more than a problem. That's a catastrophic disaster.

"You always do," Robert flirted back. He did set a new record, holding cum for twenty minutes. "Let's go again!"

"Um... hello?" Yolo said reminding him of her call. She frowned up wondering if it was as gay as it sounded. "My book? *Lady and The Beast.*"

"Oh yeah, yeah. That was okay, we need to read the whole thing," Robert replied with his lying ass. If she sent that book today it would be on E-book by the morning. No edit or nothing. Just a cheap book cover with the same stock photo models on a hundred other covers.

"Can we talk in person? I'll be in Atlanta in a few days," she purred seductively. He may suck dick but he still enjoyed screwing his authors. Both literally and figuratively. He had a woman at home but she looked like a baby hippo with a crooked wig. "Sure, sure. Call me when you get to town."

"See you soon," Yolo smiled knowing she would be the last person to see him.

Chapter 13

"Mm hm," Sincerity hummed suspiciously as she watched Killa getting dressed to go out. The sly grin on his face said he was up to something. Who could blame him, good pussy is something to smile about.

That's not to say Sincerity didn't possess a pot of gold between her legs because she did. However, variety is the spice of life; especially when it comes to vagina. He only saw Yolo every couple of months and eagerly anticipated her insides.

"What?" Killa asked trying his best to wipe the smirk off his face. That only made it worse and he smiled broadly.

"Got time for back shots before you go?" she asked. This was a test.

"Actually..." he paused to check his watch. "I don't," he replied failing the test. Had he been picking up his homeboys form the airport they would've had to wait, but he couldn't, wouldn't have his kids standing around in the terminal waiting. Even Grandma would've had to wait a few minutes for back shots.

"Mm hm," she repeated and mentally marked an "F" on his test. Since when didn't he have time for back shots? She held her tongue and watched him dress and leave.

*****

"Put it down! Stop touching stuff. Boy if you don't stop!" Yolo fussed at her busy son, son. Meanwhile the little diva Shyne was looking at herself in every mirror and glass window that they passed on their way through the airport.

"I got him," Christi said and scooped him up. He squealed in delight and tried to get loose.

Christi shed two tears over her mom's death and then was over it. She was officially a part of the family. Little sister to Yolo and big sister to the twins. The girl blossomed from raggedy to a cute and confident teen. She was secure in her skin and natural hair. Best of all her eyes were fixed firmly on the prize. High school, college, and then on to med school. There was no time left for boys or turning up.

"Daddy!" Shyne shouted at the sight of her beloved. She snatched away from her mommy and took off towards her father.

"Sell out!" Yolo quipped. She was slightly jealous but understood that daddies are a little girls' first loves. That relationship can affect every other relationship in their lives. A girl is either going to want a man just like or nothing like her daddy.

"You too, huh?" she asked when Sun ran ahead to greet his dad as well.

"You are my Sun-Shyne, my only Sun-Shyne," Killa sang as he scooped his children. They squealed, Christi cheesed, and Yolo fought back the tears.

For the first time in her life, Yolo knew exactly what she wanted. A family. Sure killing bad people was good fun but more than anything she wanted them to be together. Anyone in her way was in serious danger.

"Sup yo," Killa greeted with a sly smile. He'd never admit it but he was happy to see his baby mom as well. He and Christi exchanged a mile and a head nod.

"Sup with you?" Yolo replied hoping her panties didn't get all squishy wet like they do whenever she's around him. "Damn it!"

"What?" Killa frowned at her muted outburst.

"Nothing," she said, cracking a fake smile as her panties squished under her cute skirt. She followed him out to where he parked on the concourse. Killa strapped the twins in the back with Christi while Yolo took shot gun. Literally since Killa kept a shot gun under the passenger's seat of the luxury vehicle.

The Killa couple carried on two separate conversations at the same time as they rode towards downtown. The first was verbal as they chatted about and with the kids. The second was a tacit exchange of body language that spoke volumes. Christi peeped it but was too young to understand it.

Killa bit his bottom lip to say 'I'm gonna fuck the shit out of you'. Yolo smiled in agreement then clenched her jaws tightly. That meant 'I'm suck yo' dick so hard you gonna beg me to stop'.

"Ya'll crazy," Christi cracked up at the two of them. Soon they pulled up to a swanky downtown hotel. Killa grabbed their bags and handed them to the bell hop before leading the way inside.

"Welcome to Atlanta!" the pretty clerk said with a smile and bat of her fake eyelashes at Killa. She was so smitten by him that she didn't even notice his family come up behind him.

"Bet if I punch her in her throat she won't be so flirty," Yolo told Christi loud enough to be heard by the clerk. She was right too and the truth wiped the smile off her face.

"Your keys, Sir" she said with a submissive bow and handed Killa two sets of key cards.

"Why two rooms?" Yolo asked with a disappointed pout on her face. Killa thought about biting that poked out lip, but let it pass.

"One for y'all, one for us," he replied and bit his own lip once more. "Get settled and I'll fall back through to take you guys out."

"Settled? I have a set of terrible two twins, ain't no getting settled!" Yolo protested. Christi co-signed by nodding her head up and down. The twins took off down the hall in different directions to help prove the point.

"So... an hour or so?" Killa surmised.

*****

"Oooh!" Sun, Shyne, Yolo, and Christi all exclaimed as they stepped into the Georgia Aquarium. Killa felt the same every time he walked into the place.

"I know right!" he agreed and scooped his daughter up in his arms. Sun wanted up so he scooped him up as well. Yolo alternated between watching him, the kids, and the fish.

A deadly silence fell over the family when they reached the shark tank. They arrived just as it was feeding time. The handler nodded his head at Killa to say 'what's up'. Killa nodded his head and cracked a warm smile.

"You know him?" Yolo asked despite it being obvious.

"Yeah, that's my man Wali," he replied as Wali tossed in a large piece of fish.

"Oooh!" The twins cheered as a feeding frenzy ensued. Shyne pushed out of her father's arms and fell to the ground. She popped right up and rushed to the tank.

"Same one who worked at the zoo?" Yolo pondered with her mouth twisted in thought "Who fed the lions?"

"That's the one," Killa replied with a chuckle. "What are you up too?"

"I have a date with my publisher later," she said with a mischievous grin that meant someone was going to get murdered. "Wanna make it a double since he has a bodyguard?"

"Bodyguard! Why the fuck would a publisher need a bodyguard?"

"For protection from all the single mama whose books he stole!" Yolo replied with a snarl. The activity in the tank turned her snarl back into a wicked smile.

The family enjoyed dinner at the aquarium before heading back to the hotel. Christi and the kids were beat from the long day, but the killers had some killing to do.

Chapter 14

"Mm, mmm, mmph!" Robert moaned when Yolo approached on him out on the restaurant's patio. The silky mid-thigh dress clung to her body showing off the fine frame. A soft wind pressed it firmly against her baring witness that she didn't have on a bra or panties.

The dress was too skimpy for a bra but Killa was the reason she was going commando and not wearing any panties. By the time they reached the restaurant they were soaked from being so close. She wrung them out and tossed them into the backseat. Killa picked them up and sniffed them as she walked away. With his nasty ass!

"Hey," Yolo sang and giggled so sweetly that it appeared as if she wasn't there to murder the man. She glanced around and spotted his bodyguard nearby. He looked relaxed form the blow job the dick sucking publisher had given him.

"Looking good!" he cheered, throwing his arms open for a hug while puckering his lips for a kiss.

"Thanks," she said slapping him '5' instead. Second hand cum is worse than second hand smoke any day as far as she was concerned. Another glance didn't reveal Killa's position, but she knew that he was there.

"Should detonate both of y'all right now," Killa growled as he peered at the publisher and his bodyguard through the rifle scope. It wasn't part of the plan but he wanted to hurry up and get Yolo back to the hotel. She had him rock hard and he couldn't wait to get inside of her. It's true that crazy girls have the best pussy and Yolo was a fucking Lunatic!

"So, did you send your manuscript?" Robert asked eagerly. If so he would upload that bitch on the spot from his phone.

"Not yet. I wanted to read over the contract first. Don't want to get screwed you know? I prefer to get fucked."

"I wouldn't screw you, but I would fuck you," he said licking his lips. The same lips he had just given his bodyguard head with. "A lot of these publishers steal books, royalties, and errthang. You gotta be careful!"

"I heard," Yolo replied forcing a smile instead of throwing up. She imagined reaching across the table and stabbing him with her fork. "You wanna get out of here?"

"Hell yeah!" he shouted. Robert liked to fuck his authors before he fucked them out of their money. "Let's go!"

"As long as we can go by the aquarium. I'm leaving tomorrow and don't want to miss it. 'Sides, all that water makes me wet."

"Check please!" Robert rushed Yolo towards the door with his bodyguard on his heels. He jumped in the front of the used Lexus while Robert and Yolo got in back. "Georgia Aquarium?"

"That's closed now a..."

"Just go there!" Robert shouted with the same lips he just used to suck the man off. At least he'd try to take and then they could go fuck.

Yolo sat silently ad if she didn't know that the place would be open for them. As if she didn't know that Killa was somewhere behind them with murder on his mind.

"Awe man, it's closed," Robert pouted and poked out his dick suckers. "Well, we tried. Let's hit my condo!"

"Pull around back," Yolo suggested. The driver started to protest until Robert sucked his teeth urging him on.

Wali was waiting with a side door ajar. He waved them over when they pulled around.

"You can come too," Yolo urged when the driver didn't get out.

"Who is that?" he asked continuously and got out of the car. He looked the door so at least the car would be safe. It would be the only thing because these two were in grave danger.

"My uncle," Yolo said over her shoulder as she led the way. Robert locked his eyes on her ass bouncing around under the dress and was literally led away to slaughter.

Wali nodded at Yolo and company as he held the door open for them to enter. Once they were all in he pulled it up but left it unlocked since he was expecting more company.

"Let's go see the sharks!" Yolo said leading the way. Both men followed submissive with the hopes of getting some head. Killa had the same thing on his mind as he entered the building.

"That's a Great White. That one is a White Tip, and that's a Hammer Head," she said since she had gotten the tour herself earlier in the day. The men were so into the tour that neither heard as Killa crept in. no one heard the silent slug that tore through the bodyguard's spine.

"What the fuck?" the large man grunted as he went down. Robert screamed like the bitch that he was when he turned and saw the man with the gun.

"Wait!" Yolo shouted when Killa pointed the gun at his tonsils. "Let's finish him first and maybe ol' Robert might want to make things right."

"Make what right? Yeah, I'll make it right!" he pleaded desperately.

"First things first," Yolo growled and turned her sights on the bodyguard's.

"Soups on!" Killa laughed and joined her. Together they stripped the man down to his tiny whiteys. Sharks don't like denim.

"This fucka is heavy," Wali grunted as he and Killa lifted him up and dragged him towards the shark tank. He tried to put up a fight when he saw where they were taking him.

"Help me Rob! Don't just stand there! Hel..." he screamed until a punch to the throat shut him up.

Robert didn't help but instead stood helplessly as his bodyguard got tossed in the water. The Great White frowned like 'yeah right' when he saw the person in his tank. He wondered everyday what those people outside the tank might taste like and now was about to find out.

While he debated the Hammer Head swooped in and took his foot. One of the Reef Sharks swam by and bit off an ass cheek. The blood in the water set off another frenzy as they all took bites of the man. His struggles ended when the Great White bit him in half and swam away.

"You owe me a grand!" Killa said pointing at the puddle of piss the publisher stood in. "Told you he was pussy!"

"You did," Yolo agreed. "Now let's see if he wants to make good on his debt."

"What debt? Who I owe?" he asked. He had no clue since he shitted on everybody, authors, graphic designers, editors, and pretty much everybody else that he had ever done business with.

"Go into your phone and pull up your royalty reports. The real ones!" Yolo shouted in his face. The man was so scared he dropped his phone. She kicked him in his ass when he bent to pick it up sending him sprawling on the floor.

"This is why I brought popcorn!" Wali said excitedly as he watched the show.

"Gimme some," Killa said holding out both palms to get as much as he could.

"Here it is. The real one!" Robert said pulling up his distributor sales record. Yolo took one look and kicked him in the ass again.

"You could have paid those girls and still had plenty of money fo' yo'self! Free money!" Yolo growled when she saw how much he had stolen.

"I, I, I can pay them now," he offered hopefully looking for a way out.

"You think," she said sarcastically and watched as he sent electronic payments to the authors for their hard work. Afterwards he gave them all back the publishing rights that he stole.

"Can I go now?" Robert asked as if it was a possible option. Like if a bank robber gave back the bag of money he wouldn't have to go to jail.

"Sure, just one more thing. Swim across the tank and then you can leave," Yolo offered generously. It was generous considering she was about to shoot him in his head and then have him thrown in the tank.

"I got a grand that says he don't make it halfway!" Killa said willing to wager the money he had won when Robert peed his pants.

"You're on!" he said accepting the bet.

"I got five that he don't last ten seconds!" Yolo dared. Both men looked at each other as if she were crazy. They knew that the sharks would investigate and procrastinate before they ate.

"Bet!" They both cheered at the easy money.

"And I can go when I make it across?" Robert asked for confirmation. He swam just as well as he sucked dick so he believed that he could make it across before the sharks realized what they missed.

"Yup, swear by Allah," Yolo said and didn't even cross her fingers. It wouldn't have matter if she had anyway because I covenant with God must be kept. Besides, no way was he making it across. She was sure of it.

"Ouch!" Robert yelled louder than the silent shot that sent a slug into his calf. He was yelling form the pain when Yolo kicked him into the water. Now he was in even bigger troubles.

"That's not fair!" Wali protested as he stood.

"One, two, thr... Two seconds!" Yolo laughed as the first shark took the first bite. They smelled the blood from his calf and pounced instantly.

"Guess that's the end of that chapter," Killa joked and got booed.

"I'll take it from here," Wali offered, clearing the way for them to leave. He saw the look in their eyes and didn't want to cock block with the clean-up.

Chapter 15

Yolo and Killa returned to the hotel in a seductive silence. The desire to fuck left them both speechless. All that needed to be said would be said as soon as they got into bed.

Yolo couldn't help but put her ear to the room's, that sheltered her children, door as they passed by headed for the one next to it. The three snoring kids inside couldn't be heard, so she kept on moving. Reaching their room Killa used the key card to open the door and then stepped aside like a gentleman so that she could enter. That was as gentle as he would be for the night. Once the door closed it would be straight Animal Planet.

They took opposite sides of the large bed to come out of their clothes. For Yolo that meant lifting the skinny straps off of her shoulders causing the dress to fall to the plush carpet below. She then stepped out of it and climbed onto the bed.

Killa momentarily forgot how to unbutton his shirt when he looked over and saw a naked Yolo. The slight baby pouch that was previously there had been replaced by a rock hard six pack. Her breast hung full and heavy and were topped by big brown nipples. Her neatly shaved vagina glistened with wetness before the first touch.

"Oh yeah," Killa said when he once again recalled how buttons worked. He quickly peeled off his shirt, showing that he had been working out as well. Had Yolo still had her soaked panties they could have been washed on his wash board abs. His pants and boxers came off together in one motion, leaving his hard dick pointing straight at him.

Killa then climbed onto the bed and went straight into the 69 position. Since he was on top he lowered his dick down into Yolo's throat until he heard her gag. Once she felt the tip of his dick hit the back of her throat she took over from there while his tongue went to work between her swollen lips.

The 69 position is supposed to provide mutual pleasure, however, in reality one of the parties was always cheated during the act. Yolo noticed that the activity on her enlarged clit had ceased as Killa's moans increased. But that didn't stop her from sucking, kissing, and stroking his dick.

"I'm getting ready to cum," Killa warned politely, giving her the option to pull away or keep her mouth wrapped firmly around his manhood. Yolo chose to stay and gagged once more when he exploded on her tonsils.

"Mm mmm," Yolo moaned as she swallowed all he had to offer. When his spasms finally subsided she spit his dick out of her mouth and laid her head on it like a pillow as Killa threw his tongue into overdrive.

Yolo writhed, wiggled, cursed, and came again and again filling his mouth with her sweet nectar. Killa planted soft kisses on her inner thighs while she regained her composure.

"Rodeo time," Yolo happily announced as she flipped him over and mounted him backwards. She was so wet that he slipped easily inside of her allowing her to sink slowly down until he hit her cervix.

"Mm," Killa moaned as she rocked to and fro making circles with her hips. He then took her by her small waist and held on as she rode him up and down, in and out, and side to side.

"I'm on the pill," she reminded him when she noticed his toes curl up.

"Good!" Killa grunted as he exploded all over her cervix. Good thing that she really was on the pill because he came in her twice more after that.

The killer couple laid on their backs and basked in the post climatic bliss of good sex. Killa's phone beeped and vibrated breaking the silence.

"Probably your other woman," Yolo spat jealously. She tried to make it sound playful and nonchalant, but failed.

"Nah, that's the Killa site," he replied, reaching for his phone.

"You got an app for that?" she asked, really jealous now.

"Had to! You keep taking all the good ones!" he shot back, as he pulled up the latest request and began to read it aloud.

'Dear Sir or Ma'am...' he began.

"Ma'am please and thank you," Yolo giggled and threw her leg over his. He just shook his head and continued.

'Dear Ma'am... My name is Sam Jenkins and my wife, well ex-wife, really deserves to die. This woman, Maryam, had nothing when I met her. She had less than zero, counting her just below average looks. She had no skills, no education, and was toiling away at a low paying job when I met her. I wanted to help her, to give her a better life.

She pretended to be this sweet damsel in distress and promised to be a good wife so I married her. I bought her clothes, a car, and paid off all her credit cards. I even took a second job to buy us a house when she got pregnant.

Not only did she cheat on me she also aborted my baby and then left me. Her excuse for it all was that I was never home. I blame myself for ignoring the signs and buying her feeble excuses. While I was busting my ass to pay all the damn bills she was out fucking and sucking some cop she met. I found his number, called him, and asked him to leave my wife alone. He just laughed at me and said I sounded like his wife.

One day while I was at work Maryam packed up and snuck off to be with him. Kill her! No, kill them both! Do it just like the bible says, 'stone the adulterers'.

"My pleasure!" Yolo growled hotly. The heart felt plea of the oppressed man had her heated. The site received plenty of request from woman wanting cheating husbands, baby daddies, and boyfriends murdered. However, further investigation into those request prove that those women knew that the man in question was a dog to begin with. Most had started off as side chics and just couldn't accept karma when it came back around.

"I got this one. I hate cops!" Killa cut in on her thoughts.

"Ooh, I know! Let's do it together!" Yolo suggested so they could spend more time together. "They're here in Atlanta, and we don't leave until next week."

"Let me think about it," Killa replied knowing that would get him more pussy.

"Well, let me help you think," Yolo offered as she began kissing her way down his body. Somewhere during the blow job she gave him he made up his mind.

*****

"You may as well get a costume since you're super hero," Sincerity said sarcastically. She knew him well enough to tell when he was getting dressed to kill.

"Eh," Killa replied since it wasn't like he had never thought about it. "Nothing with a cape or anything, but a mask would be cool."

Sincerity just shook her head as she continued to watch him. She had no idea that Yolo was in town, but she did notice the effects. It was a given that he got out of town pussy when he was out of town, but she was used to having his full attention at home. The goofy smile on his face made her even more suspicious of him.

"Want some back shots before you go?" she asked for different reasons. First she wanted to see if he would turn it down and two because she was horny and really wanted to get hit from the back.

Killa had been stingy with the dick since Yolo had arrived in town. The sex between the two was intensely insane and left nothing for Sincerity when he got home.

"Rain check?" he pleaded. Even he heard how feeble his words sounded. After all, who begs off of back shots?

"I see," she said, nodding her head in confirmation.

"You see nothing. I'm just caught up with a few assignments," he said, as if he had an actual job. "After Saturday you'll have my full attention again. Promise."

"Okay, Mr. Man," Sincerity agreed. Not that she believed him, but because it was what she wanted to hear.

*****

"Daddy!" the kids shouted as they raced towards their father when he entered the room. Yolo wanted to scream daddy and rushed into his arms too but instead she let the twins have him first. Once they went to sleep he would be all hers.

"Sun, Shyne," Killa greeted his son and daughter with a hug and kiss. "You track our friends down?" he said in greeting to their mother.

"I did. Everything is in place," she smiled wickedly. Christi frowned as she tried to decipher what they were talking about.

"Old testament?" Killa asked hopefully. Lord knows that the adulterers deserve it.

"Mm hm!" she nodded happily. "Let's get the show on the road."

Killa drove his second family over to Six Flags over Georgia amusement park. It was deja vue since he had just been there last week with Sincerity and their two boys, Xavier and Rico. Christi tore off running the second Killa parked at the amusement park. Yolo smiled proudly at the young girl. It was so refreshing to see a kid who was content with being a kid.

"Um... you got them right?" Killa asked hoping to be spared form the kiddie rides.

"Yeah, go on and..." was all Yolo was able to get out before Killa ran off to catch up with Christi so that they could ride the roller coasters together. They all met at the food court for lunch and then separated once more. By the time they left all parties were completely pooped.

"I'll drive," Yolo offered since Killa was yawning. By the time she pulled out of the parking lot she was the only person still awake. She let her family slobber and snore until they reached the hotel.

*****

Yolo took a cat nap while Killa and Christi took the kids to get dinner. Killa was amused to see Yolo's traits in their children. It was obvious that she had also rubbed off on the young girl as well. They had only picked up her good traits which was a good thing.

"A-yo?" Killa called out when they returned to the room. The steam pouring out from the open bathroom door answered him before Yolo did.

"In here," she called out as she cut her bath time short. She stepped out and let the plush towel literally suck the water from her skin. After moisturizing her body she slipped into a pair of jeans tight enough to show she had an ass but loose enough to kill in.

"You ready?" Killa asked when she finally emerged.

"Yup," she replied and kissed her children. The first stop was the room next door. That's where Yolo stowed tonight's party favors.

"Whatcha got?" he asked eagerly when he saw the items laid out on the bed.

"Let's see... tie down straps, nail gun, heavy duty sling shots, and of course stones," she said sounding like a sales person. "Since he's a cop and they live in the suburbs they think it's safe to leave the backdoor open."

"Thought wrong!" Killa laughed as he loaded the stuff in the bag into the trunk along with a few choice items of his own.

*****

The licentious couple had just settled in front of the fire place. Maryam poured shots of cognac as liquid foreplay. She planned on sucking the cop off real good in hopes that he wouldn't want some pussy afterwards. It was already swollen and sore from the afternoon romp she had with the next door neighbor.

"Mmph," the cop grunted when the liquor hit his throat at the same time as his dick hit the back of hers. That's exactly how Killa and Yolo found them when they eased inside the room.

"No, don't get up," Killa said and fired. The tranquilizer dart that he fired hit his victim squarely in the thigh, putting him to sleep in seconds.

"Ugh!" Yolo grunted as she hit Maryam with her own kind of tranquilizer. The brass knuckles she wore knocked out a couple of her teeth as it put her to sleep as well. Luckily for her she wouldn't need the teeth anymore after tonight.

"Nail gun, duct tape..." Killa ordered like a doctor performing an operation. Yolo quickly handed over each item like an operating room assistant. Once they had the two all prepped and ready all that was left to do was to wait for them to wake up.

"That was some blow job she was giving him, huh?" Killa suggested.

"Mm hm," Yolo replied while twisting her lips up to let him know that she saw right through him. "If you want your dick sucked just say I want my...,"

"I want my dick sucked!" he blurted before Yolo could finish her sentence. "Please."

"My pleasure," she said with a smile and knelt down before him. Pleasing him was pleasing to her so she was down for whatever he wanted.

"Mmmph?" the cop asked as much as one can ask while nailed to the wall. Killa had used the nail gun and straps to secure the couple to the wall. Both of them had been stripped completely naked just like their morals. Duct tape was used to mute the screams that the two killers were sure was to come.

"Give me a minute if you don't mind," Killa said politely as Yolo continued to work her head giving him head.

"Mmmph?" Maryam wanted to know too when she awoke in the middle of the blow job.

"I'm about to cum," Killa warned. This time Yolo pulled away and finished him up with her hand. Neither of them worried about the DNA he skeeted on the carpet since it would be destroyed in the fire.

"You're worried about the wrong thing, girlfriend," Yolo quipped when Maryam frowned about the cum on her carpet. "You'd probably be sucking your teeth if they wasn't over there!"

"You too stupid!" Killa said as he cracked up. The two killers high fived and cracked more jokes on the future decedents. That's what's called adding insult to injury. Now that the jokes were out of the way it was time for the injuries.

"What the hell! What are these? I thought we were 'posed to stone them to death!" Killa asked as he hooked the high powered sling shot around his wrist.

"Well, I couldn't find a bag of rocks, so marbles will have to do," Yolo replied and loaded one onto her sling shot.

"Bet you can't hit him in the head," Killa dared as Yolo lined up a shot to his face.

"A yard says I can!" she said lowering the device so it aimed between his legs. She pulled the marble back as far as she could to get as much velocity as possible and let it go.

"You owe me a hundred bucks!" Killa cheered as the marble tore through his nut sack. The cop let out a loud scream under the duct tape.

"Double or nothing!" she shouted and fired again. This shot split the head of his dick wide open.

"My turn!" Killa said, wanting in on the fun. He fired a high velocity marble that put a sickening dent in the cop's forehead.

The two killers were in a zone as they fired missile after missile at the couple. Each shot broke whatever it hit as they cried out in pain from behind their gags. The cops tape slipped off from blood and saliva. Yolo fired just as he opened his mouth to scream again. The fired marble passed through his mouth and entered his brain.

"He's dead!" Killa surmised when he slumped over. They then turned their full attention towards Maryam and stoned her to death as well.

Killa then took the liberty of lighting a candle near their mutilated couple. Once the gas reached the flame they would be on the express train to the upper room.

Chapter 16

"Yolo, Yolo," Christi whispered urgently as she simultaneously tapped on and entered Yolo's bedroom. "Yolo, wake up!"

"What? Huh? And why are you whispering?" Yolo grumbled and pulled the comforter over her head to stop the intrusion.

"There's a car in the driveway!" Christi whispered again. She knew it wasn't Killa because she would have heard them having sex all night. She also knew he was the only man in her life so no one else would be here.

"Here," Yolo grunted passing Christi a pistol from under her pillow.

"What am I supposed to do with that!" she asked reeling back away from the gun.

"Kill them. Aim at their foreheads and pull the trigger!"

"Kill? Me? I can't shoot nobody!" Christi whined at the notion.

"Well, here then. Take it for a spin instead," Yolo said handing her the keys. "Happy birthday sweetie!"

"It is my birthday!" The girl suddenly remembered. She had been so occupied that she had lost track of the date. "You bought me a car! I got a car! Thank you! Thank you, thank you!"

"You're wel... ugh!" Yolo replied and grunted when Christi dove on her for a hug. "You deserve it. I'm very proud of you."

She had every reason to be proud of the girl too. Christi excelled both in school and at home. The young girl couldn't name any of the top rappers, but she knew Algebra, Geometry, and Physics. She'd also taught the twins, who weren't quite four yet, how to read, write, and do basic math problems.

"Did you get a car when turned seventeen?" Christi wondered.

"No, I got a... um," Yolo paused and then decided not to tell her about Mr. Grimsley's idea of a birthday present. Not many girls could appreciate a rocket launcher anyway. "Yes, now go on out and look at it. I'm right behind you."

Christi kissed Yolo's face once more and then ran from the room. Yolo climbed out of bed and slipped into the comfortable sweats she wore around the house. By the time she reached the driveway Christi was hugging the brand new Charger. Sun was inside pretending to drive while Shyne looked at herself in all the mirrors.

"You like?" Yolo asked despite the obvious.

"Like? I love it!" Christi replied bouncing with joy.

"It comes rules. Lots of them!" Yolo warned then began to recite them, "No boys, no car full of friends, no drugs, no booze, and stay off the block! Use Lindenhurst!"

"Okay, okay, okay..." Christi agreed, since she had no interest in any of the above anyway. At seventeen the only thing a boy could offer was his penis and she had absolutely no use for one. The neighborhood girls no longer teased her but they were far from friends. Cordial nods and fake smiles were all that they got out of her. One of the four girls already had a baby, another one was pregnant by the same dude, and the other two were fucking him behind the first two's backs.

Soon Christi was driving herself to and from school. It cut into her research time, but saved her from the ratchet conversations and after school fights. She also ran errands and helped shuttle the twins around. It was all good until it went bad.

*****

"There's nothing to eat in here!" Christi whined from inside of the full refrigerator. Yolo saw right through the girl, since she had just gone grocery shopping the day before.

"Ooh, I got an idea!" Yolo said as if she didn't know what the girl was up to. "Why don't you run out and get us all something to eat?"

"I can. I mean, I don't mind going," she nodded thoughtfully. She waved Yolo off when she reached for her purse. "No, no. I got it. It's my treat.

"Okay. Well, take the twins with you because it's dark," Yolo said. It was only a little after 6pm but the short winter days ended and the nights rolled in at five.

"I'm doing my hair!" Shyne protested. She put her hand on her imaginary hip and rolled her eyes, like her mother was a punk.

"Girl, I'll...," Yolo growled and stood. Shyne quickly took off up the stairs to avoid getting popped.

"She's been watching *Bad Girls' Club*," Christi explained. Yolo just shook her head and grabbed the remote.

"Won't be no more of that," she declared as she blocked its channel. She should have blocked fifty more to prevent all sorts of negative bullshit from entering her house and children's minds.

"I'll drive," Sun offered and got laughed at. He twisted his lips and squinted at Yolo and Christi cracking up at him.

"Or not! Come on!" Christi laughed and led the way out to her car. The dilemma began as soon as they got outside.

"Hey Christi! Sup Girl! What's good Ma?" The ratchet girls called out as they walked by.

"Sup y'all," Christi replied. She couldn't help but notice the greasy paper bag each girl held. Knowing that they contained some of the best chicken wings on Long Island made the girl's mouth water. She wanted some. Only problem was that the restaurant that served them was in the strip mall on The Block.

Christi was loyal, trustworthy, and obedient, but she was also a teenage girl. The most impulsive creature in creation. She reached the turn off and debated on whether she should go right to Lindenhurst or left and into the heart of Wyandanch.

"It'll only take five minutes. I'll be in and out," she convinced herself and turned left. She passed a legion of zombies as she headed into the wrong direction towards the wrong side of town.

"In and out, without a doubt," Sun rapped. Lately he'd become addicted to rap music. Every time he learned a new vocabulary word he used it in a rap instead of a sentence.

"Your mom need to block those music channels too," Christi fussed. She certainly wouldn't miss them.

"A-yo son, peep that shit," Chicken told his partner Blade when the shiny new car pulled into the run down lot.

Most of The Blocks traffic –be it automobile, foot, or bicycle– came looking for crack, weed, or coke. The dope boys in the plaza did as much business as the legitimate stores. The stores didn't mind since it drove business to them as well. When a nigga buy weed he's also going to need cigars, lighters, and beer. Once he got high he's gonna have the munchies and need something to munch on, hence the long line at the Chinese spot's counter.

"I see it!" Blade said. He was licking his chops already at the car until Christi hopped her cute ass out of the car. They saw Sun with her and assumed that he was hers. That meant that she was fucking. "Let me go bag dis bitch."

"A buck say you don't," Chicken dared as he approached.

"Bet!" Blade called back over his shoulder before tapping Christ on hers. "What's good Ma? How you doing? What's yo name? You stay around here? By the way I'm Blade, who you be?"

"Fine," Christi replied and kept it moving. Even if she was into dudes it wouldn't be a drug dealing thug with red eyes, black lips, and grey gums from chronic weed use. What could he offer her? Nothing! All he had to share was some weed, dick, and a bleak future. No thanks, she could and would do good all by herself.

"Yoooo! That bitch played you!" Chicken laughed at his partner's rejection. "Pay up! Pay up!"

"Bitch gay," Blade explained. What other plausible reason could she have for turning him down. He took out a wad of drug money and counted out a hundred dollars. "Bout to get it right back from her car, anyway."

"Hells yeah!" his grimy partner agreed as he peeked inside the car and saw all the leather and wood.

"I better get your mom a double order?" Christi figured hoping it would make amends. It's hard to chew someone out when you're chewing on crispy wings.

Mistake number two came when Christi pulled out a roll of money from in her purse. The dope boy/robbers had discounted the designer bag as worthless since most of the chics around their way rocked fake ones. They did, however, zero in on the real cash though. Sun eyed them both suspiciously but was too young to make any sense of his sense of impending danger.

"Thank you," Christi smiled, stunning the confused clerk. The elderly Chinese lady had never heard not one customer utter those words before.

"Um..." she stammered trying to recall the proper reply. She was use to customers coming in and making fun of her and her speech. They would make orders for cat lo-mien or shr fri ri in robster sauce. "You relcome."

Sun got confirmation to his feelings of danger as soon as they stepped outside. He was first to see the two thugs wearing masks rushing towards them.

"Give up them keys, cash, and that phone!" Blade demanded from behind a cheap little pistol.

"Quit playing," Christi ordered back. She just knew he was joking since she knew who he was. He'd just introduced himself as she walked into the store so pulling his shirt up over his face didn't do much to disguise his identity.

"Ain't nobody playing bitch!" Chicken shouted. He ran up and snatched the purse from her shoulder. After digging out the cash, keys, and phone he tossed it on the concrete. "Knock off shit."

Christi was in a daze as she watched her car pull out of the parking lot. These fools just carjacked Yolo's little sister and son. Definitely two of the wrong people to fuck with.

Chapter 17

"Mommy, the police are at the door!" Shyne called out when she saw the squad car pull to a stop in front of the house.

"The who?" Yolo frowned even though she heard her clearly. That's why she pulled a pistol from the pasta container and got ready for whatever. "Earthquake!"

"Okay," Shyne replied to the code word, before rushing upstairs and climbing into the bathtub as trained.

Yolo peeked out the window and shook her head at what she saw. She knew that it was only a matter of time until the police brought her son home but she didn't think he would be this young. She tucked the gun into the small of her back and went to answer the door.

"What's going on? Where is your car? Did you have an accident? Are you okay?" Yolo asked Christi as if the cops were invisible.

"She was carjacked down on straight path,' the older of the two cops replied as she let them in.

"That's not possible because she's not allowed on straight path!" Yolo said staring at Christi who stared at the ground.

"I'll let you tow work that out," the younger cop said curtly coming close to getting shot. "Here's the police report."

Next it was the older cop's turn to almost get shot as he looked around the front room of the house. It had been completely flipped and updated but his eyes flashed in recollection. He snapped his thick fingers when it came to him.

"This is the old Brown residence!" he nodded in agreement with himself. "There used to be a hole in the wall over there. We would stick our... um... She-ra. She-ra Brown! She had the twins Larry and Harry!"

Yolo visibly flinched upon hearing Harry's name. Her mind flashed back to being dragged inside a bathroom and molested. The thought made her spit on the hardwood.

"What's wrong?" Christi asked seeing the sudden and drastic change in her.

"Nothin," Yolo blurted and turned to the cop. "Whatever happened to them?"

"Beats me. She-ra and Larry disappeared, and Larry's on death row. He's 'posed to get the needle next month." He said nodding again, this time in approval.

"Don't expect the car to be found. More than likely it's at the chop shop being parted up as we speak," the young cop announced.

"That's what insurance is for," Yolo said with a stoic shrug and let the cops out. Christi braced herself for the ass chewing to come.

"I'm sorry. I..." she said but got cut short by a wave of Yolo's hand.

"Don't worry about it. Hopefully you've learned your lesson. Now you see why I don't want you over there," she responded eerily calm.

"Yes, yes, and yes!" Christi said sincerely. She was on the verge of tears form letting her mentor down.

"Oh yeah, and the next time you get in trouble don't call the cops, call me."

"I would have, but they stole my phone," Christi whined. She then broke down crying at the loss of the pictures and videos of her and her family.

"They did? Great!" Yolo cheered and rushed over to the computer.

"It is?" Christi asked with a frown as she followed her.

"Sure is. I put a tracking device on your phone," she explained as she pulled up the software.

"You bugged my phone?" Christi asked indignantly.

"Girl, yes. Your phone, car, and your bedroom," Yolo laughed. She then smiled broadly at the flashing red light that indicated where the phone was. She jotted down the address so she could go pay the thief a visit.

"Oh okay. Oh yeah, the guy's name is Blade!" she remembered.

"You know him?"

"No. He told me his name before he robbed me," she recalled.

"How exactly does that work? 'Sup Ma, I'm Blade. Break yo self!" Yolo chuckled. "These kids today are fuckin retards!"

"Pretty much," she agreed. Being smart made it hard to find real friends and she was too smart to settle for fake ones.

"Who's Harry Brown? You got pale when the officer said the name."

"Nobody! Go to bed!" Yolo spat.

"Bed? It's not even late! Plus we didn't eat," Christi pouted.

"Well, fine. Cook something and then go to bed," Yolo shot back and rushed into her bedroom.

Yolo made sure to lock the door so no one could walk in and see her crying. Cry she did as her fucked up life ran through her mind. She couldn't help but wonder who or where she would be if not for She-ra and her sons. Who was her mother, where was her father were questions that squeezed more angst from her soul. A had a good cry from all the bad memories.

It took a while but Yolo finally ran out of tears. Now all that was left was anger. A rage that could only be quenched by blood. Lots and lots of blood. Somebody was about to get fucked up.

Yolo got out of the bed and got dressed to kill.

"Welp, y'all wanted a monster and now y'all got one!" Yolo told She-ra's memory. She accepted it and went out in the night to do what monsters do.

Everyone was in there rooms as Yolo passed through the house. The kids now had separate rooms, both were awake behind their closed doors. Sun could be heard rapping while Shyne was in the mirror as usual. Sounds of keyboard strokes could be heard coming from Christi's room.

Tonight was special so she retreated to the seldom used basement. In it was enough guns, ammo, knives, and bombs to kill the entire town. Her first choice was a sawed off shot gun along with huge hollow point slugs to go in it. A glance on the wall spread a smile on her face.

"Well, it is a chop shop," Yolo reasoned and took the two machetes off the wall. They were already sharp, but she still took them to the grinding wheel. Once she was done with them they were honed to a razor sharp edge.

*****

Yolo drove over to the train station and parked in the short term parking lot. She grabbed her gear and walked over to the long term parking where she kept a car for occasions such as this. The non-descript vehicle flashed its lights in response to its remote control. The GPS gave turn by turn direction to the address she had typed in. the flashing light on the tracking app said the phone was elsewhere but that didn't matter.

"It's a chop shop alright," Yolo confirmed from the criminal activity she witnessed. A couple of goons whipped in and hit their horn. A man came out and then opened the roll up door. A few minutes later the two goons walked out counting money.

"You Blade?" Yolo asked as she drove slowly passed the two men. The thieves checked out her car before answering. They decided that Chico wouldn't pay much for it and declined.

"Nah, he probably on The Block," one replied in passing.

She repeated what she had seen them do as she pulled up to the garage's door. Again a man came out to answer the car horn. He squinted at the vehicle, scrutinizing it to decide on whether or not he would take it. It was worth a couple of thousand in parts so he decided to offer her a few hundred for it. He stepped back in and once again rolled the door up.

Yolo was pleased to see the door roll down behind her. That meant no one was would get away. Chico did a double take when she jumped out of the car.

"Yo you're a girl!" he declared. He was certain of it since he had locked his eyes on her breast.

"Uh... yeah," she replied like 'duh'. "Who else is here?"

"Just me, Manny, Flaco, and Paco," he answered pointing to each man busy stripping someone's stolen car. Paco was finishing up on Christi's charger so he would be last.

"Excuse me," Yolo said politely as she reached back into the car. The request was polite but what she was after was rude as a mother fucker. Chico moved closer to get a good look at her good looking ass. Good thing he enjoyed the sight because it would be his last.

"Argh!" Yolo grunted as she pulled out a machete and swung it with all her might. The blade caught Chico right under his Adam's apple and passed clean through his neck. His head did a back flip as it came off and landed on the ground behind him. The headless body crumpled to the ground after it with a loud thud causing Manny to look up.

"What the fuck?" he demanded trying to make sense of what he was seeing. However, there was no time for contemplation with Yolo running at full speed towards him with a machete in each hand.

He lifted an arm to ward her off while blocking himself and got turned into a one armed bandit for his efforts. Manny let out a scream so loud that it alerted the other men in the chop shop. It was cut short along with his body. He tried to run but that required two longs and Yolo's last swing subtracted one. Manny was in so much pain that he was relieved when she killed him.

Yolo chopped into the top of Manny's head killing him instantly. The blade got stuck in his thick skull. As she stood with one foot on his head as she attempted to pull it out she heard the unmistakable sound of a round being chambered into a gun. She spun around just in time to see Flaco aiming at her face.

"Shit!" she said dropping down a split second before getting shot. She then rolled and dodged as he fired wildly at her again. He probably would've had better luck had he aimed.

"Uh oh!" Yolo laughed when she heard the gun click harmlessly, signaling that it was empty. Hearing the sound she popped back up and rushed him before he could even think about reloading. She swung both blades simultaneously, turning him into Puerto Rican confetti.

Paco had seen more than enough and decided that he would flee, but not before he ran the intruder over. He turned a stolen SUV in her direction and stomped on the gas pedal. The tires squealed and spun giving Yolo just enough time to get out of its way. The truck slammed into another vehicle leaving the driver shaken like a martini.

"Missed me bitch!" Yolo growled as she ran over to the truck. She thrust a blade into his neck so hard that it came out on the other side. She decided not to behead him and let him die a slow death instead.

Paco made a gurgling noise as he choked on his own blood. He wrapped his hands around his throat in a futile attempt to keep his blood inside of his body. It certainly couldn't do him any good in his lap. Losing the battle he stared off into space at whatever it is that dead people stared at.

Yolo looked around and smiled proudly at the carnage and said, "Now this is a chop shop!"

Chapter 18

"And in National News police report a violent night in the Long Island town of Wyandanch. The mutilated bodies of four or five men were found in a garage suspected to have been used as a chop shop. Body parts along with car parts tied to multiple recent car jackings were found strewn all over inside.

"And... just how is that funny?" Sincerity wondered as Killa giggled at the gruesome news cast. "Whoever did that must be a complete lunatic!"

"I bet," Killa agreed, knowing exactly who the lovely little lunatic in question was. He was due for a visit, but the sudden report of violence made him decide to move it up a little.

"Turn," Killa said as he positioned Sincerity on her side and lifted one of her legs towards the ceiling fan. He then slid inside of her like a baseball player sliding safely into home plate.

Knowing that Sincerity would protest his sudden departure he used his patented side winder stroke. He laid some serious pipe causing her to cum over and over again.

"I gotta go up top in the morning," he announced while she was still in throes of her orgasm.

"Okaaaay!" she sang just like he knew she would. His motto was fuck first and divulge information last. Works like a charm. "H-h-have a safe trip."

*****

The next afternoon Killa landed in Newark, New Jersey. A short train ride later he was in New York City. A cab ride later he was dropped off at one of his cars parked up in The Bronx. He crossed the Throgs Neck Bridge and headed to the Island.

"Daddy!" the twins cheered at the sight of their beloved patriarch as he walked into the house. They dropped their toys and bum-rushed him.

"Hey Sun...ugh... Shyne," he grunted when the twins jumped into his arms. He smiled at Christi who was smiling back at him.

"Hey Killa!" she cheered sounding just as happy to see him as the kids were.

"Sup lil' mama. Where's big mama?" he asked as he looked around.

"Still in bed," she replied, twisting her mouth at the oddity. Yolo rarely slept during the day, but the bad memories of her childhood had her in a funk.

"She is?" Killa frowned. He tussled with his babies for a few minutes before going up to check on their mother.

"Come in," Yolo moaned in reply to the knock at her bedroom's door. She was still feeling down but put a little extra on it when she saw her part-time man walk in the room. Part-time beat no time, for now.

"What's wrong?" he asked as he plopped down beside her on the bed. Yolo scrambled over into his arms and cuddled up under him. It felt so good to be held that she began to cry once more.

Killa knew all he could do was hold her and let her get it all out. She sobbed so hard that snot was running from her nose. It took almost a full hour for her to get it all out.

"Sooo, I saw you on the news. Chop shop, huh?" he asked.

"It is now!" she laughed and filled him in about the carjacking, police visit, Blade, and finally Harry Brown.

"So where's this Blade at now?" Killa asked ready to do what Killa does.

"Let's see..." Yolo said reaching for her laptop. She pulled up the program and spotted the flashing light that showed the location of

Christi's phone. "Looks like he went shopping on Jamaica Ave, to the weed spot, to White Castle..."

"Hope he had fun," Killa growled. Christi was family and you don't fuck with family. "Got heat?"

"Do I have heat? What's my name?" Yolo laughed and pulled a pistol from under her pillow. "Bam!"

"Nah, too neat and clean. I'm wanna make a mess of this dude!"

"Follow me," she said as she bounded out of bed. She pulled on a thick house coat, slipped her feet into some house shoes, and led the way. The door to the basement was on the outside of the house. It was a useful inconvenience that kept her bad ass kids from getting a hold of any of her weaponry.

"Oh wow!" Killa said, feeling his knees buckle at the sight of all the guns, knives, and other killing accessories.

"I know right!" Yolo giggled. She made several suggestions for his use, but in the end he found what he was looking for.

"Here we go! This will make a real nice mess," he said picking up a street sweeper along with some hollow point slugs.

"Excellent choice sir," Yolo said with a little curtsey.

*****

It was too cold for Daisy Dukes so Yolo squeezed into a skintight pair of jeans instead. A short leather jacket and a pair of matching Tims completed her outfit. She was dressed as bait.

"I'd fuck you!" Killa nodded by way of compliment.

"You say the sweetest stuff," Yolo spat sarcastically. "Now let's hurry up and kill these dudes, so we can come back and fuck!"

Killa drove into the heart of town and dropped Yolo off a block before The Block. Cars honked at her switching her ass like a worm wiggles on a hook. Bait.

"There go one!" Chicken announced when Yolo reached The Block. He got a real kick out of seeing his partner in crime get shot down by the ladies. He was really about to get shot down tonight.

"A-yo! Yo ma! Over here!' Blade yelled waving his arms to get her attention.

Yolo scrunched her face up scrutinizing the man. He kinda fit the description Christi had given her, but she wasn't absolutely sure. This is until he told on himself that is.

"I'm Blade ma, who you?" he asked and assumed a B-boy stance.

"Yolo," Yolo replied with a genuine smile. She had her man and his side kick. "Who's your friend?"

"That's my nigga, Chicken. We call him that cuz he got little skinny legs," Blade explained, as if she cared.

"Let's go somewhere and chill. Where's your car?" she asked, as she dipped her hip. Again, like a worm on a hook; bait. "Let's go to the park!"

"Let's bounce!" Blade said leading the way to his hooptie. Chicken was so happy to be included that he could hardly contain himself.

"We gon' run a train on her!" he whispered loudly. Yolo fought the urge to pull the pistol form the small of her back and shoot them both in the back of their heads while they rode to the park.

"Over there," Yolo directed, pointing to the back of the lot. As soon as they parked she pulled. "Out! Both of you, out now!"

No one likes to argue with a pistol in their face so the men complied. Killa whipped up to a screeching halt as soon as their feet hit the ground.

"Which one is Blade?" Killa demanded, moving his shot gun back and forth in front of their faces like a news reporter does a microphone.

"Him!" They both shouted, pointing at one another. Yolo settled it by nodding towards the real Blade. Killa paused to come up with a cute punch line, but drew a blank.

"Oh well," he shrugged and gave the trigger a squeeze. The heavy slug nearly took the thug's head off.

"Heeeeelp!" Chicken screamed and took off running.

"I know that's right!" Yolo laughed. "Run, Forrest, Run!"

He didn't make it too far before Killa fired the street sweeper twice more. The first round opened a hole in his back so big the second one passed straight through. Chicken kept right on running. Faster even, since the large hole made him more aerodynamic.

"You see this shit?" Killa chuckled. He raised the gun higher and fired once more. The slug knocked his fitted cap off with half of his head still inside of it. Yolo raised her eyebrows waiting for a joke but none came.

"I got nothing," he shrugged and turned back to the car. "Let's go!"

Killa and Yolo could already hear sirens approaching as the sped out of the park with their lights out. A few back streets and quick turns later he flipped them on and slowed down.

"I am so fucking horny!" Yolo shouted. She then reached over and fumbled to pull his dick out. The car swerved when he felt her hot mouth engulf him. She felt him grow long and hard inside of her mouth. He tried to focus all his energy on making it to the house as she sucked him off.

"Fuck this!" Killa decided and pulled to an abrupt stop. The couple quickly scrambled to get their pants off in the front seat. Yolo got one leg out before spreading her legs wide.

Killa pulled his pants down to his knees and rolled over and inside of her. Yolo planted both of her feet up on the roof of the car so he could get in deep and get it all. She offered it all and he took it all too using long hard strokes.

"God I love you!" Yolo shouted. It came straight form the heart so her brain had no chance to stop it. "It, I love it!"

"Mm him," Killa agreed with her excuse and kept right on giving her the business. A young couple stopped to watch as they were passing by. It was all good until Killa's mind began to wander.

He wanted to love her back. As a matter of fact, he was almost sure that he did. She did give him Sun and Shyne after all, but she had also taken away his first born son. He had forgiven her because he hoped for God's forgiveness for his own transgressions, but he just couldn't forget.

"What! What's wrong?" Yolo asked urgently as she felt him going soft inside of her. "You need me to do something? Anything?"

Nothing. I'm cool," he replied as he rolled back into his own seat. They fixed their clothes and rode the rest of the way back to the house in complete silence. She halfway expected him to drop her off and keep it moving, but to her relief and delight he followed her inside.

"We made a fort, Daddy!" Sun proudly proclaimed when they came in.

"I see," he said inspecting it. "Nice!"

"You gotta spend the night in it with us," his fussy little diva demanded.

"Okay," he eagerly agreed. He and Yolo said nothing, but shared a glance that spoke volumes. She was satisfied just to have him under her roof so she went on to bed.

"So you wanna be an architect when you grow up?" Killa asked his son, who was making adjustments to his structure of blankets and pillows.

"Nope, I'm going to be a rapper!" he shot back confidently.

"Uh oh. I guess you gonna wear skirts and twerk," Killa teased.

"Nuh uh! I'm a New York rapper! We don't twerk!"

"True," Killa nodded and turned to his daughter. "I guess you're going to be his backup singer?"

"No, security!" the little girl shot back like she meant it. She looked so much like her mama that he didn't doubt it.

Chapter 19

"Are you sure you don't want me to come?" Christi asked once more as she watched Yolo pack a bag. Her stoic demeanor was a stark contrast to her usual upbeat personality which concerned Christi.

"Yes, for the tenth time!" Yolo shot back not meaning it as harshly as it came out. She loved Christi and knew that the young girl loved her back. They were the only family that either of them.

"Well, you sure you want to take the kids? You can let them stay home with me," she offered.

"Nah, they need to see this," Yolo replied after a moment of contemplation. Her and Christi loaded the twins along with their bags into the car and then exchanged hugs. "No wild parties while I'm gone!"

"Aww man!" Christi fussed as if Yolo had ruined her plans. In truth her only plans involved her getting ready to go off to college.

It was a long ride to the upstate prison where the execution was being held. The children filled the time playing games, watching movies, and answering quizzes. Yolo was amused as she listened to their conversation. The four year olds sounded like adults talking about kiddie stuff with their large vocabularies. Their conversation was also splashed with Spanish and Arabic as well thanks to Christi.

"I wanna talk to my daddy!" Shyne suddenly demanded. Yolo hit speed dial and passed her phone back to her daughter.

Shyne's end of the conversation was all smiles and giggles. Daddy was a rock star in her eyes and she was delighted to have him for her dad, even if she did have to share him. She sucked her teeth and rolled her eyes when Killa finally asked to speak to Sun.

Yolo shook her head as she listened to her son spit his latest verse to his father. She looked for a rest stop so that she could pull over and wash his little mouth out with soap. Luckily for him the next one wasn't for miles.

"Daddy wanna talk to you," Sun said passing the phone forward.

"Hello," Yolo barely got pass the huge smile on her face. It had been a month since he was last in town and she missed him desperately.

"Sup yo. Where you headed? The kids said you been driving for a hundred years already," he said stifling a smile at their exaggeration.

"Sure seems like it. I'm headed upstate to watch Harry take his last breath," she said causing the line to go quiet. She wanted to murder the man herself but had to settle for watching the state kill him instead.

"I feel you," Killa admitted after thinking about it. He knew the role Harry played in Yolo's whole life story, so he understood. Knowing that she was in a vulnerable place he kept her company for the rest of the ride.

They took a break once she reached the hotel. Yolo fed and bathed their kids and put them to bed. After a taking a relaxing shower she got her boo back on the line.

"Man I wish you were here," Yolo sighed as her hand slipped down into her panties.

"Oh yeah. Why is that?" Killa asked dropping his voice an octave to make it sound even sexier. He knew full well where she was going and planned on helping her get there.

"So you could do this for me," she moaned as she made circles on her swollen clit. She was so wet that her pussy squished loudly enough for him to hear it over the phone. "It's talking to you, Daddy."

"Mm, I hear. Just pretend that your finger is my tongue," he growled. Yolo came instantly. His work was done. "Night, night."

"G-g-g-go-good n-n-night," Yolo stuttered, rolled over, and went to sleep.

"Who you talking to?" Sincerity demanded with her 'what you talkin' about Willis' scowl.

"No one," he lied truthfully since he was no longer on the phone.

"Mm hm," she hummed skeptically when she saw the bulge in his pants. She came closer and gave his erection a squeeze.

Killa let out a sigh of relief when she unzipped his pants and set his dick free. She held it tightly in her hand and gave it a few strokes. Sincerity didn't have on any panties under her t-shirt, so it made it easy to sit on it. She wriggled the swollen head inside and sank down.

"Shit!" Killa cursed at the sights, sounds, and feel of his woman riding him. Her vagina fit his dick like a glove, just like Yolo's did. Two hands two gloves, and one very lucky man.

*****

"Where we going, Mommy?" Shyne fussed and frowned as Yolo put lotion on her face.

"To watch the bad man go bye-bye," she explained which explained nothing to the child. Once she finished her she moved on to her brother, like an assembly line. Teeth and heads were brushed, faces were washed, and lotions applied now it was time to go.

Yolo made sure she arrived at the prison early to insure that she got to view the execution. Although she was early she still barely made it. When she got there the room was already filled with family, reporters, and morbidly curious spectators. She recognized Jane's parents in the front row. Little did they know their child's real killer sat in the row two seats behind them. Still, the guest of honor Harry Brown was the cause.

"Mommy! Watch my hair!" Shyne fussed when Yolo instinctively put her arm around her and Sun.

A door opened and the condemned man shuffled inside wearing shackles on both his wrists and ankles. Yolo held her breath in fear, before realizing that he was no longer scary at all. Harry looked nothing like she remembered. He looked nothing like a monster at all. A dense beard now covered his face and a crisp white kufi covered his head. Like many men before him, he made a connection with his maker while in prison. Sometimes it takes the worst to happen to bring out the best. Harry had the calm demeanor of someone who had accepted his fate and was content with it. Actually he was eager to meet his Lord.

It wasn't until he was strapped onto the gurney that he finally turn his head and look around the spectator's room. He knew where the family was sitting and turned directly towards them.

"I'm sorry," he offered. They turned or lowered their heads in reply. Apology not accepted.

Harry scanned the room to take in the sights before he left here for the hereafter. His eyes passed right over Yolo before they shot back. He squinted trying to place the face. A small smile appeared on the corner of his mouth when it came to him. Again he said, "I'm sorry."

Yolo, like Killa knew that she needed, wanted, and hoped for God's forgiveness so she forgave Harry. With a nod of acceptance she was finally able to breathe again. Although she forgave him the state didn't.

"Any last words?" the warden asked as the death doctor installed an I.V into his muscular arm.

"La illaha illAllah!" he said loud and proud. The executioner hit the switch that started the deadly cocktail flowing to make sure they were his last words.

"What's that mean?" Shyne asked her mother.

"Only one God," Sun answered for her.

"Yeah, there's only one God," Yolo muttered as she watched Harry drift off to an eternal sleep. The deepest of all sleeps.

Chapter 20

"I don't know Yolo. I think I should just stay in New York. Just go to S.U.N.Y," Christi said trying to punk out once again.

"I hear you but it's going to be hard moving around campus with my foot in your ass," Yolo offered in reply.

That had been the debate all summer as Christi tried to figure a way to stay with her beloved family. She had accepted a full scholarship to U.C.L.A but now that it was time to go she was trying to stay.

Yolo wouldn't hear of it. As much as she loved her she wanted her to have the full college experience. The girl was smart, focused, and in no danger of losing her damn mind once she got out on her own.

Her new car had already been shipped to her new apartment and she was all set to go. Now Yolo just had to get her on the plane, which was turning out to be easier said than done; especially when it came to leaving the twins.

"And just where do you think you're going young lady?" Yolo asked when Shyne came down the stairs with her little bag packed.

"To college!" she said rolling her eyes and shaking her head.

"How about we start with Kindergarten first," Yolo suggested.

"Don't worry, Shyne, I'll call every day!" Christi assured her and picked her up.

"Promise?" the little girl pleaded and squeezed.

"I promise!" came Christi's reply as she carried her little sister out to the car. The ride to the airport was jovial until they got there. Reality of separation really hit home once they reached the terminal. The moment of truth came when the plane began to board. Christi said her good byes to her siblings and then Yolo.

"I love you," she her as they embraced. It's said that what's understood doesn't need to be explained, but that's some bullshit! If you love someone you should tell them. Every chance you get.

"I love you too," Yolo replied. There wasn't a dry eye in the place when Christi boarded the plane. A whole lot of drama considering she would be back for Thanksgiving, Christmas, Spring and Summer breaks.

The family waved at the plane as it lifted off for its six hour flight to California. Yolo then led her children to over to the next terminal and took a seat.

"Why we staying here!" Shyne demanded with a hand on her imaginary hop. Yolo looked around for any child protection workers before she popped her.

"Cuz I said so," Yolo growled the typical parental answer. The real answer came an hour later when Killa's plane landed.

"Daddy!" the twins shouted as the rushed their father.

"That's right, you know I wouldn't miss your first day of school!"

*****

It's hard enough getting two children dressed but her rubbery legs from having multiple orgasms all night made the task that much more difficult. Killa had fucked her the previous night like the world depended upon it. Luckily for her he pitched in and helped her this morning by fixing breakfast and filling lunch boxes.

Their nostalgic father had bought them throwback metal lunch boxes for the school. They had no idea who Wonder Woman and Aqua Man were but loved them none the less since they came from their father. Once they were dressed and fed the proud parents walked them to the bus stop.

They were the only parents in sight. Most of the other kid's partner were at home sleeping soundly. They were turned out form turning up most likely. Yolo made a big fuss when the kids boarded the school bus. She waved, blew kisses, and cried as they pulled away.

"Come on! Let's follow them!" Yolo shouted and rushed back to the house. Killa had to run to keep up with her. She hopped in her car and followed the bus to the school. Once her children were safely inside she went back home.

Once Killa and Yolo were back at home they dove back into her bed and fell right to sleep. They were both worn out from a long night of long stroking. As soon as they woke up, a few hours later, they were back at it again.

Just as Killa got settled inside of Yolo her phone began to ring. She screwed her face up like 'what the fuck' and continued to plant kisses on Killa's face and neck. He had just slid his tongue into her mouth when her answering machine came on.

"Good afternoon Miss Jackson. This is Principal Hunter at Wyandanch Elementary and I was calling to inform you that there's been a slight incident at the school..."

"Get up!" Yolo shouted and shoved Killa out and off of her. She jumped up and scrambled for her phone. "Hello, hello! What happened? Are my babies okay?"

"Yes, they're fine. They got into a fight and..."

"I'm on my way!" she said as she leapt form the bed. She took off out the room with Killa on her heels calling her back. "What! I need to get my babies! They need me!"

"I know, but they also need you to put some clothes on too," he said bringing attention to her nakedness. Yolo twisted her lips up and marched back up the stairs. They dressed quickly before heading out to the car.

"I'd better drive," Killa decided. He knew Yolo would speed which could lead to them getting pulled over which could lead to a cop getting shot in the face. Yeah, it was best that he drive.

Yolo leapt form the car before Killa could come to a complete stop. She sprinted into the school while he calmly walked in behind her. They entered the principal's outer office where the twin's sat on a bench.

"What happened?" Yolo demanded as she burst in staring everyone down.

"We got beat up!" Shyne cheered as if she'd had a good time. She sported a busted lip and a pair of knots on her head that looked like horns. Yolo turned to Sun, who was pretty much unscathed.

"You too?" she asked.

"He ran," Shyne said which explained his lack of injury.

"Ran? You little..." Yolo growled and went after him. Luckily his father stopped her before she could get her hands on him.

"Just like a rapper," Killa said shaking his head.

"Excuse me, Mr. and Mrs. Jackson?" Miss Hunter asked looking directly at Killa. She knew that children's last name was Forrest but wanted to hear the magic words.

"We're not married," Killa explained. His eyes scanned her fine frame in the tight mid-thigh skirt and jacket. He got an eyeful when she turned around to lead the parents into her office.

"What happened?" Yolo demanded. She was already hot but the woman's flirting had her breathing fire.

"Kid's stuff, nothing to be concerned with. Kids fight you know," she said smiling at Killa as if Yolo were invisible. "Your daughter actually started the fight. Some boys were teasing your son about his lunch box, and your daughter jumped on them."

"And he ran," Killa said shaking his head once more. "Well, we'll take them home and try again tomorrow."

"That's fine," Miss Hunter said, batting her eyes at him. Killa heard Yolo growl and couldn't help but to laugh.

"Go 'head babe. I need to ask Miss Thing, eh, I mean Miss Hunter a quick question," Yolo said quite pleasantly.

"Sure," Killa said. He took a final look at the pretty principal just in case it was the last time she looked like that.

"How can I help you?" Miss Hunter asked, as if speaking to a child.

"Oh, I was just wondering if I was going to have to fuck you up about my man? Not my baby daddy, my man!" she stressed. It was hard enough sharing space and time with Sincerity so she'd be damned if there'd be a third wheel.

"Absolutely not!" the woman insisted.

*****

"Take me to Home Depot!" Yolo demanded when she joined her family in the car.

"For what?" Killa asked frowning up. What could she possibly want to build at a time like this he wondered.

"So I can get one of those big ass pots, like witches use."

"A cauldron?" he asked to see if that's what she meant.

"Yeah! A cauldron so I can cook those fucking kids who put their hands on my babies and feed them to their dead beat ass parents before I kill them and..."

"Eh em," Killa cleared his throat and motioned to the backseat with his eyes. Yolo turned to see her children eyes wide with shock from her violent outburst.

"Fix it!" she told their father, knowing that he would.

Fixing it was exactly why he bypassed Yolo's street and headed to the Long Island Expressway. A couple of bridges later Sun read the sign that said 'Welcome to The Bronx'.

Chapter 21

"Where are we?" Shyne demanded when they pulled into the University Homes Projects. She crinkled her little nose up like the place stunk. It did but she hadn't smelled it yet.

"This is where your daddy grew up!" Yolo said proudly. She felt a sense of connection to the grimy projects that raised her boo.

"It is?" Sun said staring around in utter fascination. He took in the colorful people amongst the bleak grey backdrop. He saw dope boys and ratchet girls along with working men and women.

"Why are we here?" Yolo finally asked, as Killa lead his second family through the courtyard.

"To see him," he replied pointing upwards. There was Karate Joe practicing moves on the rooftop.

"Good idea!" Yolo smiled and walked faster.

"Eww!" Shyne squealed when they stepped inside a pissy elevator.

"Smells like you," Sun giggled and cracked up.

"I know you ain't talking Carl Lewis," Yolo quipped. The revelry was cut short once they reached the top floor. Killa lead them up a flight of steps onto the roof.

"Killa-son," Karate Joe greeted with a bow.

"Sup yo," he shot back minus the bow. Killa bowed to no man. "This is Miss Jackson, Sun, and Shyne."

Yolo cut her eyes at him upon hearing the genealogically insufficient greeting. She saved her protest for later since they were on a bigger mission. The kids giggled and bowed at the karate man in his karate clothes and his karate shoes.

"They need to learn how to fight," Yolo interjected impatiently. "Especially him!"

"All children should know how to fight. Let's see what they know," Karate Joe announced and took a swing at Shyne.

"Stop it!" the girl spat as she blocked the blow. The teacher nodded in approval and tried her brother. Sun stood there and got popped upside his head. He began to cry and tried to take cover behind his mother.

"Un uh!" Yolo said and pushed him away from her. "How long will it take to teach them?"

"Letha or decaff?" Karate Joe asked.

"Lethal!" Both lethal parents replied simultaneously as one, as parents should.

"Hmm..." the old man hummed as he sized them up. "Her, a year. Two at the most. Him about ten years."

"Mm mm mph," Yolo said shaking her head at her goofy son. "Well, let's get started."

Karate Joe started with the basics and taught the kids how to block. Months would be spat on defense before they threw a single punch or kick.

"So," Yolo began once she and Killa were off to the side. "Who exactly is he?"

"Him? Karate Joe!" he replied as if it were a silly question and then braced himself for the rest.

"I know that. Who is Karate Joe?" she asked through clenched teeth.

"The best karate teacher in New York, who just happens to be Sincerity's father. But this ain't about her, you, or me. It's about Sun and Shyne!" Killa said all in one exasperated breath.

"Oh, okay," Yolo said. What else could she say?

*****

Training went far better than anyone expected. Yolo trained along with her kids each weekend and then practiced with them all week. By the time they returned the following weekend they had mastered the last lesson.

The kids still got their asses kicked once a week, but they both fought back. Yolo refused to run to their rescue again so they had to fight. Every loss made them go harder to learn how to win. By the end of the school year they were ready. Not yet lethal but there would be no more ass kickings.

"Uh oh, here comes Dumb and Blind!" a hefty first grader name Bo-Bo announced when the twins entered the lunch room. The large boy hated them for wearing clean clothes and having all kinds of good foods in their lunch boxes. He was the leader by default since he had beaten everyone else up.

"Dumb and Blind! Dumb and Blind!" the chant erupted as usual. Shyne smiled wickedly at her brother since she knew what was coming. The twins vowed not to be touched or teased ever again and they meant it.

"Wait for it... wait... for it," Shyne said as Bo-Bo approached. He liked to taunt them by sticking his face inches form theirs and blowing his government cheese breath in their face. Both tightened the grip on their metal lunch boxes. Metal lunch boxes would be forever banned after today thanks to Sun and Shyne.

Bo-Bo stuck his face out just as Sun swung an Aqua Man uppercut. Now in Sun's defense those front teeth were about to come out anyway the lunch box just helped speed up the process. Shyne swung a Wonder Woman hook that left the bully shook. He did what all bullies do when confronted, he turned and ran.

"Un uh," Sun said and clipped him before he could get away. Down he went and the twins stomped and kicked him like he was on fire.

"Do something!" a teacher shouted to the school's security guard.

"I am!" the man laughed and kept watching. Why not? He'd had to watch the first grader bully kids for the last three years. He was going to enjoy the show like everyone else. Once the twins finished beating him to a pulp he then escorted them to the principal's office.

"Kid's stuff, nothing to be concerned with. Kids fight you know," Yolo said sarcastically, throwing Miss Hunter's words back at her when she called to report the beating. She then hung up and waited for the school bus to drop them back off at home. She had a huge surprise waiting for them.

Yolo breathed a sigh of relief when she heard the school bus come to a hissing stop up the street. She never could relax until her babies where safely inside the house.

"Hello, Mommy... Christi!" they twins cheered and rushed to their big sister. The semester had ended and she was home for the summer.

"Hey guys!" Christi yelled back as they rushed over to embrace her. It wasn't until they pulled away that she saw the blood on their clothing. "Is that blood?"

"It ain't ours!" Sun said proudly.

"We had to put the smack down," Shyne explained. "Oh Mommy, we need new lunch box."

"I bet you do," Yolo laughed to herself. "Now go change so we can all go to Chuck E Cheese!"

*****

The family settled into a booth in the restaurant. Not for long though because when Christi returned with tokens the kids took off to play games.

"Sooooo... how was your first year of college?" Yolo asked once she had Christi alone.

"Great! I aced all my classes! Mid-terms, finals, everything! I have a perfect 4.0 grade point average! I made the Dean's list, who's who among freshman...," Christi replied enthusiastically. She would've went on for an hour about her accomplishments if Yolo hadn't stopped her. She did because that wasn't what she was asking about.

"Yeah, yeah but are fucking?" Yolo wanted to know. She got her answer when the girl turned beet red from embarrassment.

"What! Me? No!" she said clutching invisible pearls.

"So, no boyfriend?" Yolo dared.

"Nope," Christi said shaking her head.

"Girlfriend?"

"No! Eww!" she said turning an even darker shade of red. She was proud to have made it through with her morals and hymen intact while so many girls lost theirs.

"I met a lot of cute guys but they all want one thing!"

"Your lunch card?" Yolo quipped.

"Sex crazy! All of them. Nice guys, bad boys, nerds, athletes, stoners, professors, janitors, lunch...,"

"Wait! Back up. Did you say professors?" she asked feeling a homicide coming. She had been so busy with the twins she had no time for 1-800-Killa. Her baby daddy was having all the fun.

"Yup. Male and females! They sleep with students for grades, but I ain't with that. First of all, I can get good grades on my own and secondly you raised me better than that!"

"I did!" Yolo replied proudly. She was proud of Christi as well as herself. Killa was the only man she had ever slept with and she planned to keep it like that. "Isn't that um... what's her name? From The Block."

"Who?" Christi asked scanning the restaurant. It took her a second to realize the woman with child with a child was one of the girls who use to tease her. She felt no satisfaction seeing the girl was struggling. She was feeding her child a grilled government cheese sandwich before sending him to play on the jungle gym. That made the foray absolutely free which was great since she was absolutely broke. "I should go say hello."

"You should," Yolo agreed. She watched as Christi approached then turned to watch her kids. After Christi gave her all the cash from in her purse she returned with a scowl.

"Men!" she huffed, like the word had left a bad taste in her mouth. She went on to relay what the girl told her about the dead beat dude who had fathered her kids.

"Well, what do expect when you mess with little dope boys?" Yolo shrugged.

"Actually, her kid's father is a grown man with a job, house, and everything. He just refused to take care of his kids. He says it's not his problem. The kids would be better off if he was dead. At least she would get S.S.I for them," Christi explained.

"Facts," Yolo nodded and smiled. She just had a reason to kill. You can't just turn that shit off you know.

Chapter 22

"Sup Pops!" Sincerity said smiling into her phone.

"Daughter," Karate Joe greeted with a bow as he began a video chat session with his beloved child. Once a week they chatted it up so he could stay in contact with her and his grandsons.

Yolo had reached the roof but ducked back inside before she could be seen. Killa's words rushed into her head, this is about the kids.

"My students have arrived," Karate Joe announced and gave a parting bow.

"Okay Daddy," Sincerity laughed. She thought it was cute him training anyone who came by and calling them students. "Same time next week."

"Greetings," Yolo called out as she came back through the door after the termination of the call. Karate Joe bowed to Sun first, then Yolo, and finally Shyne.

"Have you been practicing?" he asked peering at Yolo.

"We all have!" she assured him.

"Good. Today, you learn the ledge," he announced and started walking over to the roof's edge.

"I'm not letting my babies play on the edge of no damn roof!" Yolo shrieked. She had to snatch Sun by the collar to prevent him from following him.

"Not them. You!" the teacher demanded. He had no idea she had been trained to fight by the Black Mob's in-house killer Mr. Grimsly. All he knew was that she had mastered every move he taught the children second hand.

"Oh, okay!" Yolo cheered and rushed over. She stepped up onto the ledge and turned towards her teacher. They bowed and eased into karate stances.

The sparring session started off light so she could get her balance. Then Karate Joe threw off speed strikes that she easily swatted away like gnats.

"Hmp!" he huffed and increased the speed. She blocked 98% of the strikes only twice. She had a busted lip and a lump on her head to show for it. Then, to everyone's surprise she caught him with a blow of her own.

"Yay Mommy!" Shyne cheered and clapped like the cheerleader she would never be able to be. Picture Killa allowing his only daughter to dance, turn flips, and do flips in a little bitty skirt and panties in front of men. He was too old school for that.

Karate Joe frowned at the unfamiliar feeling of being hit. It had been a lifetime ago since the last time anyone got passed his defenses. Not even his daughter/best student had ever managed that feat. He touched his finger to his lip and looked at the blood. Karate Joe began to smile and bowed.

"You now know the ledge."

*****

"Daddy's here!" Sun shouted, stating the obvious when they got home from training.

"Duh," Shyne teased since everyone could see his car parked in the driveway. That led to a karate chop, followed by a kick, and then the twins went at it again.

Yolo turned a blind eye to the daily sparring sessions even though she knew someone was going to get hurt. To her it was like lion cubs practicing hunting on each other. She walked in the house and found Killa being pummeled by Christi and her college stories.

"Hey there," he said coolly though his eyes screamed 'save me!'

"Hey mister man," Yolo sang like a school girl. There was no chill whenever he was around. She was hopelessly in love with the man and couldn't hide it if she tried. "I hope you plan to grill?"

"You want me to?" he asked licking his lips like he was LL Cool Killa.

"Mm hm! You know I like it hot off the fire," Yolo grunted.

"Oh boy!" Christi laughed. "Guess I better take the karate kids to the park."

"No need, I'll let them help me cook," Killa said. He rustled up his kids and took them into the backyard to light the grill.

Yolo joined them a few minutes later with hamburger patties and hotdogs ready to go on the grill. Sun was trying to mimic his dad's every move while Shyne stared at the flames.

"Does she always do that?" Killa asked watching his daughter watching the fire. It was like Shyne was in a trance as she watched the dancing flames.

"Yes! That child scares me," Yolo admitted. She had an obsession with fire.

"She scares you!" Killa exclaimed then got a peek at what Yolo had changed into. "What are you wearing?"

"Bait," she giggled and jiggled under the tank top with no bra. A tiny pair of shorts was hiked up into her crutch letting her ass cheeks hang out the back.

Killa shrugged and turned back to the grill as she went to her car. He was sure she would fill him in on whatever she had going on. Yolo drove a block away from her victim and walked around the block.

Smoothe was out front washing his pussy mobile when Yolo turned on the block. He was downwind and lifted his head and sniffed the air. He could actually smell new pussy and whipped his head from side to side to spot it.

"Mm, mm, mph!" He frowned and zeroed in on Yolo's crotch from half a block away. It seemed to get fatter and fatter with each step.

"Fuckin' clown," she mumbled to herself as she approached. He was too damn old to still be so fascinated by sex. There's nothing worse than a grown ass man behaving like a child.

"Sup lil mama? I'm Smooooove," he said stretching his hand out as he stretched out his name.

"Smoove?" Yolo snapped then caught herself, "hey Smoove, nice truck."

"Sure is," he beamed proudly. The decked out SUV was almost ten years old but the fresh paint job and rims made it look new. New enough to trick gullible young girls out some ass. He spent all his money on the truck, so none of his kids got a dime of child support.

"Can we go for a ride?" she giggled.

"As long as you can ride," Smoove said grabbing his crotch so there wouldn't be any misunderstanding. Make no mistake he was trying to fuck something.

"My mom goes to work at eleven," she said setting the trap.

"Want me to come pick you up?"

"Nah, I'll come back through," Yolo said and departed. She put a little extra swing in her hips and felt his eyes palming her ass until she turned the corner.

*****

"You sir, have done it again!" Yolo proclaimed once she could speak again.

"Thank you, thank you," Killa said with his face practically dripping from pussy juice. He kissed his way up from her vagina and stuck his tongue in her mouth.

"Wait!" she protested when he attempted to push inside of her. The clock was close to eleven and she had a date. "I gotta go help some kids get their S.S.I started."

"At this time of night? And what I'm 'posed to do with this?" Killa asked holding his erection in his hand.

"Keep it hard, I'll be right back," she said getting out of the bed. Killa watched her sip into a pair of shorts and t-shirt. She grabbed her D.C 2000 from closet and hit the door.

Smoove was waiting impatiently when Yolo arrived. He was going to let her keep the roach of the blunt after he fucked her but she fucked that up.

"Sorry, I'm late," she said sounding sincere. "I was feeding my baby."

"Mm hm," Smoove hummed sounding salty. He liked young bitches but obviously had a little bitch in him as well.

"I'll make it up," she offered soothingly as they pulled away.

"I want my dick sucked real good!" he demanded. "What is that?"

"This is the D.C 2000. It gives the greatest head!" she dared.

"It does?" he frowned at the wire contraption. Men love regular head so great head was too much to pass up. He pulled to a hasty stop and pulled out his dick.

"Okay, here we go," Yolo said putting the ring over his head. He actually leaned over to help her out.

"What do I do now?" he asked since he didn't feel anything.

"Die," she replied and hit the switch. His head popped off and fell into his lap. His dick ended up in his own mouth when it dropped. It wasn't quite what he had in mind but at least he got his dick sucked.

So did Killa. Yolo rushed home and returned the favor of good head. The blowjob was the prelude to another sleepless night filled with steamy sex. Lunatics have the best pussy.

Chapter 23

Time flies whether you're having fun or not. Luckily for Yolo she was having fun watching her children grow bigger, stronger, healthier, smarter, more beautiful, and more dangerous by the day.

By age nine their training with Karate Joe was complete. They were both certified black belts in karate. Killa had been taking them to a private gun range for the last year and they were crack shots with a variety of weapons.

Sun studied dictionaries and the thesaurus every day in his quest to be a rapper. His parents humored him by buying him a computer program that made beats and let him record his raps.

Shyne was a super model in training with a fetish for fire. Her first real ass whipping, from Yolo, came when she set the woods on fire. Now her mother shook her down daily for match books and lighters.

Killa was still juggling two families with expertise. He kept a rotation that should have kept everyone satisfied but didn't. Yolo still longed to be the only one in his life, and pressed the issue on his next visit.

"I gotta go down and see my grandmother," Killa announced after laying some pipe. He knew from experience that she was easier to deal with after he dicked her down real good. Not today though.

"Are you taking the twins? Don't you think it's time that they meet their great grandmother? What are you ashamed of them? Are your other sons better than them? Oh, what cuz I'm your side chic they your side kids? They 'bout to turn ten years old and..."

"You're right," Killa admitted. What more could be said. She was right. He had kept them separated to avoid having to deal with Sincerity on it.

"I know I'm right! That's why... wait, you said I'm right?" Yolo said feeling silly. "So, make it right!"

"I will. As soon as I get back things will change. Promise."

"And I can have you to myself? We, can have you?" she challenged.

"Yolo, you know the situation. If it wasn't for her, we would have that," he said. This is one of those times where he should've chosen his words more carefully.

"I understand," Yolo sighed in relief. What she heard was, kill Sincerity and we can get married.

*****

"Spit something for me," Killa told his son once they were all inside the car. It was a good ride to the airport and he didn't want to deal with Yolo the whole time. Little did he know she was done with the conversation. She heard all she needed to hear last night. That's why there was a machete in the trunk.

"Okay, Daddy!" Sun eagerly agreed. "He turned to his sister and said, "Hit it!"

Shyne put her hands to her mouth and started beat boxing. Sun nodded to the beat and then went in. Yolo scrunched her face up like 'damn' as her son rapped better than most of the wack ass rappers on the radio. He spit non-stop from the driveway until they reached the airport. Both children were out of breath when she pulled into short term parking lot.

"Can we go with you?" Shyne pleaded like only a four year old can when they reached the gate. She'd done it just like her mommy had told her to.

"Next time. When I get back I'm gonna take you two to meet your great grandma," he replied, cutting a knowing side eye at Yolo. She was content now because Killa does what Killa says. He hugged and kissed his twins before turning to their mother.

"That'll be done when you get back," she announced triumphantly.

"Um... okay," he agreed since he had no idea what she was talking about. They shared a hug and peck on the lips before he departed.

"Come on guys. We're going to the Museum of Natural History!" Yolo cheered as she led the twins through the airport.

"Yay!!!"

*****

"Now look!" Yolo demanded like she did anytime she had to leave her kids somewhere. "Stay together, don't touch nothing, and don't talk to strangers!"

"Cuz anything you say can be used against you in a court of law!" Sun warned his sister. Yolo pressed her lips together tightly to prevent herself from laughing.

"I'll be back in a few minutes," she said backing away.

"Okay Mommy," the kids said holding hands. They waved with their free hands until she was out of sight.

"See ya!" Sun shouted and snatched his hand away the second Yolo was gone. He took off in search of trouble while Shyne looked for something flammable.

Meanwhile Yolo drove towards The Bronx. She was so excited about the prospect of being a wife that her panties got soggy. All she had to do was lure Sincerity out in the open and murder her. That's why she was going to see Karate Joe.

Yolo had almost become a regular in the projects so she didn't get a second look as she passed through. Even if she did have a machete in her hand.

As usual Karate Joe was on his roof top gym. He had no students so he was surprised when the roof top door swung open. A smile spread on his face when he saw one of his best students.

"Miss Jackson," he said with a humbled bow. It would be his last because Yolo swung the blade from behind her back and chopped his head clean off.

"Karate Joe," she said bowing to his head as it rolled away. She went into his pocket and retrieved his phone before picking up his severed head.

"Daddy?" Sincerity asked hearing her father's persona ringtone. She silently hoped the off schedule video chat wasn't bad news. "Hello?"

"Hello Sincerity, I'm Karate Joe," Yolo said through clenched teeth like a ventriloquist as she held his head up to the phone's camera. "Guess who killed me? I did!" Yolo growled as she tossed his head aside and putting her own face to the screen. "Now what are you going to do about it!"

"Nooooo!!!!" Sincerity howled realizing that her father was dead. The fact that it was Yolo who did it lit a burning rage in her heart. "Stay right there bitch! I'm on my way!"

"Oooh, I'm so scared!" Yolo laughed. "No can do, but I'll meet you at this same spot at the same time tomorrow. Oh and bring your kids."

"Bitch I...," Sincerity yelled until she realized that the chat had ended. She scrambled to go get her children together for the ride to New York. She had to go bury her father and kill his killer.

*****

Yolo rushed downtown to pick up her kids before they got into too much trouble. She had only been gone for an hour but was fifty minutes too late for that.

"Excuse me, ma'am?' a security guard inquired as Yolo came rushing into the museum. She took one look at his uniform and shook her head.

"What did he do?" she asked assuming it was Sun who cut up. She was half right.

"Well, he climbed into the Native American exhibit and shot the bow arrows. She... well, do you smell that smoke?"

"Can't take you anywhere!" Yolo snapped via the rearview mirror as she drove back out to Long Island.

"I tried to tell him Mommy," Shyne said hoping to deflect the attention away from herself.

"Tell him how? With smoke signals!"

Chapter 24

"Okay look!" Yolo began from in front of the monkey enclosure at The Bronx Zoo. "Mommy has something very important to do. I need you two to behave yourselves. One hour, can you do that for one hour?"

"Yes!" the twins said nodding their cute faces up and down. They weren't lying because they really thought that they could pull it off, behaving for an hour.

"You! Keep an eye on your sister!" she demanded before she hugged Sun tightly.

"Okay Mommy," he agreed. She released him and embraced his sister.

"Keep him out of trouble," she whispered in Shyne's ear. "Love you guys!'

"We love you too," the twins sang in chorus. They waved at their mom until she was gone.

"I'm going in," Sun announced looking at the monkeys swinging from the trees. There's no way this could turn out well.

*****

Yolo raced over to the projects once again to kill as she had the day before. Today she brought a couple of guns to go along with her machete. A standard issue 40 caliber, as well as a two shot derringer that she hid in the small of her back.

She was halfway through the courtyard when she felt something strange. The air seemed absolutely still and despite it being full of residents it was eerily quiet. She glanced around at the faces of the project's dwellers and saw doom. She looked up and saw the reason for it.

"Don't stop now, bitch!" Sincerity called down from the roof. The glint from the razor sharp machete was almost blinding.

"I'll be right up!" Yolo assured her and rushed inside. The elevator seemed to take half a second to get to the top floor. A second later she emerged onto the roof.

It was billed as a sword fight but as soon as Yolo hit the roof both women began firing at each other. The highly trained combatants both ducked, dodged, and dipped as they ran full speed towards each other while shooting. They both did a roll and came up face to face. Both guns clicked empty an inch away from the opposing woman.

"Ugh!" Sincerity grunted as she swung her machete at Yolo's neck. A split second faster and it would've all been over.

"Touché," Yolo said feeling the spot where the blade had removed an inch of her hair.

It sounded like something out of a gladiator movie as the blades clinked together. Sparks flew as they jousted and chopped at each other. Sincerity smiled as a blow cut through Yolo's pants and drew blood. It was just a flesh wound that didn't slow her up.

The victory was short lived as Yolo scored a similar flesh wound on her arm. She was tempted to pull the gun and end it but that would be way too easy. She wanted to punish the girl. Sweat mixed with the blood leaving both women dripping in red.

"Let's put these down and fight, unless you scared," Sincerity dared.

"I ain't never scared!" Yolo said and tossed her machete over the edge. "Been wanting to beat that ass!"

"Well, now's your chance. Hope you know the ledge," she said stepping up to the edge of the roof.

"Let's get it," Yolo said and joined her.

"Right here, Sin! Nah, throw her to me! Represent!" the project dwellers called from below.

Neither bowed before the fierce bout of hand to hand combat began, that would put most karate movies to shame. Having been trained by the same teacher made for an even match. There was a counterstrike for every strike, an answer for every question, and a re-action for every action.

"I see my daddy taught you well," Sincerity said through a busted lip.

"Best student he ever had, have him tell it," Yolo laughed. Sincer-ity knew that that was a lie. She was his best student followed by the Dope Girl herself. He'd taught his daughter moves that he'd taught no one else.

The fist fight just like the sword fight and gun fight before was on its way to being a draw. Both women were lumped up, bruised up, bloody, and frustrated. Both women had an ace in the hole and they both decided to use it.

"Fuck this!" Yolo announced and went for her gun. Sincerity was thinking the same thing and also made a move.

She dipped low and faked a kick knowing what her defense would be. When Yolo hopped over the fake kick the real one caught her square in her chest.

Yolo saw her life flash before her eyes as she struggled to catch her balance. She saw both She-ra and Casper along with Grimsly and Killa, and lastly both Sun and Shyne. She recalled Harry Brown's last words as her foot came off the ledge.

"There's only one God!" she proclaimed triumphantly knowing she was going to meet him. She wasn't going alone though. A smile spread across her face as she pulled her gun.

Sincerity could only watch as she quickly fired off both rounds. Both found their mark making neat little holes in her forehead. She lost her balance too, as dead people tend to do, and came off the ledge right behind Yolo.

"Oh shit!" the projects shouted as the women hit the ground with a sickening crunch. Both bodies were twisted and mangled from the thirteen story fall.

"You think they're dead?" a teen asked in disbelief.

"As fuck!" Little Villian replied. He was the only one in the projects with Killa's number. He slowly pulled his phone and gave him the double bad news.

Chapter 25

"What we gonna do with them?" A security guard asked his supervisor. The zoo was about to close and no one had come to claim the twins. They had been in the office since Sun was rescued from the monkey cage. Announcements over the PA system had yielded no results. Yolo couldn't hear it from where she was.

"Beats me? May have to call Child Protective Services. You guys want that? Huh? Wanna go to foster care?" he shouted, hoping to get them to talk. They hadn't said one word since they were picked up.

Shyne pointe at the desk's phone still refusing to speak. The monkeys had their phone so she dialed the only number that either of them had committed to memory. Both Sun and Shyne knew their mother's number, but relied on their contact list for everyone else.

"Dial 9 first," the guard said as he handed her the phone. He took a step back but still stayed close enough so that he could snatch it once she had a parent on the line.

Shyne took a deep breath and braced herself as she dialed. She just knew she was in trouble for letting her brother get in trouble. Poor thing had no idea how much trouble they were both in.

"Hello?" an officer asked as he answered Yolo's phone. There was no identification on the mangled body so they hoped the phone found in her pocket would lend a clue. They couldn't get passed the lock and the SD card only contained dick pictures.

"What?" Sun demanded when he saw his sister turn pale and drop the phone.

"Mommy's dead!" she announced. No way would anyone else be answering her phone. No way would she have left her babies and not come back for them. Sun broke down into heavy sobs as the guard spoke to the police.

"Stop crying. You have to take care of me now. We have to find our father!" Shyne ordered.

"Okay," Sun said, turning off the tears immediately. After that the two would never say another speak another word in public.

An hour later a social worker came and picked up the lost children. She took them to a downtown facility and entered them into the foster care system, but that's another story...

*****

"Nothing yet?" Killa asked when Christi picked up the phone. She had been come home from grad school to help find the twins. She'd moved back into Yolo's house hoping that they would show up.

"No," she moaned to the same question he asked her several times a day every day when he called. It had been weeks and still nothing. "Is she really... gone?"

"Yeah," Killa croaked. He disconnected the call and leaned back into his chair.

He was in a dangerous mood. It was mixed with anger, guilt, and confusion. In a blink of an eye he lost almost his entire family. He was dirty, unshaven, and losing weight from not eating. Something had to give. If he didn't catch himself he could very well self-destruct. Someone had to die. He needed to kill in order to live.

He pulled up his 1-800-Killa app in search of someone who needed to die. In search of some relief. It didn't take long for him to find it.

'I need some help. My entire family has been destroyed by our pastor. He's fucked my whole family. My wife, my daughter, and even my son. He got the little nigga floating around my house humming gospel songs. The preacher! He's raping and pillaging the entire congregation...'

"Lithonia, Georgia," Killa read aloud placing the Atlanta suburb in his mind before moving on to the next one. It really caught his attention since it was from the same place.

'My name is Mother Josephine Jackson from Greater First Baptist Church in Lithonia, GA. We are having major problems with our preacher! This man throwing the dick like he Luther Campbell! Spending our tithes on silk suits and pussy. He probably got at least ten chillen running 'round the chuch now. Oh, and I hear he like boys too, but you ain't hear that from me. Anywho, can you send someone down here to kill this blasphemous bastard!'

"Sure can," Killa nodded. "Time to go pay this Reverend Cash a visit."

Meanwhile, he wondered what would happen to his children...

CHAPTER 26

"The Stevensons are a very nice couple. I'm sure you will love them as much as they will love you," the social worker said hopefully. She knew that new foster homes and foster parents could be scary, but truth be told the two children in her backseat scared the shit out of her.

Aesthetically they were gorgeous kids, but something about them just seemed odd. The little girl had a pair of pretty hazel eyes that could look right through you; right down to your very soul. She had locked her eyes on the social worker the moment she arrived and hadn't blinked since. The social worker had been told that the little girl was playful and a bit sassy, but today she appeared to be dead serious.

The boy's eyes were the same shade as his sister's and also had a faraway gaze of someone in deep thought. They never spoke aloud but moved in unison, as if they were communicating via mental telepathy, the distinct synchronization of the highly trained.

What was even scarier was the unexplained blaze that had destroyed the last foster house that had housed the two. The fast moving fire killed both their foster parents along with two other teenaged foster kids. Only the little boy and girl made it out alive. They didn't call for help and were found a mile away briskly walking.

The two had been in foster care for only a short while. They had been placed there a few months earlier after the brutal murder of their mother. They looked alike, however, the slight height advantage of the boy gave the impression that he was older. He wasn't. Sun and Shyne were ten year old paternal twins. Of course, the social service staff didn't know that nor did anyone else since they hadn't uttered a single word in front of anyone. Their bond was so tight that they became extremely violent when the staff tried to separate them, so they thought it was safer to leave them together. Which was ironic really because they were dangerous as fuck.

Sun favored his murderous father in many ways. He inherited his quick wit along with his killer smile. Like his father he was also extremely protective of his family and watched out for his mother and sister. He had become the man of the house while still a boy and took his role seriously. The death of his mother had the same effect on him that his grandfather's death had on his father. It created a slow burning rage.

Shyne was just as much like their mother as Sun was like their father. The little girl was pretty just like her mother. Like her mother she was also sassy, girly, and rough and tough, and ready to tumble. Although Shyne was a lot like their mother she also had some of her father's qualities as well. She had inherited her father's high IQ along with some of his other traits. She also was extremely protective of her family which is why she had burned their last foster home to the ground. The older teens that also lived there had tried to bully her brother, and it had cost them their lives. Their foster parents got if too for not stopping them.

"Well, here we are" Ms. Davis sang as she pulled into the driveway of the Stevenson's home. She sprang from her care anxious to get the twins away from her. Every time she peeked through the rearview mirror she saw Shyne glaring back at her. The child hadn't even blinked.

Sun and Shyne looked up at the modest home for a second before looking around in all directions. They were already planning their escape. The front door opened grabbing their attention.

"Well, look at what we have here!" Mrs. Stevenson squealed with delight. The 300 plus pound white lady smiled a yellow smile and clapped her pudgy hands.

"Mm hm," Mr. Stevenson agreed while locking in on Shyne. He looked at her as if she was a piece of candy that he could pop in his mouth and suck all the flavor out of. He didn't blink either, so he and Shyne engaged in a staring contest. Shyne would eventually win since he probably wouldn't be alive much longer. Good thing he had so much fun on his last birthday because it would be his last birthday.

"This is David and Dawn," Ms. Davis introduced. The agency had to give them names since they refused to speak. "He's ten and she's nine."

"So tender at that age," Mr. Stevenson moaned. A line of drool escaped his mouth and ran down his chin and onto his stained t-shirt. From a distance it looked like tie-dye but up close it was just nasty. Ms. Davis knew that she shouldn't leave the kids with the couple, not with all the complaints and citations, but to not leave them meant putting them back in her car.

"So, have fun!" the social worker grunted as she rushed back to her car. Her tires tossed up gravel as she tore out of the driveway.

"Come on in guys. Let's take a look at your bedrooms," Mrs. Stevenson sang as she held the door open.

"Take a look," her husband mimicked as he glanced down at the starter nubs on Shyne's chest. He was stared so hard that he missed the murderous glare from her brother.

The twins linked hands and walked inside. The pair of pedophiles high fived behind the twin's backs once they entered. They were ecstatic that the New York foster care system had once again donated to their sick cause. However, unbeknownst to them the joke was actually on them.

"Pink for her and blue from him," Mrs. Stevenson said when they reached the upstairs bedroom. Sun walked into the room with his sister close behind.

"No, you guys have your own rooms," she corrected and took Shyne by her hand. She led her into the pink room and sat her down. "I'll get dinner!"

As soon as the squeaky stairs announced her reaching the bottom Shyne got up and crossed the hall. She joined her brother in the blue room and finally spoke.

"What's the plan?" she asked. Usually she was the brains to his brawn but the roles interchangeable.

"Same plan, find our father," he stated plainly. "Mr. is going to be a problem."

"Nah, just give me some matches," Shyne giggled. She was a lovely little lunatic, just like her mama.

But, let's go back, to the beginning.

CHAPTER 27

"Where in the hell am I?" Sun asked as he blinked in the darkness.

"I was wondering the same thing," Shyne said from behind him.

"You can hear me?"

"Of course I can, stupid. I'm in here with you!" she shot back, sassy from the start.

"No wonder I'm so cramped in here!" Sun said as he pressed his back against hers to try and free up a little space.

"Hey!" Shyne protested as she shoved back.

"If I didn't know any better...I'd swear that I had twins in here!" Yolo said, feeling the commotion going on inside of her. Looking down at her swollen belly, she saw the movement going on inside.

"Please, no!" Killa prayed with his hands clasped together. One child with the lovely little lunatic was more than enough.

"Chill, yo! We in here together so we may as well try to get along," Shyne reasoned, since the shoving match wasn't going her way.

"I guess. What's your name?" her brother asked.

"Um...I don't know? How about you?"

"I don't know, either. I guess those two we keep hearing will tell us sooner or later."

The twins spent the rest of their time in their mother's womb bonding with each other. The humorous, sarcastic, but loving banter of their parents served as a backdrop to their growth and development. They were born prematurely and spent months in an incubator together. Their parents were off murdering the Black Mob so all they had was each other. The two formed a bond that each would kill or die to protect.

****

"Just relax and breathe," the delivery nurse said soothingly.

"Relax? Bitch, I got a whole person trying to come out of my vagina! How the fuck I'm 'posed to relax?" Yolo shot back. She glanced around the room for something to kill her with, but luckily nothing was in reach.

"You're three months early...something is weird with this heartbeat," the doctor announced as he checked on the baby.

Yolo memorized his full name. She was going to do something weird to him if anything happened to her child. "You sure you know what you're doing? Last time I gave someone an epidural, she felt it when I cut off her foot," Yolo asked as the nurse performed that procedure.

All movement in the room paused to process the statement. In the end, they shrugged it off as labor pains.

"Just rel...uh...I...um..." the doctor stammered as he prepared to go in and get the premature baby.

"Can we wait for my boyfriend?" Yolo whined, causing the nurse to snicker. Quite a few mothers made that same request when they arrived and most ended up giving birth alone and raising their child alone.

"If I had a dollar for every time I heard that, I'd..."

"Be a dollar short today!" Killa said as he walked into the room.

"Hey, there, little fellow," the doctor said happily as he pulled a tiny baby boy from Yolo. He was small and underweight, but healthy. "He'll have to go into an incubator to cook for a couple of months."

"Cook! No one's cooking my baby!" Yolo shouted, trying to sit up.

"Relax, it's just a figure of...Doctor, you missed one," the nurse said urgently.

"One what?" both Mom and Dad shouted together.

Neither got an answer because the doctor was too busy pulling their daughter into the world.

"Oh my," Killa said and sank into a chair.

"A boy and a girl!" the nurse announced with glee. "Have you given any thought to names?"

"You do it," Yolo said in exhaustion.

Killa got up and went over to look at the fraternal twins. Even though the babies were premature, they still had classic Forrest features.

"Sun...and Shyne," he announced, looking from his son to his daughter.

"Sun and Shyne...I love it," Yolo repeated and fell asleep.

Chapter 28

A couple of weeks before the twins were to start kindergarten, Yolo decided to take them on a field trip. They were headed to an Upstate New York prison to watch a man die. She wanted to teach them about life's truest reality; death.

It wasn't just any man. It was the man who'd sent her life into the darkness of death and destruction. It was his fault that she'd turned out like she was and now he was finally going to pay for it.

"Where are we going, Mommy?" the fussy little diva demanded to know from the passenger's seat. Both she and her brother had begun to grow restless from the long ride.

"To watch someone get what they deserve," Yolo replied, speaking of the long overdue execution of Harry Brown. Ironically, he was being put to death for a murder that she committed, but it was still justice.

Yolo never understood why it took so long for the condemned to actually be put to death. When she decided someone needed to be dead, their ass was dead. There were no appeals, no pardons, and no mercy. Fuck up and you got fucked up on the spot.

"I need to say bye-bye," Yolo smirked wickedly. It pleased her to no end that her face would be among the last faces that Harry saw in his life.

"He ain't got no phone? Why you ain't just call and say bye?" Sun demanded to know from the backseat.

Yolo just shook her head at her son through the rearview mirror. Just like apple trees produce apples, smart alecks beget smart asses. The car swerved slightly, alerting Yolo that she had gotten stuck staring at her son's handsome face instead of watching the road. He'd gotten that from his dad, along with a few other traits that would manifest later in life.

"I wanna talk to my daddy," the daddy's little girl pouted.

"Go 'head!" Yolo spat jealously. It seemed as if she had to compete with the little girl for Killa's attention.

"Don't let me find out you hatin'," Shyne mumbled under her breath as she went into her phone.

Both twins had their own cell phones already with their parents and Christi's numbers locked in on speed dial. Without realizing it, their parents had handicapped them by not allowing them to memorize important numbers the old fashioned way. It was all good now but it would come back to haunt them later.

Shyne's end of the conversation was all smiles and giggles as she gushed over her daddy. She sucked her teeth and rolled her eyes when he asked to speak with her brother.

"He got his own phone," she fussed and hung up.

"No, you didn't!" Yolo laughed. She meant to check the child but it was just too funny.

Sun found 'Daddy' in his contacts and pressed 'send.' "Daddy, Mommy won't stop driving!" he tattled when his father took his call.

"Snitch!" mother and daughter called out at the same time and high fived.

"I don't know who he call himself telling on. Your father ain't the boss of me!" Yolo told her daughter who scrunched her cute little face up in disbelief. The girl witnessed how her mother acted around her father so she knew damn well the he was the boss of her.

"Daddy wanna talk to you," Sun said in a smug 'take that' tone as he passed the phone forward.

"Hello," Yolo sang through the wide smile on her face.

"Sup, Yo? Where you headed? I heard you been driving for a hundred years," Killa said, stifling a laugh at the colorful exaggeration.

"Seems like," Yolo agreed with a sigh. The low rumbling bass of his voice eased her frustrations instantly. "Goin' upstate to watch

Harry get put down like a puppy at the pound. I have to see him take his last breath."

The line went momentarily quiet as Killa answered all the questions that popped into his head for himself. He knew her story so he understood perfectly. He also wondered why she'd take the kids but he figured that out on his own as well. He concluded that she was in her feelings so he verbally kept her company for the rest of the ride. Now it was Sun's turn to get in his feelings since he couldn't get his phone back.

"'Bout time," Sun mumbled when they finally pulled into a motel. His mother twisted her lips at him as she gave the dead phone back.

"What you guys want to eat?" Yolo asked once they were comfortably inside their room. She handed them the menus from the local restaurants that delivered.

"Hamburgers! Chinese food!" Sun and Shyne cheered. She added pizza to the mix and made the call.

The combination of the long ride, their full bellies, and hot baths put the five-year-olds to sleep like five-year-olds with full bellies, after a long ride and a hot bath. After taking a hot shower of her own, Yolo got into the bed and got her boo back on the line.

"Sup, Ma?" Killa answered in his sexy South Bronx accent that drove her wild.

"Man, I wish you were here," she sighed as she slipped her hand into her panties.

"And why is that?" he asked, dropping his voice an octave and making it sound even sexier. He'd clearly heard the arousal in her voice and knew where she was going with her statement. It was his job to help her get there even if he was eight states away.

"So you could be doing this for me," she moaned as she alternated between rubbing little circles on her clit and slipping a finger in and out of her slippery box.

"Well, just pretend like your finger is my tongue and..." he growled before being cut off by the sound of her cumming instantly. "I see my work is done."

"G-g-goodnight," Yolo stuttered before she hung up and rolled over to sleep like only a good nut can make one do.

"Who you talking to?" Sincerity demanded as she rushed into the room. She'd heard him using his sexy voice and came to investigate.

"No one," Killa shrugged. Technically, it wasn't a lie since the call had already ended. That still didn't explain the erection that bulged in his pants.

"Mm hmm," she said as she twisted her lips up skeptically. She moved in closer to inspect it and gave it a squeeze to test its hardness. Obviously it passed the test because she unzipped his pants and set it free.

She was naked under her t-shirt so she climbed onto his lap and straddled him. Once she wiggled him inside of her, she sank down as far as she could go. The couple kissed softly as she rode him until they both came hard. Killa had satisfied both of his women for the night, proving that they didn't call him Killa for nothing.

****

"What is this place, Mommy?" Sun whined as they entered the prison.

She usually checked him for whining but made an exception this time due to how dreadfully dreary the place was. Being in prison was worse than death because it's kin to being buried alive.

"I wanna go home," Shyne pouted as well.

"Be easy. We won't be here too long," Yolo said. A glance at the wall clock proved her right since its time said that the execution was only thirty minutes away.

They'd barely made the cut to witness it as the room filled with the victim's family, members of the media, and people with morbid curiosities. Yolo recognized the victim's family as they sat in the front row hoping for closure that would never come. The death penalty was about revenge, not closure. It was an eye for an eye, and ain't nothing wrong with that.

The dead girl's mother let out a gasp as Harry Brown was led into the death chamber. He looked around, blinking his eyes to make sure that it was real before he calmly laid atop the gurney and was strapped down. It was only then that that he allowed himself to turn toward the viewing window. He faced it, knowing that his alleged victim's family would be on the other side.

Turning in their direction, he mouthed, "I'm sorry," since they couldn't hear him through the thick glass. The mother snapped her head away, which translated to 'apology not accepted.'

Curiosity caused the condemned man to scan the faces in the rooms as an IV was started. The innocuous saline drip attached to his arm would soon be infused with poisons. His gaze swept right over Yolo until his mind processed the face and caused him to shift it back and lock gazes with her. He remembered telling his lawyers that it had to have been her who'd strangled his alleged victim and hid her body in his room. He knew he deserved his fate so he offered her a half smile as he again mouthed the words, "I'm sorry."

Yolo gave a slight nod as a sign of her acceptance of his apology. There was no need for her to continue to hold a grudge since he was paying for what he'd done to her with his life. Besides, with all the wrongs that she'd committed, she knew that one day she would need forgiveness of her own.

"Any last words?" the warden asked, hoping that he would say no. The last man he'd asked the question had begged, pleaded, slobbered, and cried for fifteen minutes.

"La illaha ill Allah," Harry replied confidently like a man who was ready to meet his Lord.

"What does that mean?" Shyne whispered to her mother.

"It means there's only one God," Sun answered for her.

"Yeah, that there's only one God," Yolo muttered. She wasn't big on religion and had only gone to church to kill the crooked clergyman, but that much she did know.

The spectators watched Harry as his eyelids fluttered and he fell into a deep sleep as his chest moved up and down slowly with each of his last breaths. It rose and fell one final time before he moved on from the here and now into the hereafter.

"Come on, y'all. Let's go home."

****

"Is that man dead, Mommy?" Shyne finally asked as they drove home. They'd been riding for over an hour in the silence of death before the she spoke and broke it.

"As a doorknob," Yolo chuckled in amusement. Harry had really gotten off easy as far as she was concerned. Had it been left up to her, he would've had a slow and painful death. "That's what he gets for touching me!"

"Did you get pregnant?" Shyne asked, eyes wide with fear.

"Huh?" Yolo asked, fighting to control the car.

"If a boy touches you, you'll get pregnant, have a baby, and die!" Shyne repeated urgently.

"Wha-, wh-, who told you that?" Yolo demanded. She knew good and well that the girl she'd adopted from next door hadn't, she was too smart to say something so dumb. It came to her at the same time that her daughter answered.

"Daddy! He said not let a boy touch me because I'll get pregnant and..."

"Hello!" Yolo yelled when Killa picked up. He knew from the tone of her voice that he was in trouble. He was right too because Yolo read him the riot act.

"What's wrong, Mommy?" Shyne asked, hoping that she hadn't gotten her daddy in trouble.

"Nothing. Your father is right. Don't let no boy touch you or you gonna get pregnant and die!"

Chapter 29

"One more time! Let's go again!" Yolo cheered, breathless from an orgasm. Killa had swung into town for his children's first day of school. Yolo, of course, had greeted him with open legs.

"Look what time it is," he reminded. The excuse was valid, but truth be told, she'd put it on him.

"Okkkaay," she pouted and let out a sigh. "Get her, I'll get him."

Killa smiled and gave himself a mental pat on the back when he saw Yolo wobble upon standing. Her legs were rubbery from the multiple orgasms from the multiple positions he'd sexed her in. He'd fucked her like the world depended upon it. And of course, Killa had saved the world.

"Knock, knock," Killa called out as he eased Shyne's bedroom door open. She'd chewed him out the last time he'd entered without formal permission. To his surprise, she was already up and sitting, fully dressed, at her vanity fussing with her afro puffs.

"Would you make Mommy let me get a perm, a lace front, or something cuz..." Shyne fussed.

"Uh...no," her father laughed then frowned. "What's that on your lips?"

"MAC lip gloss!" the little diva said, pulling her shiny lips into a smile. "How does it look?"

"Well, let me see," her father said, drawing closer. When he was close enough, he used the palm of his hand to un-gloss his five-year-old's lips. "Much better!"

"Daddy!" Shyne fussed and stomped her little feet.

"Yeah, I know. I see you got this so I'll go fix breakfast and lunch," Killa said on his way out. Yolo wasn't faring much better with their son.

"Wake up, handsome. You don't want to be late for your first day of school," she sang in a motherly voice as she entered his messy room. It looked like a toy store's dump truck had backed up to it and emptied its load.

"I'm not going. I'm just gonna get my G.E.D," Sun explained quite reasonably and pulled the cover over his head. He'd researched alternatives to school on his computer and decided it was the best course of action.

"I...uh...you...," Yolo stammered at a loss for words. "Okay, I'm about to get my B.E.L.T!"

"Okay, Mommy!" Sun called out as he rolled out of bed. Both he and his sister could read, spell, and write very well thanks to their big sister, Christi. He knew B.E.L.T spelled ass whooping and wanted no parts of it.

****

"Breakfast is served!" the proud papa announced when his gorgeous kids entered the eat-in kitchen.

The eggs, waffles, and turkey bacon spoke for themselves. It was the strange metal boxes that had the smart kids confused.

"What's a Wonder Woman?" Shyne asked, scrunching her face up like whatever it was stank.

"Wonder Woman!" Killa replied, like the name itself was self-explanatory. "And Aqua Man for Sun."

"Who?" Sun asked, frowning up at the strange figures on the metal boxes.

"Eat," Yolo demanded, since that would be easier than trying to explain the ancient super heroes.

Eat the kids did. Then it was off to the bus stop. If Yolo had her way, she would've dropped her children off and picked them back up in an armored truck. However, their daddy insisted that they ride the bus with the other kids.

"Damn, we're the only parents out here," Yolo exclaimed. She was right, there wasn't another parent anywhere in sight.

"They've probably been turning up all night and had to turn in," Killa guessed. He was right, too. A few minutes later, a school bus pulled to a hissing stop and the kids boarded.

"Bye-bye! Love you! Muah! Muah!" Yolo called out as she blew kisses at her children as the bus pulled away with them on it. "Come on!"

"Where?" Killa asked as he ran to keep up with her.

She hopped into her car and followed the bus all the way to the school.

****

"Good morning, class. I'm Miss Cranford," the teacher greeted. She turned and wrote her name on the blackboard, giving Sun a chance to watch her booty.

"Born...God...Supreme...Williams?" she struggled as she looked around for the raised hand.

"Peace, Earth. I'm the God Supreme," a little Five Percenter called out.

"You're not God!" Shyne said with a disgusted scowl upon her face. She knew that there was only one God and he wasn't it.

"The Black man is God," he replied, rattling off the bullshit his Five Percenter parents had filled his little head with.

"If you God, then why didn't you comb your hair and why you ashy? You God, but you couldn't find no lotion?" Shyne wanted to know.

"Sun and Shyne Forrest. Twins!" Miss Cranford cheered, bringing unwanted attention to the two.

"Sun and Shyne? Kinda names is that?" a wannabe bully wanted to know. Little William Johnson was a runt but had a dozen cousins at the school to back him up. "They moms must be on crack!"

"My mother isn't on crack!" Shyne stood and declared.

She had no idea what crack was but was pretty sure that it wasn't something good. Little William, on the other hand, knew exactly what it was since his mother was on it. Picking on other kids helped him forget about the rumbles of his empty stomach.

"Sit down, Shyne!" Sun warned when he saw a few kids coming near. Shyne, however, was too busy going in to see the danger. He knew his sister had no chill so it came as no surprise when she reached out and slapped dust from the other child. The cousins jumped in and Sun took off. "Run!"

But Shyne didn't run. She stood and fought. She got her ass whipped, since four on one isn't much of a fight and she was quickly subdued, but she didn't run. Miss Cranford moved in to break it up and then sent all the kids to the principal's office.

"Already?" Miss Hunter exclaimed at the first fight of the school year. The sexy principal wasn't quite thirty yet, but was already running her own school. "I'm calling your parents!"

"You better yell loud cuz we ain't got no phone," Little William laughed. His mother was sitting in a crack house somewhere, with a belly full of semen, getting high.

****

"Ssss," Yolo hissed as Killa slid inside of her. They had taken a quick nap when they'd gotten in but now it was time to fuck again.

"Ssss is right," Killa agreed as he entered her hot box.

He had just got a good stroke going when Yolo's phone began to ring.

"Pst, yeah right," she huffed at the call that was about to be ignored.

Killa slipped his tongue into her mouth just as her answering machine app kicked in. The app served as an old school device, allowing callers to be heard as they left their message. It was actually the first form of Caller ID.

"Good afternoon, Miss...Jackson," the principal said, noticing that the kids had a different last name, "This is Miss Hunter, the principal over at Wyandanch Elementary. There seems to have been a slight incident at school..."

"Get up! Get up!" Yolo shouted as she shoved Killa up and out of her. He rolled over and off the bed as she scrambled to catch the call before it ended. "Hello, hello! What happened? Are my babies okay?"

"Yes, they're fine. They got into a fight and...,"

"I'm on my way!" Yolo shouted and tore out of the room.

"Wait! Hold up! Yolo! Yo...lo!" Killa yelled as he ran behind her.

"What? My babies need me!" She yelled back over her shoulder as she reached the front door.

"Okay, but they need you to put some clothes on first," Killa said, alerting her to her nakedness. "It's not show and tell!"

"Ha ha," Yolo quipped, twisting her lips as she marched back upstairs to slip into a sweat suit. Killa lagged a step behind to watch her ass jiggle since she hadn't bothered to put on panties.

"I'll drive," Killa suggested once they got outside. He knew that she would speed, which could lead to some cop pulling them over, which could lead to that same cop getting shot in his face.

Killa pulled into the school's parking lot and before he could bring the car to complete stop, Yolo bolted from it. She sprinted into the school while he calmly walked in behind her. Sun and Shyne were seated in the foyer of the office when she burst in looking like a crazy lady.

"What happened? Huh? Huh?" she demanded, getting all up in the secretary's face.

"We got beat up!" Shyne said happily. She was lumped up and bleeding, but she'd still had a good time.

Yolo turned to Sun, who didn't have a mark on him. "You too?" she asked her son.

"He ran," Shyne said and shrugged with her palms up.

"Ran? You little..." Yolo growled and went after him. He ran again and ducked behind his father just as he entered the office.

"Excuse me, Mr. and Mrs. Jackson?" Principal Hunter asked as she came out of her office. She looked at Yolo then at Killa and got stuck.

"We're not married," Killa explained, the words sounding like music to the principal's ears. He quickly scanned her from head to toe while Yolo silently fumed.

"Follow me," she said and spun around to lead the parents into her office. She made sure to sling her ample ass from side to side, knowing he would watch. He did, and so did his son.

"What happened? Why does my daughter have knots on her head, looking like she has horns?" Yolo wanted to know.

"Looking like a young sheep," Killa cracked and cracked up. "Yolo had a little lamb."

"And just how is this funny?" she demanded of him before turning back to the educator and asking again, "What happened?"

"Kid stuff, nothing to be too concerned about. Kids fight, you know," Miss Hunter said, sounding slightly condescending.

"Nothing to...Do you have kids?" Yolo asked.

"No, I have no children," she replied to Killa as if he'd asked the question. "From what I gathered, a few boys were teasing your son and your daughter jumped on them."

"And Sun ran," Killa said, shaking his head at his son through the window. "That's enough for the day. We'll take them home and try again tomorrow."

"I understand," the principal said, batting her eyelashes as if Killa's baby mama wasn't in the room. Killa couldn't help but laugh when he heard a low growl emanating from Yolo.

"Go 'head, babe. I need to ask Miss Thang...um...I mean Miss Hunter a quick question."

"Sure," Killa replied and started for the door. He stopped, turned, and took one last look at the pretty woman, knowing that there was a good chance that she might not look like that anymore after dealing with his baby mama. She was known for giving reverse facelifts.

"And just how may I help you?" Miss Hunter asked in a tone reserved for the children.

"Oh, I was just wondering if I was going to have to fuck you up about my man?"

"Absolutely not! I just try to make sure that the dads realize how important they are at this stage of their children's development," she explained.

"Oh, well, okay," Yolo said, buying the bullshit that the lady was selling. She cracked a smile then exited the office to catch up with her family.

"And then I fuck their brains out!" the principal laughed behind Yolo's departing back. Luckily for her, she was out of ear shot or Wyandanch Elementary would be needing a new principal.

Chapter 30

"Here we go," Killa grumbled to himself when he saw Yolo come marching out of the school like a North Korean soldier.

"Mommy is mad," Shyne observed from the backseat.

"Take me to Home Depot!" she demanded as she joined them in the car.

"Home Depot? For what?" Killa asked.

"I need one of those big ass pots! You know, like the ones witches use in the movies."

"A cauldron? For what? What you tryna cook?"

"Yeah, a cauldron! I'm about to cook those fuckin' kids and feed them to their parents, then kill..."

"Eh em," Killa cleared his throat and motioned towards their kids in the backseat with his head.

Yolo turned to see what he meant and saw her twins sitting wide eyed with shock from her violent outburst. "Fix it! I want you to fix this," she demanded.

Killa had just turned the signal on to turn on their block, but quickly clicked it off and kept straight instead. He headed straight towards the Long Island Expressway. A few bridges later, Sun read a sign that said 'Welcome to The Bronx'.

The scenery changed from bleak to bleaker the further they went before finally taking a turn for the worse as Killa pulled into the projects.

"What is this place?" Shyne whined. She wrinkled her nose up as if the place stank.

"This is where your daddy grew up," Yolo said proudly.

"I wanna grow up here," Sun declared.

"You wouldn't grow up here. This place would chew you up and spit you back out," Killa said as he found a parking spot. He wrote the word 'Killa' on a piece of paper and put it in the window before getting out. Yolo furrowed her brow in question and he replied, "Car alarm."

"Why are we here?" Yolo asked as he led his family through the courtyard. The kids marveled at the lights, camera, and action of the project life.

"To see him," Killa said and pointed up to the roof.

As usual, Karate Joe was up there practicing his moves.

Karate Joe was an odd little man who wore karate clothes and karate slippers. He walked slightly bowed with his arms folded behind his back. When he spoke, there was slight delay between his words and the movement of his mouth like an old karate movie. He was a bit of an oddball, but he was dangerous as fuck.

"Good idea," Yolo nodded when she understood. Karate lessons were just what her children needed.

"Ewww! It smells like pee!" Shyne squealed when they stepped into a pissy elevator.

"Smells like you," Sun teased and cracked up.

"I know you ain't talking, Carl Lewis!" Yolo snapped in defense of her daughter. "We probably should've taken the stairs."

"You think the elevator is bad," Killa exclaimed. He knew you could find a body in the stairwell since he'd left plenty of them there himself back in the day. Once they reached the top floor, they got off and walked a flight up to the roof.

"Killa-Sun," Karate Joe greeted with a bow that Sun found amusing. The boy snickered and gave a bow of his own.

"Sup, yo," Killa replied, minus the bow. Killa bowed to no man, but he did shake hands. "This is Miss Jackson, Sun, and Shyne."

Yolo snapped her eyes towards him hearing the greeting that lacked any hint of their family ties. She decided to save it for later since they were on a mission to save their children from any further ass whoopings.

"They need to learn how to fight. Especially him! He runs from fights," Yolo snarled in her son's direction.

"Runs!" Karate Joe reeled. He walked over to Sun and looked him up and down before suddenly reaching between his legs and cupping his little package. "No vagina, no run!"

Sun looked to his mother who looked to his father who shrugged his shoulders. Sun nodded up and down and got his package back.

"All children need to learn to fight; especially girls!" Karate Joe said and took a swing at Shyne.

"Stop!" the girl protested as she swatted the blow away. Karate Joe nodded his approval at the block and tried her brother.

"Ouch!" Sun cried when he got popped upside his head. He tried to take cover behind his mother but she wouldn't let him.

"Un uh! No vagina, no run!" Yolo repeated, pushing him back. "How long to train them?"

"Lethal or decaf?" Karate Joe needed to know. There was a difference between learning karate for self-defense and learning it to fuck people up.

"Lethal!" the parents said in unison.

"Let's see," the teacher said as he sized the two youngsters up. "Eight hours a day, every Saturday...her, about a year. Two at the most. Him, ten years!"

"Mmm mph," Yolo said, shaking her head at her goofy son.

It amazed her how much he looked like his dad, yet acted nothing like him. Not yet anyway, but he would because he was most definitely his father's son in every way. He was just too young for it to show as of yet.

Karate Joe started with the basics, teaching the twins how to block and deflect blows. Months would be spent on defensive training before they would be allowed to throw a one single punch or kick. Both kids smiled broadly as their first lesson began. Yolo saw it as her opportunity to question Killa and took it.

"So, who exactly is he?" she asked.

"Who him? He's Karate Joe," Killa replied as if that summed it all up. He knew she was digging for more information, but wasn't going to help her.

"I know that, but who is he, exactly?" she asked again through clenched teeth, just like she did with their son.

"Karate Joe is the best karate teacher in New York. He also happens to be Sincerity's father, but this ain't about her, me, or you. This is about Sun and Shyne!" he laid out.

"Oh, okay," she agreed since he'd summed it all up.

****

Killa had to leave during the week so Yolo had to take the twins to their next lesson alone. She took a gun along with her just in case she spotted Sincerity. That would put an end to living the side chic life.

"Are we ready?" Karate Joe asked when his students arrived on the rooftop.

"Yes," Sun and Shyne chimed as Yolo stepped aside.

"You too! You here," Karate Joe demanded of Yolo.

"Me?" the mother asked slightly impudent.

"Yes, you! You must learn too so that you can practice with them during the week," he explained. This would allow the twins to master a lesson by the time they returned the follow week.

"Makes sense," she agreed and joined the lesson. By November, they'd mastered blocks and graduated to blows. One day, after a lesson on various strikes, Yolo took a detour on the way home.

"My daddy coming home?" Shyne asked when she recognized the route to the airport.

"Dick rider," Sun remarked from the backseat. The whole family vied with each other for Killa's attention, but the girls seemed to get the majority of it.

"What did you say?" Yolo asked her son with a confused smile. She thought she'd heard him, but wasn't sure.

He misunderstood her smile and therefore made the mistake of repeating himself. "She's a dick rider. A cock jockey! Always 'daddy, daddy, my daddy!'" Sun mocked.

"That's what I thought you said," Yolo said through the same smile right before she attacked. She gripped the steering wheel with one hand and tried to hit her son with the other.

Sun blocked the blow as he'd been taught and scrambled behind her seat so that she couldn't reach him. The car swerved violently as she took swipes and swings at him.

"Grab the wheel," Yolo told her daughter as she unbuckled her seatbelt.

"No, Mommy!" Shyne shouted as if Yolo was crazy. "Your exit is coming up!"

"I got you, buddy! Go to sleep," Yolo warned as she turned back to the road. Luckily for all, Killa was already standing on the curb at the concourse when she pulled in.

"Sup, guys?" Killa cheered as he jumped into the back with their son. Both Yolo and Sun were out of breath and Shyne was still shook up from them nearly having an accident. "What I miss?"

****

"Very nice!" Killa applauded when his children demonstrated their newest karate moves. They'd already showed off the A's they'd received in the time since his last visit.

Yolo glanced at her watch and smiled. It was almost their bedtime and she'd have Killa all to herself. She counted down the minutes while her loved ones wrestled on the floor. Ten, nine, eight, seven, six, five...

"Bedtime!" Yolo cheered causing her kids to groan. "Daddy will read you guys a story while I fix him something to eat."

Killa smiled wickedly and carried the twins up to their rooms. Between karate class and Yolo refusing to let them take a nap, neither lasted to the end of the story.

"I thought you were fixing me something to eat?" Killa asked as he entered her room. Yolo was butt naked, striking a pose in the center of the bed.

"I did," she replied and spread her legs wide. Her bald vagina looked like a fresh juicy nectarine. Killa liked nectarines so he moved in for a taste. He peeled off his clothes as he approached and took position at his plate.

"Mmm," Killa moaned as he tasted her sweet nectar. Yolo moaned even louder as she reached the first of many orgasms.

"Put it in!" she demanded after he'd sucked a third nut out of her juicy box. She pulled him upward and guided him inside. Killa didn't last a full minute inside her quivering box before he came.

"Damn it, man!" he shouted at his premature ejaculation.

"Don't sweat it, good pussy will do that," she assured him. It ain't bragging when it's the true, so Killa just nodded in agreement. They cuddled up and enjoyed the warmth of each other's body heat.

"I brought you something," Killa remembered.

"I know," she giggled and reached for his dick. "My favorite."

"Well yeah, that too, but I got a hit from the hotline that I think you'd enjoy. There's a dastardly dentist who desperately needs deadened."

"It would be my pleasure!"

Chapter 31

"Just a little prick. You won't even feel it," Dr. Alexander assured his patient as he administered the sedative. A simple anesthetic would have sufficed but then he wouldn't be able to spend quality time with his sexy young patient.

He had been treating sixteen-year-old Amy since she was six and he'd waited and watched as she grew. He figured since he waited until his patients were sixteen or over, that he wasn't a pedophile. That was debatable, but he was definitely one sick dude. Volunteering in a low income clinic provided a steady flow of disposable victims.

Black and Latina girls had been complaining for years about their suspicions, but no one listened. During that time, he'd deflowered dozens and impregnated dozens more girls as he molested them while they slept. Nope, no one listened except Killa.

"I thought you said I just needed a filling?" Amy asked, but it was too late since he'd already sedated her, causing her to doze off and miss his nefarious answer.

"You don't even have a cavity," he chuckled as he pulled her pants off, "but you're about to get filled, though."

The dentist snapped a few pictures of the young girl's privates to share publicly. He then leaned in gave her a few licks as foreplay, leaving saliva behind to ease his entry.

"Oh, another virgin!" he exclaimed as he struggled to get inside. The girl frowned in her sleep from the pain of being raped. When she awoke, she was fully dressed and sore.

Amy went home and found blood and semen in her panties. Shock and embarrassment sent her rushing into the shower to scrub away any traces of what happened. She called the police but Detective Alexander told her that she'd probably dreamed it. And without any evidence from a rape kit, she couldn't prove it. It was all bullshit but he wasn't going to arrest his own brother.

Amy decided to go to the 1-800-Killa site to vent. She'd reported the dirty dentist as well as the crooked cop. Now Killa and Yolo were on the case and they were both in trouble.

****

"Doctor, your three o'clock is here," the clinic's receptionist announced into the intercom. She turned her head to point out the way and Yolo shot her in the neck. Luckily for her and her next of kin, it was just a tranquilizer. By the time she awoke, Yolo would be done and long gone.

Taking the last appointment of the day meant that the office would be empty. Now no one would be able to hear the doctor's screams, and he was definitely about to scream. Yolo loaded another dart into the tranquilizer gun and crept forward. The receptionist had dozed off before she could tell her which room the doctor was in, so Yolo had to hunt him down.

"Helllllooo, Doctor Alexandeeerrrrr," Yolo sang as she peeped into an examination room. The room was empty so she moved on to the next. Three rooms later, she finally located the dentist looking at the fake X-ray she'd sent in. The teeth were perfect but the file said that she was seventeen so she was getting put to sleep.

"Miss Jackson?" Dr. Alexander greeted with a smile. She looked a little older than seventeen but she was still pretty, so nothing changed. Then everything changed as she whipped up the gun and shot him in his neck too. He felt the effects of the tranquilizer immediately and knew he was in trouble. "Uh oh."

"Uh oh is right!" Yolo laughed as she rushed in and quickly prepped him for surgery.

****

The Alexander brothers obviously hadn't gotten enough attention from their mother as children. This resulted in them both preying on women and young girls as adults. The dentist put young girls under while the cop was a bully with a badge. He routinely patrolled lower income areas in search of prey. The tables had finally turned and today, he was the prey.

"Jackpot!" Detective Alexander cheered when he saw Joyce walking down the street. He'd arrested her several times already for turning tricks without a pimp. The local pimps paid a tax in cash and flesh, but Joyce felt like she was exempt since she was free agent.

"Ain't nothing happenin'! I'm just goin' to the store," Joyce insisted when the cop pulled up. She was liar, but this time she was actually telling the truth. Her last arrest had gotten her sent to rehab and she was now clean.

"Sure you are," he said as he hopped out of his car. He then came around it and performed an illegal search for drugs.

"I tol' you I ain't doin' nothin'!" she challenged when his frisk came up empty.

All he'd gotten was a free feel and he wasn't satisfied with that. "Oh yeah?" he chuckled and went into his pocket. He fished around until he found a small bag of crack. "Well, what is this then?"

"That's that bullshit is what it is," Joyce groaned.

The cop unbuckled his cop pants and whipped out his little cop cock. Joyce let out a sigh as she sank down slowly to her knees. His penis was so tiny that she'd have to suck it like it was a straw.

"That's it," Detective Alexander laughed as he thrust into her face.

He was having a great time, until alone came a killer.

****

"Yeoooow!" Doctor Alexander yelped when he was abruptly awakened.

Yolo had given him a diluted dose of the tranquilizer so he wouldn't sleep as long as his receptionist. The dull pain of getting his dick cut off had snatched him from his slumber.

"I bet," Yolo giggled and dangled his dissected penis in front of him.

The doctor squinted at the familiar penis then glanced down to confirm that it was indeed his. "Yeoooow!" he screamed again upon confirmation. A raggedy void between his legs gushed blood in sync with his every heartbeat. Luckily for him, he didn't have many heartbeats left. He tried to get up but discovered that he'd been securely strapped in place.

"In we go," Yolo sang as she stuffed his dick into his mouth. He tried to move his head from side to side to prevent its insertion. The movements reminded her of when Sun was a baby and she'd fed him split peas. "Your patients didn't want it in their mouths either!"

"Mph ghrb," he protested when his dick reached tonsils. His struggles slowed along with his heartbeat, then they both suddenly stopped, putting an end to the sexual predator.

****

"Mm...mm...mm," Detective Alexander moaned as he drew near his climax. He was so close; too bad he wouldn't make it. "What the..."

"Fuck?" Killa laughed at the cop's reaction to getting doused with the cold liquid. He made a move for his gun but it was down at his ankles. Joyce jerked away, managing not to get any of the liquid on her in the process.

"Gas?" the cop asked when he processed the smell.

"Yup, premium. Only the best for you! Gonna send you away in style," Killa replied.

"Away? Where am I going?" the cop asked. It was a rhetorical question designed to keep the man talking. He needed a second to make another play for his gun.

"To hell, you son of a bitch!" Joyce growled. She saw an opportunity to spit in his face and took it.

"Actually, we don't know where he's going. God is so merciful that he could actually be forgiven. That's why I'm gonna burn his ass now!" Killa growled. The wise man understood that God's mercy triumphed and prevailed over his wrath.

"Let me!" the rehabilitated woman demanded. Killa shrugged and tossed her the lighter. The cop ducked as the lighter sailed in the air and went for his gun. He didn't make it.

"Yeooow!" the cop wailed when the fire engulfed his head and torso.

The spectators cheesed widely as he danced along with the flames. The burning man took off running, which only caused the oxygen in the air to fuel the flames. Finally, he fell face first and finished burning to a crisp. Killa and Joyce shared a silent nod that spoke volumes and about-faced, going their separate ways.

Later that night, Yolo and Killa giggled at their handiwork on the nightly news.

Chapter 32

Bo-Bo Creekmore was the school bully. By the age of nine, he was still in the first grade. The man-child was as tall as a fifth grader and already had peach fuzz under his chin. His mother Mia was M.I.A in the streets, so he had no lunchbox full of food, no clean clothes to wear, and no pencil or paper to write. He was a have-not, so he took from those who had. Sun and Shyne had, so he set his sights on them.

"Here we go again," the school's security guard groaned. He had been keeping an eye on the bully so he saw him as he approached the twins. The boy would fight him too when he attempted to stop him from beating up the other kids.

"Here he comes," Shyne warned when she saw Bo-Bo moving rapidly towards them.

He liked to tease and taunt the twins by sticking his face in theirs while calling them names. The names didn't bother them as much as his tart, government cheese smelling breath did.

"Good," Sun growled. Karate Joe had just taught them how to make a weapon out of regular, everyday items. A newspaper rolled tightly rolled up became a nice Billy club. Glass bottles became knives, and metal lunchboxes were just that, metal lunchboxes. Which is exactly why their father had bought them.

"Dumb and Blind, Dumb and Blind," Bo-Bo taunted. It was actually the start of what would one day be a successful rap career, but not today. Today he was gonna get his ass whipped.

"Wait for it. Wait...for...it," Shyne giggled as the bully drew near.

The point of no return was marked by an invisible line. Bo-Bo didn't see when he crossed it but he damn sure felt it.

He leaned in as Sun swung an Aqua-Man uppercut. The 'clang' of metal meeting teeth rang throughout the crowded cafeteria. Bo-Bo's front teeth somersaulted in slow motion through the air. Shyne followed with swing of her lunchbox that landed a Wonder Woman hook that left the bully shook. The bully was now totally confused since no one had ever stood up to and fought him back before. He whipped his head around in confusion. Seeing the security guard, he took off towards him for help.

"Un uh," Sun said, and clipped him before he could get away. The twins proceeded to stomp and kicked the bully into submission.

Karate Joe had taught them that a half-kicked ass had the same effect as no ass kicking at all, so the twins made sure that they kicked his ass thoroughly. The bully curled into a fetal position to escape the brunt of the onslaught.

"Do something!" one teacher shouted to the security guard.

"I am!" he laughed and kept right on watching. He even pulled out his phone to capture the beating. He had been pulling the bully off other kids for years so he figured he had it coming.

"I'm sorry! I won't mess with y'all no more!" Bo-Bo pleaded. Sun looked over at Shyne who shook her head no and continued the beating.

"Okay, that's enough," the security guard reluctantly said. He then radioed for the nurse and took the twins to the principal's office.

****

"I need to speak to your father! What's his number?" the principal demanded. Shyne peeped that she'd picked up her personal cell phone to make the call instead of the school's phone, but was too young to figure out why.

"He doesn't live with us all the time," Sun blurted before his sister kicked him in his leg. That was family business and not to be shared.

"We don't know his number," Shyne cut in. It was true since their wanted father changed phones and numbers frequently. Their mother made sure to keep his number updated in their phones so that when the pushed the contact named Daddy, it was Daddy.

"Well, I guess I'll have to call your mother," Miss Hunter sighed and picked up her desk phone.

"Hello," Yolo said when she answered. She braced herself just in case it was bad news. Killa had made her promise not to run up to the school every time the twins had a problem.

"Mrs. Forrest, your children got into another fight! They jumped on another student and beat him pretty badly," the principal said with far more attitude than necessary. She'd purposely used the children's last name to remind their mother that she wasn't married to their father.

"Nothing to be concerned with. Like you said, kids fight," Yolo said, throwing the principal's words back at her. It was no big deal when her children had gotten beat up, now she wants to be concerned. "Ta-ta!"

"Hello? Hello? No this bi-," Miss Hunter said, and stopped when she saw the twins staring at her. "Go to class! And when you get home, tell your mother that metal lunchboxes are no longer allowed at school!"

****

Yolo breathed in a huge sigh of relief when she heard the hissing brakes of the school bus. She could never relax until her babies were safe and sound at home. After all, she had cooked a few kids in her day.

Sun and Shyne bounded happily inside of the house. They were always elated to see their mother, but their big sister Christi was home for the summer.

"Hello, Mommy...Christi!" the twins cheered and pounced.

"Ugh! Hey, guys!" Christi groaned under their combined weight. She squeezed her beloved siblings then pulled away when she saw the blood. "Is this blood?!"

"It ain't ours!" Sun said proudly.

"We had to put the smack down," Shyne explained. "Oh, Mommy, we need new lunchboxes. And they have to be plastic!"

"You're not going to say anything?" Christi exclaimed. She couldn't believe how nonchalant Yolo was about her children coming home with blood on them.

"'Bout what?" Yolo shrugged.

"Um, about these two jumping on kids and beating them bloody with their lunchboxes, maybe?"

"Oh, yeah. You guys go to your rooms! Get changed so we can go to Chuck-E-Cheese," the proud mother proclaimed.

****

With Christi home for the summer, Yolo enrolled her in karate class. Karate Joe was delighted to have another student and Yolo was relieved she would learn self-defense. Once class was underway, Yolo eased off to do some exploring. She crossed the courtyard and entered the building Sincerity once lived in.

"I should have killed you when I had the chance," she sighed. She was inside with her but had spared her and her children.

"Can I help you?" the new tenant asked when she opened the door and saw Yolo standing there drooling.

"Huh? No!" she said, embarrassed, and took off.

"Where you been, Mommy? You missed it," Shyne pouted when Yolo reappeared.

"We learned how to do a fake kick, then come up with the real one," Sun declared.

"I'm sure it won't kill me to have missed one lesson," Yolo replied. She was wrong, dead wrong.

Chapter 33

"Nope," Sun protested when Miss Hunter tried to put him and Shyne in separate classrooms at the start of first grade. "We stay together!"

"Why, because your mother said so? Well, your mother does not run this school! I do, and..."

"Actually, our dad said we have to stay together," Shyne said as she checked her reflection in the glass.

"Your father?" the principal gushed, batting her lashes and smiling. "Well, that's a different story."

The worst thing that she could do was have the teacher put one in the front and the other in the back of the room. Shyne was a teacher's pet anyway so she rushed to a seat in the front of the class. The bad boys played the back, so Sun headed on back. This way he could goof off in peace.

Sun saw an empty desk next to a new kid in the class. The handsome boy had thick cornrows running down to the middle of his back. He seemed unimpressed and unconcerned with what was going on in the class as he sat drawing pictures in his notebook.

"Don't sit next to him. He's artistic!" a small time bully named Antron warned.

"He is?" Sun asked, looking at the stick figures on the paper. "If that's artistic, then I must be Picasso."

"Who?" the bully asked, as if he would have understood the answer.

"Nobody," Sun replied and went to work goofing off.

He tried to anyway but the bully's taunts began to piss him off. The victim didn't seem fazed by the wisecracks, but Sun, on the other hand, didn't like it one bit. He was taught to mind his business, but he'd also been taught that oppression was worse than slaughter.

"Leave him alone!" Sun growled. He was ready to take it wherever the bully wanted it to go.

"Sun Forrest, would you like to come up to the board and solve the problem?" the teacher dared since she saw he wasn't paying attention.

"Okay," he shrugged. He walked to the chalkboard and easily solved the math problem. Shyne snickered since they had been taught math by their big sister. He saw the new kid watching when he returned and introduced himself.

"I'm Sun," he said, extending his hand like his father had taught him to do. The other boy scrutinized it for a second before he took it.

"I'm Asad, nice to meet you," he replied and turned back to the lesson.

They liked each other immediately and a life-long friendship was instantly formed. Sun tried to introduce his new friend to his sister but it didn't go well.

"This is Asad," Sun announced to Shyne once class ended.

Asad smiled and stuck out his hand, but Shyne wouldn't take it.

"Un uh! You not getting me pregnant!" Shyne shouted and took off. The two friends shared a WTF look before shrugging it off and hitting the playground.

Sun hit the monkey bars where he was king. He spun and flipped while Asad stared in amazement. Shyne was too busy playing in her hair to watch, but she could still hear.

"That boy is artistic! Artistic!" Antron teased.

"That's autistic, stupid!" Shyne fumed. The new word was just as confusing as the name Picasso to the little dummy.

Autism is a brain condition characterized by having difficulties with social interaction, verbal and non-verbal communications, and repetitive behaviors. That explains autism but what the fuck is wrong with bullies?

Asad was on the low end of the spectrum, which allowed him to not only attend regular classes, but to excel in them. He kept to himself and followed all the rules, making him a target for bullies like Antron. Only now, he had a new friend who hated bullies.

"Who you calling stupid?" Antron demanded, balling up his fists for a fight. Sun saw the impending show down and flipped off the monkey bars. He did a perfect double backflip with a half twist that caused him to miss the whole fight.

"Ha-ya!" Shyne shouted before kicking the bully between his legs. The force of the kick lifted him off his feet. When he landed, he had a beating waiting for him. Luckily for the bully, a teacher rushed over to break it up before Sun could get a lick.

"To the principal's office!" the teacher shouted to Shyne and before turning to Sun. "Both of you! Now!"

"Me? But I didn't even touch him!" he protested.

"Snitches get stitches!" Shyne grumbled and marched back into the school.

****

"You two again!" the principal said when she saw the twins. She decided to try her luck and asked, "I'm going to need to speak with your father!"

"He's home now, call him," Sun dared. He wanted to go home anyway so he could spend time with him. Miss Hunter huffed and dialed their home number.

"I need to speak with Mr. Forrest," she insisted when the call was answered.

"Mr. Forrest," Christi announced as she extended the phone to Killa. Yolo frowned up, wondering who would be calling there for him.

"Who was that?" she demanded in a whisper so that she could still listen to Killa as well.

"The school," Christi said and shrugged before turning back to her laptop.

"Mr. Forrest, this is Principal Hunter. I need you...to...cum...down to the school to discuss your children's behavior," she said, amused by her wordplay.

"Is that right?" Killa replied with a chuckle. He was amused as well, but for a different reason. He knew that Yolo was hot about her flirting and hoped she had up-to-date dental records because she was going to need them. Unable to take another second of it, Yolo snatched the phone from Killa.

"Hello! Sup? Huh? Sup?" Yolo spat.

"Oh, it's you. Well, your children jumped on another student..."

"No, we didn't! I got him myself!" Shyne corrected in the background.

"I'm on my way!" Yolo shouted and hung up. Killa was next to get barked at when he stood to go with her. "Un uh, you stay here!"

"Uh oh," Christi laughed at Killa and the kids.

"What I do?" Killa whined.

****

"I'm sick of this bitch flirting with my man! It's bad enough I gotta share him with his other baby mama. Glad his first baby mama dead," Yolo grumbled as she drove to the school. "I'm tryna be patient and mature about the shit, but I really wanna cut the bitch's head off!"

Yolo pulled into the same spot she always pulled into when her kids got in trouble. The school really needed to reserve her a spot of her own. She passed by the lumped up child sitting in the office and shook her head.

"She did it this time," Sun said when his irate mother entered the principal's office.

"Snitches get stitches," Yolo reminded and turned to her daughter as if the principal was invisible. "What happened?"

"He was picking on our friend Asad," she said, sticking her chest out proudly. "You fu-...um, mess with him, you mess with me!"

"Us!" Sun corrected, causing Miss Hunter to delete the report she was entering into the computer.

"Good job!" Yolo agreed and high fived her daughter. She took their hands and marched them out of the building without saying a word to the principal.

"She who laughs last," the educator laughed as Yolo stormed out. She loved frustrating baby mamas before fucking their baby daddies.

"Can Daddy cook out for us?" Shyne pleaded as they left the school. She tried to play the sweet little girl role, but Yolo saw right through it.

"Damn pyromaniac!" she laughed, knowing her daughter loved fire. She loved her boo's jerk chicken, though, so she agreed. "Sure, let's stop by the store."

Chapter 34

"Let me do it, Daddy! Please, pluh-leeeze! Come on, Daddy, let me! Let me!" Shyne pleaded, hopping from foot to foot like she had to pee. She dropped down and clasped her hands together like she was praying.

"You're scaring Daddy," Killa admitted, but still gave in and gave his daughter the box of wooden matches. "All you have to do is... Damn!"

Shyne didn't hear one word her father said once she got the matches in her hands. She struck one and put it in with the rest. Once the box flared up, she tossed it into the grill. The charcoal, soaked in liquid fluid, made a loud 'woomf' as it exploded.

The little girl stand frozen in place, mesmerized by the dancing orange flames. A crooked smile turned up one side of her mouth as she watched the fire.

"Yolo! Yolo, come get her!" Killa shouted in bemusement.

"Don't cheat!" Yolo demanded as she paused the video game she and her son were playing.

"Who, me?" Sun exclaimed as if the notion was preposterous. As an afterthought, he dug into his pocket and pulled out a card and extended it towards his mother. "Give this to Daddy."

"What is it?" Yolo growled, despite the fact that she could read the principal's name embossed on the card.

"Miss Hunter said to give it to Daddy," he said with a shrug.

"Sweet boy," she cooed and kissed her son's forehead.

The sweet boy resumed the game the second she left the room. He scored a quick touchdown to even the score before putting the game back on pause.

"What's the emergency?" Yolo asked, but saw it for herself as she noticed Shyne standing fixated on the fire. "Oh my!"

"'Oh my,' is right! Look at this!" Killa replied as he passed his hand in front of their daughter's face and she didn't blink. "This is going to be a problem!"

"For somebody," Yolo shrugged. "Oh, Bae, can I use your phone? Mine is..."

"Sure," Killa said, and handed it over without hesitation. The killer kept several phones in rotation, including one for each baby mama's house. It kept his women from spying, which kept the drama and confusion down.

Yolo cupped the phone in both hands and laughed wickedly as she rushed inside and up the stairs to her room. Sun took the opportunity to score another touchdown. His team was now in the lead.

Yolo was already hot about the principal flirting with her man, so the woman trying to use her son to get to his father only served to make matters worse. The handwritten note on the back of the card she'd given Sun only served to add fuel to the fire. 'Call or text me,' it read.

"*This is Mr. Forrest; how can I help you?*" Yolo texted, saying each word aloud as she typed them. The reply came back within seconds.

"Really! Are you serious?" Yolo shouted when the principal sent a picture of her vagina. It was quickly followed by a picture of her nipples then one of her smiling face. "Grrr!"

"*Looks nice,*" she texted back, gritting her teeth while steam came out her ears.

"*Taste nice too, lol,*" came her reply.

"*Would you like to be eaten alive?*" Yolo texted and giggled. This was definitely one of life's 'be careful what you wish for' moments.

"*I would love to be eaten! But what about your crazy baby mama?*"

"*What about her?*" Yolo said aloud as she typed the words.

"*Just hoping I won't have to slap her!*" the educator replied.

"*How about I come over once she's asleep?*" Yolo texted and a date was set.

****

Sun and Shyne often waited until their mom went to sleep and got back up to sneak back down and watch cartoons. Yolo usually went to bed early when Killa was away, but he was home. The twins met in the hallway like always but were met by strange noises coming from their mother's room. It sounded like people were jumping up and down on the bed while clapping their hands. They both shrugged it off and headed down the stairs.

"I said, whose...is...it?" the aggressive lover on the top growled.

"Yours! It's yours!" Killa shouted as the rodeo girl rode him hard and fast. Technically, she shared the dick with Sincerity, but at the moment, it was all hers.

"You...damn...right...it's mine!" she said as she bounced up and down. She saw Killa's face contort into a fuck face and threw her hips into overdrive. She bounced, rocked, wiggled, and squeezed until he exploded inside of her.

"That's right, baby," she cooed as she milked him dry with her vaginal muscles.

"Mm, that was goo-," Killa moaned but was cut off by a deep yawn. He blinked, yawned again, and then fell into a deep sleep. Yolo waited until he was snoring peacefully before she got off of him.

"Works every time," she laughed at the sedative power of good pussy. On a whim, she used his phone to snap a picture of his deflating dick.

"I'm on my way," she texted under the picture before sending it to Principal Hunter.

"Mm, I can't wait," Miss Hunter texted back.

Yolo crept quietly around the room as she got ready for her mission. She blew her baby daddy a kiss from the doorway before creeping down the hall so that she wouldn't wake the kids.

"What the..." Yolo grunted when she came down and found the twins in front of the T.V.

They had popped popcorn and helped themselves to juice boxes.

"Run!" Sun shouted as hopped up.

Shyne tripped him and hopped over him to escape. He jumped back up and hit the steps right behind her.

"That's okay, I know where y'all stay," Yolo said and turned to leave.

****

"I'm here," Yolo texted as she pulled onto the woman's street. She was driving by slowly, looking for any potential witnesses when the reply came in.

"It's open," she texted back, referring to both the front door and her firm brown thighs. She'd already began playing in her box so it would be good and juicy when he arrived. It was meant to be a surprise, but it was she who was actually in for a surprise.

Yolo parked backwards in the driveway before popping her trunk. She left the motor humming quietly as she went up to the door. It was slightly cracked so she rushed inside. There was the principal, eyes closed, legs spread wide on the sofa. Yolo raised the gun and aimed it between her legs.

"Ouch! What the hell!" she groaned at the combination of pain and the sight of a dart in her vagina. She opened her mouth to say something else, but the tranquilizer had other ideas.

"Told you to leave my man alone," Yolo shrugged and got to work.

She pulled the sleeping woman off the couch by her pretty feet. She dragged her to the door and checked again for witnesses. Seeing none, she continued out to her car and put the unconscious woman in her trunk.

"It's a long ride, so here's a pillow," Yolo said, throwing a pillow at her. She was still sleep so she didn't catch it.

The ride out to Coram, New York was pretty long. The sleepy town way out on Long Island was where she kept her pets. The principal was still sleeping soundly when they arrived. Yolo dragged her out of the car and into the center of the pen before dousing her with a bucket of cold water.

"Huh? What? Where am I?" the principal shouted when she was abruptly awakened. "What's that smell? Why am I here?"

"That smell is my pigs," Yolo replied as she exited the pen and locked the gate behind her. She hit a switch that opened the doors of the pigs' cages. "You said you wanted to get eaten, so..."

"Nooo!" the principal screamed as the ravenous beasts rushed out and toward her.

She stuck her hand out to ward off the first hog and it bit her fingers off for an appetizer. It was soon joined by the rest of them and together they made a noisy, bloody meal of the woman. Yolo stood watching to make sure that they didn't leave anything behind. Once they finished their meal, it was time for her to go.

"Okay, bye-bye!" she said as she waved and headed back to her car.

Chapter 35

"Can we go camping, Daddy? Please! Please!" Sun asked as he began chanting. His sister quickly joined in and made it a duet.

"Please, please!"

"Camping? You mean like...in the woods?" Killa asked with trepidation. He wasn't scared per se, he just didn't fuck with the woods, wild animals, the dark, etc.

"Yeah. Please! Please!" the kids chanted again.

"Looks like you're outvoted," Yolo teased. "I'm sure you guys will have a great time. Meanwhile, I can relax, run a bath, sip some wine, and read a book."

"We want you to come, too, Mommy!" Sun demanded. "Please! Please!"

"Looks like you've been outvoted," Killa laughed. "I'm sure we'll have a great time."

"Oh, okay. Just make sure you get a tent with A/C, and Wi-Fi, and..." Yolo said, naming off a long list of wants as she relented.

"We may as well camp out in the den, then, for that matter," Killa cut in. "Come on, kids, let's go shopping."

"Guess I'll do a little shopping myself," Yolo said to herself once they were gone. She had no idea what kind of dangers awaited them at the campgrounds so she went to the basement to select some weapons.

"Let's see..." she said, scratching her head as she looked around the virtual armory. She began with his and her sniper rifles complete with night vision scopes and silencers. Matching Magnums and machetes filled the bill. Her shopping spree went a lot easier than Killa's and the kids'.

****

"Mm hmm," Sincerity hummed, making her 'yeah right' face when Killa called to say that he would be a few days late on his return to Georgia.

"I'll make it up to you when I get home," he vowed and hung up.

"You can't make up lost time," Sincerity sighed into the dead line. She was right, too, because once a second is gone, it's gone for good.

"Ooh, look at this one!" Sun cheered about huge tent that could sleep ten people. That was eight too many because he had his heart set on some camp-side coochie, vacation vagina, backwoods back shots.

"Too big. Your mom and I will share a tent and you two can..."

"No!" Shyne cut in with her 'something stinks' face. "I need my own tent cuz he pees the bed!"

"Well, you'll be in sleeping bags, so it'll soak it up, like a sponge."

"A pee sponge!" Shyne cracked, cracking up and taking her father with her. Sun twisted up his lips as they yucked it up at his expense.

Killa let them pick out their own sleeping bags while he found a two-person bag for him and Yolo. Unwilling to sleep directly on the lumpy ground, he bought air mattresses for them all.

"Ooh, Daddy, look!" Shyne said as her eyes lit up with excitement.

"No! No fire. You won't have Smokey the Bear messing with me," Killa protested.

"Actually, you will need a fire. It will be pitch black out there and you'll need it for heat or to cook your food," the salesman added. He, too, was a little disturbed by the look in the little girl's eyes so he offered a solution. "You can put your tent in between the fire and theirs."

"I guess," the dad sighed. "Guess we'll also take a couple fire extinguishers as well. And one of those helicopters that drops water."

****

The Suffolk County Park campgrounds were out on the east end of Long Island, not too far from where Yolo kept her pigs. She saw the exit that led to them and smiled warmly at the fond memories of the principal being eaten alive.

"What?" Killa asked when he saw the devious smirk on her face.

"Huh? Nothing," she replied, fighting the giggles. She looked back at her kids and asked, "How's the new principal working out?"

"He's mean!" the twins replied in unison. Both twisted up their little faces as if the very mention of the man left a sour taste in their mouths.

"Good!" the parents responded back in unison.

Killa finally processed all the information and shook his head. A missing principal, a lost cell phone, and Yolo could only mean one thing. "You are too much!" he said.

She shrugged and leaned in to turn the radio up.

The Killa and his family arrived at the campsite and found a spot away from prying eyes. The kids karate chopped each other while their father put up the tents and set up the rest of the campsite.

"Whew!" the sweaty dad exclaimed once he'd finally finished. He was ready for a nap but the kids had other plans.

"Let's go fishing!" Sun announced, holding up his rod and reel.

"Yeah, fishing!" Shyne co-signed. She really didn't care to go fishing but they had a deal to always support each other. It was them against the world, from the womb to the tomb.

"Oh, alright!" Killa conceded. "Come on, Yo."

"As if," Yolo laughed and went back to her tablet. The 1-800-Killa site was popping so she browsed for bodies.

****

"I got one, Daddy!" Shyne shouted when she felt a fish on her line. Before he could move, Sun was by his sister's side helping her. The proud papa smiled as he watched his children work together.

The well-stocked pond allowed them all to catch fish. Dusk began its beautiful descent and it was time to go. Yolo was still in the same exact spot she'd been in when they left. A good book will do that to you. Although she hadn't moved, she'd been all over the world in her mind.

"Look, Mommy!" Sun shouted, thrusting his fish in his mother's face and nearly getting karate chopped in the throat. "Now, you gotta cook it."

"Gotta clean it first," Killa laughed.

"Anyway, we have hotdogs and hamburgers," she replied. "Then we can make s'mores."

"S'mores!" Killa reeled in his 'I don't eat swine' voice, with a face to match. Marshmallows were made with gelatin and most gelatin was made from pigs.

"Chill, my brother, they're halal," Yolo said, holding up her fist in the sign of Black Power. "Black Power."

"Actually, Mommy, Black Power has nothing to do with Islam," Shyne explained. "Most people think that The Nation of Islam is Islam, but it's not. And neither is Isis."

"She's right," Sun chimed in. "Isis is a fanatical group that adheres to a heretical creed which is condemned by Islam and Muslims. Isis believe that it's lawful to kill anyone who opposes them, Muslims included!"

"I knew that," Yolo lied. "Anyway, let's eat!"

"Oh, yesss!" Shyne swooned when her father lit the fire. They cooked, ate, and kicked it until it was time for bed.

"I'll tuck them in while you fix me a snack," Yolo said wickedly. Her kids were saying something but she hadn't heard a word of it.

She had dick on her mind, and lots of it. She wanted Killa to pull her hair and fuck her like a cave girl. The tired kids fell asleep halfway through their bedtime story and their mother rushed off to get laid.

"Fixed your snack," Killa said, holding his thick erection in his hand.

"That's more like a meal," she said, but she didn't begin eating. Instead, she turned around and slid down his pole backwards. She rode him hard and fast until they both busted a quick nut. That was just foreplay. Now it was time to get down to business. They ran through sexual positions like a football team running different plays. Somewhere, a rooster crowed, alerting them that dawn was approaching so it was time to wrap things up. Killa called one last play and folded Yolo in half.

"Uh oh!" she giggled when he placed her legs up onto his shoulders. She gripped the sleeping bag beneath her and braced herself for a pounding. The hard strokes sounded off in the night air. They mixed with the sounds of the lover's grunts and moans of pleasure.

"Ooowweee!" Killa howled like a wolf when he finally came.

"That's right, daddy," Yolo purred softly and rubbed his back as he convulsed inside of her. He fell asleep right where he was and she let him.

****

"Good morning!" Yolo sang like a woman sings when she's been dicked down real good. She'd planned on starting breakfast, but noticed that there was something wrong with her children.

Shyne had a wide eyed look of pure shock pasted on her face while Sun was all snickers and giggles. Shyne twisted her face up and rolled her eyes at their mother while Sun smiled at their dad.

"Killa!!!" Sun cheered and high fived his dad.

"What the hell is wrong with them?" he asked of their odd behavior.

"Don't know, don't care," Yolo shrugged and began to cook. "I'm just waiting 'til night time and round...five?"

"Six," he corrected since he'd kept count. It pleased him immensely to please his family. His children got whatever they wanted and his women got multiple orgasms. It was the South Bronx way.

"Can we go hiking?" Sun asked once breakfast was eaten. "Walking after a meal aids in digestion and..."

"Okay," Yolo cut in to cut off what would be a long speech on the subject. She loved that her kids were smart and had so much knowledge, but she just didn't want to always hear it.

****

The campgrounds were a series of woods and trails speckled with clearings for tents. They explored the woods, taking pictures of things that interested them. Most of the clearings contained happy campers who waved and offered friendly greetings to all that passed by. Most, but not all.

"Look, Bae," Yolo warned as they entered a clearing. The young, shirtless, baldheaded white boys looked like nothing but trouble. As soon as one spotted the black family, he pointed them out and led the way towards them.

"Chill," Killa said, preventing Yolo from pulling her gun. She'd have gunned them all down before they'd even gotten close if he hadn't stopped her. The twins had witnessed death through Harry's execution, so the father wanted to spare them from seeing a murder. Both parents saw violence at an early age, and look how they'd turned out. "I got this."

Sun and Shyne both picked up on their parents' ominous mood swing and didn't protest when Yolo pulled them away from the clearing. They walked briskly back to camp while their father acted as a buffer. His six shots were more than enough for the five men. He decided whoever spoke first could get shot twice at no extra charge.

"What you niggers doing out here?" a Skinhead with a reddish beard asked. His partners proved he was the leader by laughing heartily at his statement.

"Just chillin'," Killa replied, gripping his pistol behind his back. They were one step away from the upper room and didn't even know it. "We really don't want any problems."

"Well..." the leader began but was cut off by a white family hiking towards them. "We see you again and there's gonna be a problem."

"Yessir!" Killa replied and turned to leave. They were right, there was going to be a problem when they saw him again.

****

"Welp, time for bed," Yolo announced after one last campfire story.

"I'll get ready," Killa said as he jumped to his feet and rushed into their tent. Shyne sucked her teeth and rolled her eyes again just like she'd been doing all day. Likewise, Sun snickered and giggled like he'd been doing all day.

"What has gotten into those two?" Yolo wondered. She turned towards their tent and saw for herself.

With the fire glowing from the opposite side of her and Killa's tent, it made it completely see through. Her sneaky kids had gotten up in the middle of the night and gotten an eyeful. A wave of shame rolled over Yolo as she recalled the previous night's events. It rolled over her and kept rolling.

"Bring y'all asses out again tonight and y'all gonna see the same thing!" she spat and then headed inside her tent to inform Killa.

"Oh wow!" was all he could say. "No wonder lil' mama been turning her nose up at me all day! Guess you better have that talk with her."

"Me!" Yolo reeled. "Why not you? Dads can teach their daughters the birds and the bees too!"

"I kinda like her thinking that if a boy touches her, she'll get pregnant and die," Killa shrugged. He would have left it just like that if it were up to him.

"I got it. You ready?" she shot back. She was definitely ready to skin some Skinheads.

****

"Wabbit season," Yolo whispered as she and Killa crept through the woods with their sniper rifles.

"Duck season," Killa whispered back and laughed. Back and forth they went until they reached the Skinhead's campsite. "Dirty, racist, Skinhead bastard season."

"Hahaha," Yolo laughed like Elmer Fudd.

They were both pleased to see that they had been joined by five more Skinheads. They were all sitting around having what they considered to be a good ole time. They were all smoking weed and meth while listening to music.

"Is that...rap?" Killa frowned upon hearing the racists listening to rap music. Actually, the dumb ass rapper used the word nigga so much that he quickly became one of the KKK's favorites.

"Watch this, trick shot," Yolo said as she lined up her targets. One Skinhead leaned in to give another one a shotgun off the weed and she fired. *Pst.*

"Nice!" Killa nodded as the large slug tore through both heads. That's called killing two birdbrains with one stone. The others didn't even notice them drop dead. "My turn!"

Killa closed one eye and peered into his scope. Two men were dancing along to the N-word off beat. He waited for...the...right...time and fired. The .223 slug passed through one man's torso and into the next. He followed it up with two quick shots to make sure the fallen men never got back up.

"The fuck?" the leader asked when he saw what was happening. His buddy opened his mouth to speak, giving Yolo a clear shot at his tonsils. Whatever was on his mind went out the gaping hole in the back of his head along with his brain.

"Un uh," Killa laughed when the redheaded one turned to run. A quiet calf shot put him on the ground. That left eight dead and two wounded when they made their approach.

"W-w-what do y-y-you g-g-guys..."

"W-w-w-want?" Yolo giggled and tuned to Killa. "You remember that song? What you wa-wa-wa, what you..."

"Um..." Killa said, reminding her of the mission at hand. "What we want is life, love, and the pursuit of happiness. Same as anyone else, but have you tell it, we can't have it because of melanin."

"Who?" the other victim asked.

Yolo put the rifle up to his head, ready to put him out of his misery.

"Wait!" Killa shouted. "Let's give them a chance. Maybe they know some funny black jokes. You know I's love me some black jokes."

"Actually...I do too," Yolo admitted. "Okay, tell us some good black jokes and we might let you live."

"Um...okay," Redhead said and scanned his vast repertoire. 'Uh, what would you call the Flintstones if they were black?"

"What?" Killa asked gleefully. He smiled brightly in anticipation of the punchline.

"A nigger," he laughed. At least he thought it was funny because his audience didn't.

"Boo!" Yolo jeered.

"I got one!" the other wounded man offered. "What did the Georgia sheriff call a black man shot 15 times...The worst case of suicide he ever did see! Get it? They..."

"Got it, not funny. You guys aren't helping yourselves," Killa advised

"Okay, okay. I got one!" Red said of his secret weapon. This joke always killed at rallies and cross burnings. "Okay, okay, okay, so I'm at the airport. The nigger in line in front is buying a ticket to Africa but he's a dollar short. He asks to borrow a dollar so he can go to Africa. I'm like, one dollar, to go to Africa? Here's a ten, take nine more niggers with you!"

"Y'all dead," Yolo shrugged and raised her rifle once more.

"Wait! You said if we told you some jokes you might let us go," the other pleaded.

"Yeah, I said might. Might expresses a possibility based on a condition being fulfilled," Yolo replied.

"Who?" he asked and got shot.

Redhead starting rapping to save his life and got shot, too.

"Da-da-da-dat's all folks!"

****

Killa gripped the steering wheel and stared straight ahead as Yolo tried to explain the birds and bees. He was a grown ass man and he couldn't understand what she was saying.

Poor Shyne looked utterly disgusted by the talk of penis and vagina while Sun giggled his ass off. By the time they made it back home, the lesson was well taught.

"Eww! Y'all nasty!" Shyne grimaced.

Chapter 36

"Can we go out and play?" Sun asked. The question was simply a formality since their mother always let them go outside. They were now nine years old and fully trained black belts, so she had no problem letting them go outside as long as they didn't get into trouble. Asad played with them most days and kept them out of trouble.

"Sure," Yolo agreed and laughed at her daughter trying to sneak by. "Yeah right, assume the position."

"Mommmmyyy!" Shyne huffed as she placed her hands on the wall and spread her feet.

"Mommmyy, nothing. Your little ass almost burned down the woods!" Yolo said as she patted the child down. Sure enough, she found a lighter in her pocket. "Un huh."

"How'd that get there?" Shyne asked, proving she had a future in acting.

"Get help, little girl, get help," Yolo said, shaking her head. "You guys be back in an hour. Your father is on his way so we can go to the zoo."

"Yay!" Sun cheered. "Can Asad come?"

"Of course," Yolo answered quickly.

He was the only friend that the twins ever bought home and was now a part of their family.

****

Yolo told her kids that their father would be there in an hour, although he'd called from up the street. It gave her an hour to bounce up and down on his dick they way they both liked before it was time to head to the zoo.

"I'm cumming!" she proclaimed and did just that. The gripping of her tight vagina as she convulsed caused Killa to cum with her. Lunatics have the best pussy.

"Mmm, that was goo-," Killa yawned and blinked.

"Oh, no you don't! You told the twins you were taking them to the zoo," Yolo reminded. She hopped off of him and pulled him up by his hand. "Come on."

"Okaay," he groaned and followed her into the shower.

The water revived them both for the trip into the city.

****

"I think that's her boyfriend," Killa remarked as he watched Shyne holding hands with Asad as they reached the zoo.

"Bae, they're just kids. He's her protector and he keeps Sun out of trouble," Yolo replied. It set the daddy's mind at ease and he left it alone.

"Daddy, can I go on the monkey bars?" Sun asked.

"Sure," his father agreed and off he went.

"You do know the monkey bars are inside the monkey's cage, don't you?" Shyne snitched.

"Oh, damn it!" Killa fussed and took off to catch his son. He got there just as Sun began his climb into the enclosure. "Not today, Sun."

"Aw, man!" Sun fussed and pouted. His father made it up at the concession stands with popcorn and peanuts. Besides, he didn't say he couldn't go in, he just said, "Not today."

After a day at the Bronx Zoo, they swung by the projects to see Karate Joe in another Bronx zoo. The karate teacher had set up a formal graduation for his students up on the rooftop. He had refreshments of chips, quarter waters, and of course, black belts.

"Sun," Karate Joe said with a bow before awarding him his black belt. He turned to Shyne and repeated the process. Yolo wondered who the last belt was for until he turned to her and bowed.

"Me?" Yolo cheesed widely, pointing at herself to be sure. She'd learned everything that the children had but didn't expect to receive a belt as well.

"You are the only student to ever draw blood," he said, touching his lip that was still puffy from their last sparring session.

"Thank you," she said with a bow and accepted her prize. She and the kids partook of the refreshments while Killa pulled the teacher aside.

"Here you go. Thank you," Killa said, passing him an envelope thick with cash.

"You know that I don't accept money for training," Karate Joe said, pushing the envelope back towards Killa.

"I do know. This, however, is for your discretion," he said, pushing the envelope back towards the other man. Sun looked so much like his father that the older man had to know that he'd fathered him, yet he'd never said a word to his daughter.

"Oh, that," Karate Joe laughed and took the money. He knew that Sincerity would have been mad and hurt about him training the side chick and her kids, but he'd had a side chick or two in his day and understood Killa's position.

"I'm still not sure how I feel about having a son who gets his ass kicked by his twin sister," Killa sighed.

"Only because he lets her," the teacher revealed. "Your son is going to be very dangerous when he reaches his full strength. He's the second best student that I've ever taught."

"Yolo is that good?" Killa reeled in surprise.

"No, but Sincerity is," Karate Joe corrected. "I would hate to see them ever come across each other."

"I got this," Killa said with a confidence that he didn't feel.

Women like Yolo and Sincerity could never be fully tamed. The two bumping heads would be the proverbial unstoppable force meeting an unmovable object. That would be a disaster and he knew it. He also knew that it was inevitable.

****

"Damn it, man!" Yolo declared as Killa sucked her vagina. He didn't eat her pussy often but when he did, he did it to death. "Why...are...y-y-y-you...b-b-being so...n-n-ice.?"

"Hmm?" Killa asked right before sliding his tongue inside of her. He hoped that it would change the subject, it did. But only for a few minutes, though, because Yolo repeated the question once she bust a gushing nut in his mouth.

"What are you up to?" she asked as she kissed her way down his chiseled body to return the favor. She opened her mouth so he could feel the heat of her mouth on the tip of his dick then stopped. "Answer me."

"I have to take the boys down to see my grandmother," he said and mourned the blowjob that got cancelled.

"Are you taking Sun and Shyne as well? They're almost ten years old now. Don't you think it's time that they meet their great-grandmother? Or are your other kids better than them? Oh wait, I'm the side chick, so what my kids don't count. Does she even know that you have twins?"

"A'right, a'right! You're right! I'll take them when I get back," he conceded. It was time to introduce them to the rest of their family.

"I know I'm right! You always...wait, you said I'm right," she giggled, feeling silly. She still had his dick in hand so she popped it into her mouth.

"Come on," Killa said, guiding her up.

He put her in her favorite position, face down, ass up, and slid inside of her. He knew he was wrong so he laid some serious pipe to make it right. He bit his own lip hard enough to draw blood in an attempt to stave off reaching an orgasm. Once Yolo got off, he finally let go.

"You need to get in trouble more often!" Yolo cheered as they cuddled.

"I know I gotta do better. Things will change once I get back. I promise," he promised.

"And the kids and I can have you all of the time? All to ourselves?" she asked, pressing her luck.

"Yolo, now you know the situation," he said, meaning Sincerity. "If it wasn't for her, we would be together."

"You for real?" she popped up and demanded. What he'd said and what she'd heard were two different things. She'd heard, 'if you kill Sincerity, we can live happily ever after.'

"Of...course, I...am," he said between yawns.

She laid back down and snuggled up against him. "It'll be done by the time you make it back. This will be the kids' best birthday ever!" Yolo sang.

"Okay, babe," Killa mumbled and drifted off to sleep.

Chapter 37

Killa had a good night's sleep and dreamt of an early morning blowjob. The alarm clock began to buzz and he opened his eyes to and realized that it wasn't a dream. Yolo was showing him what life with her could be like. She'd adored him her whole life and would do anything to make him happy. Blowjobs first thing in the morning made him happy, so...

"Good morning," Yolo sang once the blowjob ended in the way that blowjobs should end. "I guess that was breakfast. Now, I'll go fix something for you and the kids."

"Okay," Killa said as she left the room.

Ten years was a long time to put off making a choice. A week in South America would clear his mind enough for him to pick. He didn't realize how long he'd been stuck in his thoughts until Yolo called up to tell him that breakfast was ready.

"Hey, Daddy," Shyne smiled and greeted the love of her life.

"She got a boyfriend," Sun said, looking for attention.

"Snitch!" Yolo and Shyne yelled and fist bumped.

"Okay, first of all, Sun, you have the right to remain silent and you should. Everything you say can be used against you in a court of law," he informed his son before turning to his daughter, "Now, what's this about a boyfriend? Who?"

"He's talking about Asad. And he's NOT my boyfriend," Shyne said, to his relief. However, it was short lived. "He's my fiancé."

"What!" Killa yelled, coughing up his coffee.

"Relax, Babe. You know he's Muslim and Muslims don't date, so he asked her to marry him," Yolo explained.

"So, when's the big day?" the proud father asked. He actually liked the quiet kid with good manners.

"After I graduate from college," Shyne replied, causing her mother to beam brightly.

"When we going back to shoot?" Sun butted in. He liked to be the center of attention, so he jumped back in.

"Yeah, Daddy, when?" Shyne seconded. He'd started taking the kids to the range and they both loved it. Go figure, Yolo and Killa's kids like guns.

"As soon as I get back. And, we have another surprise for you guys, too!" he replied.

Yolo assumed he meant him moving in and smiled even wider. This was one of the best days of her life. One of the last as well.

****

"Spit something," Killa dared when they all got into the car. He liked hearing his son's little raps but it would also keep Yolo from pressing the issue. Little did he know, she was done with the conversation and had murder on her mind.

"Okay, Daddy," he agreed and turned to Shyne, "Hit it!"

Shyne cupped her hands and began making a beat with her mouth. Yolo failed in her attempt not to laugh and cracked up. Sun bobbed his head for a couple of bars and jumped in like double-dutch.

"Damn! He's good!" Yolo told his father. He actually sounded better than most of the rappers on the radio. His vocabulary was certainly bigger.

"He is," Killa said proudly. He scanned his memory for music business connects to hook him up with. Sun didn't stop rapping until they reached the airport.

"Can we go with you?" Shyne pleaded, making her voice sound like a four-year-old's. Just like her mother hold told her to.

"Next time. Promise," he said and scooped her up into his arms. She squealed in delight as he planted loud kisses all over her face. He put her down and turned to Sun.

"Aight, yo," Sun said with a pound and a man hug.

"Aight," Killa chuckled as they dapped.

Yolo was all smiles, knowing that she was next. The kids turned away in disgust as their parents shared an intimate kiss.

"It'll be done by the time you get back," she assured him once her tongue returned into her own mouth.

"Um...okay," he replied, still not knowing what she was talking about.

"Love you," Yolo said sadly as he walked away to board his flight.

"Love you, too," Killa mumbled to himself as he got on the plane.

****

"Get dressed, we're going out," Yolo told her children. She heard the distress in her tone and softened it, "We're going to The Museum of Natural History."

"Yay!" Sun and Shyne cheered and clapped. The little intellectuals loved learning experiences. They would choose the library over a video arcade sometimes.

"What's wrong, Mommy?" Shyne asked her troubled mother.

"If anything ever happens to me, I want you to always take of your brother. You're the strong one, so look out for him," the mother said, trying not to cry.

"Okay, Mommy," she whined, on the verge of tears. Luckily for both, Sun came in and broke it up. Shyne went to triple check her afro puffs leaving mother and son alone.

"Look, Sun, if anything happens to me, I want you to always take care of your sister. You're the strong one, so it's up to you to look out for and take care of her."

"Men are the maintainers and protectors of women," Sun said, nodding in agreement with himself.

"That's deep! Where'd you get that from?" Yolo asked knowing he didn't come up with on his own.

"Asad told me. It's in the Qur'an," he replied.

His sister joined them and they headed out to the car for the drive into the city.

****

"It's about damn time!" Diedra grunted when Killa announced that he would be bringing the twins down on his next visit. "You can leave that crazy ass girl right where she's at!"

"That crazy girl saved your life," Killa reminded. He surprised them both by sticking up for Yolo. He knew his grandmother was about to go in, so he pulled out pictures of the twins to distract her.

"Oh my God, they are beautiful!" she said, gushing over her great grandkids. "Wow, he looks just like you! And she is gorgeous with her little afro puffs."

"They are super smart, too!" the proud papa proclaimed.

"So...what are you going to do? You can't keep up living a double life with two households in two different states forever," his grandmother said.

"I know," he replied, even though he'd been doing just fine for almost ten years. Yes, both women complained and vied to be exclusive, but everyone was well taken care of. "I've made up my mind. I'm going to marry one of them."

"One of them!" Grandma Diedra reeled.

****

"Now look, stay together! Don't touch nothing! Don't break nothing! And don't set anything on fire!" Yolo briefed once they reached the museum. It was pretty much the same briefing she gave the twins anytime she had to leave them alone for more than a blink of an eye.

"Okaay," they sang as if they meant it. They may have, but it didn't stop them from touching, breaking or setting fires.

"I'll be back in a few minutes," she said, backing away slowly.

"Okaay," the kids sang once more.

They smiled and waved until she was out of eyesight then took off in different directions. Him in search of something to touch while she looked for something flammable. Meanwhile, their mother set off to murder someone.

Chapter 38

"Daddy?" Sincerity said, hearing Karate Joe's personal ringtone. It was unusual for him to call more than their weekly video chats. "I hope everything is okay. Sup, Daddy?"

"Hello, Sincerity. I'm Karate Joe," a voice other than his narrated off screen. On screen, was her father's pale face. The eyes were open but lifeless and dull. She frowned in fear and confusion at what was happening but soon got her answer.

"Guess who killed me?" Yolo said, holding her mouth still like a ventriloquist as she held the severed head to the camera. She tossed it aside and turned the phone towards herself. "I did! Now, what you gonna do about it?"

"Nooo!" Sincerity screamed at the realization of her dad's murder. She quickly regained her composure so her nemesis wouldn't have the satisfaction of her tears. "A-yo, stay right there, bitch. I'm on my way!"

"Oooh, I'm so scared!" Yolo teased. "No can do, but I'll meet you right here tomorrow. Hope you know the ledge."

"Bitch, I'm...," she growled into the empty line. She jumped up to collect her kids for the trip and remembered they went with their father. She dialed his number but hung up before it could ring. She blamed him for her father's death. He should have killed her the first time. "Want something done, you gotta do it yourself!"

****

"Oooh! Cowboys and Indians!" Sun cheered when he found the Native American display. He decided the Indians were here first, so he got on their side. He took a bow and arrow from one of the figures and began firing at the cowboys. Speaking of fire...

207

Yolo had been gone for an hour but that was fifty minutes too long. A fire truck was pulling away and she could only shake her head. Sure enough, she walked in and saw a security guard with a twin in each hand.

"What did they do?" she sighed and reached for her wallet to pay for whatever damages they caused.

"He shot arrows and she, well, you smell the smoke?" he said. The kids remained tight lipped until he released their collars. "Then they wouldn't give their names, your number, nothing. Not one word."

"Good!" Yolo quipped since that's how they had been raised. "Now, what do I owe you?"

"Insurance will cover it but...don't bring them back ever again!"

"Can't take y'all anywhere!" Yolo fussed as she drove back out to Long Island. "I have a very important meeting tomorrow."

"I tried to tell him, Mommy!" Shyne said, shaking her head.

"Tell him how? With smoke signals?"

****

Yolo felt an odd sense of dread all evening. She tried not to infect her children with it by cooking tacos and playing board games. Sincerity was no punk and killing her wouldn't be a walk in the park. She wanted to launch a grenade at her and end it but on the strength of Karate Joe, she owed her a fair one.

The night ended on pallets in the den as they all feel asleep watching movies. They awoke and made waffles together as a family, for the last time. Shortly after noon, they got in the car and went to the city.

"Can we visit Karate Joe?" Sun asked when they reached the Bronx.

"Nah," Yolo said, twisting her lips ruefully. It was as close to remorse as she'd ever felt in her life. The classic too little too late. It was a necessary evil to draw Sincerity out so she could kill her. "We're going to the zoo."

"Yay!" the twins cheered.

A short drive later, they arrived.

"Now look! I really, really need you guys to behave yourselves. Mommy has some very important business to handle and I need you to behave. One hour, can you do that?"

"Yes, Mommy," they said, nodding their cute faces up and down. They knew they were mischievous but figured they could last for an hour.

"Keep an eye on your sister, she burns things," Yolo whispered as she hugged Sun.

"Keep an eye on your brother, he breaks stuff," she said into her daughter's ear. "I love you guys!"

"Love you, too, Mommy!" they sang and waved as she backed away.

"I'm going in!" Sun declared, pointing at the monkeys swinging from the trees. "Hold the phone."

"Un uh, cuz I'm supposed to watch you!" Sun said, stomping her foot.

"Watch me then!" he laughed and climbed into the enclosure.

Meanwhile, Mommy sped towards the projects.

****

Historically, historians have called the Thriller in Manilla the best fight ever held on planet Earth, but that's only because they'd never heard of the Rooftop Romp in the Bronx. Sincerity was a highly trained and deadly dangerous while Yolo was just plain crazy.

Seeing her father in two pieces at the morgue had Sincerity seeing red. Her face was so contorted from anger that some didn't recognize her as she marched in the projects. She believed in an eye for an eye and had brought a machete to cut Yolo's head off. She had a gun as well, just in case it turned into a gunfight. Sincerity was down for whatever.

Yolo arrived in the projects shortly after Sincerity. She walked through the courtyard with a machete in one hand and a forty caliber pistol in the other. Everyone hated her for killing their beloved Karate Joe but no one said anything to her. Mainly because she had a machete in one hand and a forty caliber in the other. The eerie silence stopped her in her tracks to investigate.

"Don't stop now, bitch!" Sincerity yelled down from the roof. "Bring yo' ass on up here!"

"I'll be right up!" Yolo replied and rushed inside. She took the elevator to the top floor and got out with her gun raised. A second later, she was on the roof.

Sincerity fired at Yolo's face the second she emerged through the door. The gun fight lasted two seconds as they both emptied their clips at each other. Next came the machetes as they tried to chop each other's heads off. The clanging of the blades could be heard all the way on the ground.

"Let's put these down and fight!" Sincerity dared, "Unless you scared!"

"I ain't never scared!" Yolo assured her.

They put down the blades and put up their dukes and fought to the death. Both of theirs.

****

The monkeys all turned to the alpha male monkey when the human landed in their enclosure. He lifted his monkey paws and shrugged his monkey shoulders as if to say, 'Don't ask me.' He then walked over to confront the intruder and got even more confused.

"Hold this," Sun said, and tossed him his cell phone. The phone was far more interesting than the boy, so he left him alone.

"Oh shit! Is he...on the monkey's bars?" a security guard said, blinking at the images on his screen. "Security to Primate! Primate, pick up!"

"This is...Primate," the Primate Control Officer replied between sips on his blunt. The monkeys were hilarious when he was high so he made sure to stay high every day.

"Would you mind securing the monkeys and getting that boy out of their enclosure?" he asked casually.

"Boy? In the cage? Yeah, right! They will tear him apart and eat him," he replied as he stood to check the window. "Oh shit! There's really a boy in the cage!"

"Uh...yeah. Now would you mind moving them away so we can get him out?"

Sun had quite an audience as he navigated the monkey bars. A crowd had gathered to watch in morbid curiosity as he flipped in the air. Even the monkeys watched in awe at the strange sight. All except the one with phone, he was on YouTube. Camera phones rolled as the Primate Control Officer entered the enclosure with a tranquilizer gun. The monkeys all put their hands up in surrender and backed away. They didn't want to get shot.

"Come on, son!" a security guard urged once the coast was clear enough to enter.

Sun did a double back flip with a twist for a dismount and stuck the landing.

"Come on, Sun! Let's bounce!" Shyne shouted when her brother stepped out of the cage.

"Not so fast!" the security guard demanded, snatching both of them up. Little did he know, he had fire in one hand and lightening in the other. Lucky for him, the twins knew they were already in enough trouble. They had no idea just how much trouble. "Where is your mother?"

Both kids shrugged. Neither knew she had just fallen to her
death.

Chapter 39

"What now?" Killa sighed when his satellite phone began to ring. He was with his grandmother, so she wasn't calling. That left only his two baby mamas and a couple of solid friends. Either way, it couldn't be good news. He contemplated not answering but it really wasn't an option.

"A-yo, son?" Little Villain began in a tone that confirmed his feeling of dread. He literally felt his own life force shudder inside of him.

"What's up, yo?" he asked and braced himself for the bad news.

"Sin is dead. She got shot and fell off the roof," he explained but it made absolutely no sense. He'd left Sincerity in Georgia and no one in those projects would dare harm anyone close to him.

"Son, what the fuck are you talking about? Where is Joe? Put Karate Joe on the phone!" he barked.

"He dead, too. The same chick that killed Sin killed her, too," Villain said.

"Short, pretty chick with a fat ass and curly hair?" Killa asked, knowing who it had to be; but even that made no sense.

"Yup, that's her," he replied, looking over at the mangled body to be sure. "She dead, too. Fell off the roof, too."

It took Killa several moments to force words from his mouth. The first couple of tries only yielded pain-filled croaks. "Are there any kids out there? With the other girl?"

"Nah, yo," he answered after scanning the crowd for any new faces.

"Be on the lookout for them. I'm on my way," Killa managed. As hard as it was, he now had to deliver the news to Rico, Xavier and Grandma.

****

213

"Any of yous know who they are?" a cop standing near the fallen soldiers asked. Around there, the mantra was 'fuck the police' so most people turned their heads.

"That's my cousin, Sincerity," Sincerity's cousin moaned. She was in genuine mourning but she also wanted the bad ass sneakers her cousin had on her feet.

"What about this one?" he asked, hoping to ID Yolo as well.

No one replied because no one knew. They'd all seen her coming and going over the years but none had ever spoke to her.

The phone in Yolo's pocket began to vibrate.

"Detective."

"Hello?" the detective asked into the phone.

Shyne heard the strange man and knew her mother was gone. Not only would she never allow anyone else to answer her phone, she'd also never not come pick them up.

"What?" Sun asked, seeing his sister turn pale and drop the phone.

"Mommy is dead," she announced. She wanted to cry but wouldn't in front of the strange men. Sun, on the other hand, wailed and cried loudly upon hearing the news. "Stop crying. You have to take care of me now."

"O-o-okay," he sniffled and worked to turn off the water works. He never cried again after that day.

"Hello?" the zoo security guard asked into the open line. He shook his head as he got the same sad news. Neither could help the other so they hung up and went on about their business.

The detective noticed an SD card and popped it out. He inserted it into his phone and got an eyeful of Killa's dick. Had he shown the picture around, a few of the female residents would have recognized it. Killa had been quite the dick slinger while growing up in the projects. Instead, he kept it to himself and for himself.

"Well, if you guys still won't talk, you're going to have to go to foster care," the guard announced, hoping to scare the twins into talking. Neither said a word, so he called Child Protective Services.

"Just chill. As soon as we can get on a computer, we can talk to Christi," Sun mumbled when the guard got back on the phone.

He thought he heard talking but the twins were tight lipped when he snapped his head in their direction. He shrugged and continued his conversation. He hated sending the children into the fucked up New York City foster care system but had no other choice.

****

"Hello, I'm Miss Davis. And what are your names?" the social worker sang into their faces when she arrived. She was too close for comfort and smelled like menthols. Not to mention that she was speaking to them like they were babies. Shyne reared back to kick her in her throat but Sun caught her leg.

"They won't say nothing," the guard pleaded once more. He had begged for an aunt, sister, or someday, anybody to talk to that would keep them out of foster care.

The twins had their minds made up not to speak and wouldn't. They were Killa's kids and knew he would save them. They were Yolo's kids and figured they could handle whatever came their way until they reached the Bronx Children and Family Service building.

Sun came close to speaking when they were led into the chaotic building. The air conditioner was set on high to prevent germs but forced a shitty diaper smell down their throats when they walked in. Security guards tussled with a rowdy teen caught smoking in a bathroom.

"Are you guys hungry?" Miss Davis asked sweetly. Both were hungry but due to the smell of the place they both shook their heads no. The woman frowned, knowing that they should be after their ordeal. Their mother was listed as a Jane Doe in the same morgue as

Sincerity and her father. "Okay, let's get you to your rooms so you can get some rest. Girls are upstairs and boys down."

The twins shook their heads 'no' once more and began to back away. A security guard saw the reaction and came around behind them.

"Easy now," the guard advised as he eased up on them. Sun and Shyne pressed their backs against each other's just like they'd done in their mother's womb. Except now it was a battle stance.

"Maurice, I think you should relax. These poor children have been through quite an ordeal today," the social worker pleaded.

"Don't worry, I got them," he lied. He didn't have shit because as soon as he rushed in, Shyne savagely kicked him between his legs.

The guard felt like his balls had exploded but he didn't have time to scream. The twins spun so Sun was facing him. Being doubled over in pain put him in perfect position for a perfectly placed roundhouse. The kick to the temple turned him off like a light switch.

"Code nine in intake! Code nine in intake!" went out over the intercom. In moments, the area filled with the security guards. The twins kept their backs together and assumed karate stances.

"Wait!" Miss Davis insisted and rushed between the kids and security guards. "They just lost their mom and didn't want to be separated! I'll put them in medical for the night."

"Rules say boys downstairs and girls up," the security chief said.

"Those same rules say no fraternization either!" she shot back.

It was no secret that the handsome Puerto Rican was fucking everything that moved. A couple of female guards blushed and batted their eyelashes.

"So, medical then?" he relented and backed away.

Miss Davis waited until they scooped up their fallen comrade and left before speaking. "You guys sure I can't call anyone? An aunt, grandmother? Anyone?" she pleaded. The kids just stared at her without even blinking. She gave up with a deep sigh and said, "Follow me."

Sun and Shyne watched her walked down the hallway. He traced her panty lines with his eyes while she admired her shoes. They took each other's hand and followed her down the hall. When she held a medical door open, Sun held his sister back and peeked in first. Seeing no danger, he led the way inside.

"I'll be right back," Miss Davis said, closing the door behind herself.

"Let's go," Sun said the split second after she left. He tried the door but it was locked. "Shit!"

"Let's jump her when she gets back. Tie her up and get out of here," Shyne suggested.

"No, she's got a nice ass. I mean, she's nice, I don't want to hurt her," Sun replied. "Besides, how we gonna get out of the building? We don't even know where we are or how to get home."

"You're right, I guess. Nasty, but right," Shyne relented. No sooner did she finish than the door opened and in walked the social worker.

"It's not the greatest but better than nothing," she said of the vending machine food she'd returned with. She sat the burritos, chips and soda on the table but the kids didn't budge.

Sun signed 'thank you' in sign language. Miss Davis smiled in appreciation and backed out of the door. Once she was gone, they dug in and smashed their first meal since breakfast. Yolo was supposed to take them to lunch, but she'd died.

"Help me," Sun said, and began pushing the table against the door. It wouldn't prevent anyone from entering but it would make enough noise to wake them up.

The twins got in the one bed and pressed their backs together and went to sleep. Just like they'd done in their mother's womb.

Chapter 40

"Excuse me, sir," the flight attendant said tentatively.

The passenger had the far away gaze of someone deeply troubled. It was obvious that he'd just suffered a loss of some sort. He was handsome, though, and she wondered if a shot of her hot vagina might lift his spirits.

"Huh?" Killa asked, finally looking up from his lap.

"The plane has landed. They have to clean it," she offered softly.

Killa looked around and noticed not only had they landed, but everyone else had exited already. He stood with the creaking knees that come with getting older and retrieved his bag from the overhead compartment. "Thanks," he replied. He noticed how pretty she was and knew she had some good pussy from the tone of her voice.

When a woman has some really good vagina, it creates a slight rasp in her voice. She had it but now wasn't a good time to pursue finding out. In fact, this was the absolute worse time of his entire life.

Killa was on complete autopilot as he navigated his way uptown to the Bronx. He exited the D train at Yankee Stadium and decided to walk up the hill. Soon, he entered the project's courtyard.

"A-yo!" Villain called out when he saw his wounded mentor wander in.

Killa turned and headed in his direction. "Sup, yo," Killa greeted and plopped down next to him on the park bench. Villain didn't have any flowers or a condolence card to offer so he passed him a blunt. Killa took it and took a long pull. He held it in for just over a minute before exhaling a plume of smoke along with a question. "What happened?"

"Yo...that shit was crazy!" he replied animatedly. He realized who he was talking to and toned it down several notches. "First, they banged it out with the hammers. Then, they ran out of bullets and had a sword fight. Next, they shot a head up but nobody could get off. Then finally, they got on the ledge..."

"Who won?" Killa heard himself ask then wondered why he did.

"You mean, hit the ground first? Or...last?" Villain asked, confused at how to pick a winner when they both lost their life.

"Never mind," he said and took another pull form the blunt. Villain realized he wasn't getting it back and pulled out another one. "See you later."

"Peace," he said to his friend's back as he departed.

****

Killa headed over to his Harlem hideout instead of driving to Long Island. Once he got inside, he realized he had yet to turn on his stateside cell phone. It began to ring the moment he did. He eagerly accepted the calls in hopes of good news about his Sun and Shyne.

"Hello!" he shouted, startling a shaken up Christi even more.

"I can't reach Yolo! Shyne isn't answering her phone and when I called Sun...a monkey answered!" she moaned.

"Yolo, um...is...dead. She died," he said, finally accepting it himself. The line went silent as Christi struggled to figure out what he could have meant by dead.

"And..." was all of the question that would fit out of her throat. Her heart was already broken so any more bad news might kill her.

"I don't know," he sighed. "No answer at the house and no one has seen or heard from them."

"I'm on my way to the airport," Christi declared and hung up. She didn't even bother to pack a bag for the trip to New York. Luckily for her, she had plenty clothes at home. The next plane out of LAX wasn't until the next morning and it cost fifteen hundred dollars for the last minute purchase.

Killa smoked another blunt and fell asleep in a chair. The busy sounds of Harlem woke him a few hours later. After splashing cold water on his face and brushing his teeth, he picked an identity from the several driver's licenses he had in stock. Darius Jackson sounded like the type of guy who packed a thirty-eight, so he selected one from his cache of weapons.

The drive back over to the Bronx was a lot quicker than he remembered. Before he knew it, he had reached the medical examiner's office. As he reached the door, he saw Sincerity's aunt Rashida coming out.

"That's fucked up, yo," Rashida fussed. She was trying to maintain her South Bronx cool but finally broke down.

"I know," he replied as the woman wept on his chest. He held her and let her get it all out. It broke his heart as it was, but knowing it was his fault made it even worse.

"I'll take care of the arrangements," she offered once she regained her composure, save for a few sniffles.

"I already did. I'll text you the info," he replied and went inside.

Since no one had claimed Yolo she was in the Jane Doe section. It was the lost and found for disposable people. Most would never be claimed by family or friends, who didn't even know they had even died. Killa knew this place existed, but still wasn't ready for what he found inside.

"Wow!" he exclaimed at the rows and rows of nameless corpse.

"Looking for anyone in particular?" the clerk asked. The slim, dark haired man had the creepy disposition that the place either required or developed.

"Female, about thirty-three. Fell of a roof," Killa explained.

It was enough to light the necrophiliac's eyes. "Oh yes!" he cheered with an elation that made Killa angry. You wouldn't like him when he's angry. He snarled at the man as he followed him down the rows. He found what he was looking for and snatched the sheet away with a 'ta-dah' that would cost him his life.

"That's her," he said in a voice simmering with rage. "Yolo Jackson. I'm her...brother. I'll claim her body."

"Shucks! I mean, that's great," he said, looking the naked corpse up and down. "I'll get her ready for the funeral home."

Killa frowned at both his reaction as well as the bulge of the erection in his pants. He gave Yolo's corpse one final lustful look and signed his own death certificate. He may as well picked out a slab for himself.

"I would really like to thank you for caring for my sister. Let me send you a gift. What's your address?" Killa asked without a trace of the extreme violence coming into his voice.

"One, twenty-five Grand Concourse..." the clerk rattled off, eager to supplement his meager earnings.

"Make sure you're home tonight," Killa advised as he signed for Yolo's body. He left to go make all the arrangements for her as well.

****

"Who is it?" the coroner's clerk song in response to the ringing of his doorbell. He checked his hair in the mirror and snatched the door open without waiting for a response. It was a mistake that he wouldn't live enough to regret. Killa thrust a Taser into his neck and shocked him until he fell to the floor unconscious.

"Killa," Killa answered as he stepped inside. He dragged the man out of the doorway and locked it behind him. The satchel was opened and out came the tools.

"What? Why? Who? How?" the confused clerk asked, since waking up naked in your bathtub with a strange man standing over you is pretty confusing.

"You gotta start with the penis," Killa replied, just like Yolo would. He usually had his own technique for cutting up bodies but wanted to pay homage to his baby mama by using hers. He always wondered why she said to start with cutting off the penis and got his answer as soon as he did it.

"Yeeeooooowww!" the clerk howled in soprano. Nothing says 'shut the fuck up' like stuffing a man's own dick down his throat, so that's exactly what he did.

"You sounded like Patti LaBelle," Killa chuckled at the whimpering man. "Have you tried her pies? Not bad at all for store bought."

The dying man had absolutely no use for Killa's small talk, not when he was methodically cutting off his body parts. Every joint got separated as he worked his way up. The man was dead by the time Killa reached his hipbone. Once he finished, another Yolo memory caused a smile to spread across his face.

"It's just like cutting chicken."

Chapter 41

"Ma'am? Excuse me, ma'am, we've landed," the flight attendant said softly. The passenger was wide awake but staring off at nothing as the plane emptied in New York.

"Thanks," Christi said as she stood. The flight from California to New York had never been so short before. She turned her phone back on, expecting to receive a text from Shyne asking about haircare or fashion. She sucked her teeth loudly when nothing came through. She checked her social media accounts and still nothing.

Christi had a rental on reserve and rushed out to Long Island. She held her breath when she turned onto their street and headed towards their house. She let out a sigh of relief at the child in the yard, but it was short lived.

"Asad," she said to their faithful friend.

"Yup. Where's Shyne and Sun?" he asked in order of their importance to him. He loved them both, but he was in love with Shyne. "I keep calling but no one is answering."

"I know. I know," she said and went inside the empty house. Once inside, she began calling every agency she could think of. The police, hospitals, fire departments –for Shyne, after all the girl did like playing with fire- and even child protective services. Only problem was, she was checking in Long Island instead of New York City.

****

"What are we going to do?" Shyne asked again the following day.

Sun had an idea but didn't know how to implement it. "We gotta get on the internet," he said, knowing that he could contact Christi who could contact their father.

223

"They got computers in the office. I'll start a fire and you can sneak in," she suggested. Actually, it was a pretty good plan but really she just wanted to start a fire.

"We need a lighter...oh!" he began but she pulled one out.

"Mommy forgot to search me," she replied with a short lived snicker. The mention of their dead mother sucked the air out of the room. After a moment of silence, it was time to move.

"Good morning," Miss Davis sang as she walked into the room. Sun started to make a move but the box of breakfast in her hands persuaded him to wait.

The twins nodded a reply and stared at the food, licking their lips. The social worker sat the food down and they dug in. They scarfed it down quickly and then resumed staring at her.

"So, you guys ready to talk? Can we call your grandma? Your dad?" she pleaded once again. She knew if they couldn't find any relatives, they would end up in foster care eventually. She didn't want to see that for them.

Miss Davis gave up with a deep sigh and turned to leave. As soon as the door opened, the kids made their move. Sun shot past her and took off down the hall.

"Hey!" she called after him, giving Shyne the chance she needed to sneak out herself.

Sun led the guards on a *Benny Hill Show* chase while his sister gathered some paper. "Missed me!" Sun giggled as he slipped past another guard. He was having a ball running them around in circles. They slipped and bumped into each other as they tried to corral him. A karate chop removed any hands that reached him.

Meanwhile, Shyne stacked papers into a pile and lit them. She rolled an aerosol can in and ducked away just before it exploded.

"Isis!" Sun yelled and started a stampede towards the doors. As planned, the guards rushed to investigate the fire. He turned around and snuck into an office instead.

The plan worked and he rushed onto a computer. Actually, the plan almost worked. That was, until Sun got sidetracked. He saw his favorite video game paused on the screen and couldn't help himself. While the staff worked to put out the fire, he worked on breaking his own record.

"What are you doing in here? You can't be in here!" a social worker shrieked when she came in and found him. She called a guard who then escorted him back to the medical room along with his sister.

"Did you make it? Did you reach Christi?!" she asked once they were alone.

"Huh? Oh, um...," he stammered and stuttered just like his father.

"*Mortal Combat*," Shyne said, shaking her head.

****

"It's been a week now. What are we going to do with those two?" Miss Davis' supervisor wanted to know.

"I have no idea," the social worker sighed. It had been a whole week and neither child uttered a word in public.

Not only would they not speak, they would not separate either. The twins even showered together by turning back to back for privacy. Every day, they made an attempt to escape or steal a phone or laptop.

"Well, we may have to send them to the Wright's home. They can't just stay here."

"The Wrights! They are far too aggressive for these children!" Miss Davis shrieked at the thought.

Mr. and Mrs. Wright were an old foster couple that specialized in bad children. They could break a wild child like a cowboy broke a wild horse. Usually only disruptive teen boys were sent to them. Never children as young as Sun and Shyne.

"Find a relative or we have no choice!" the supervisor uttered with finality.

Miss Davis was set to go on vacation soon and she didn't want to have to deal with them herself.

****

"As Salaamu Alaykum, Mr. Forrest," Asad called out as he pulled into the driveway on his bike. He'd recognized his car and prayed that it meant that his friends were home.

"Wa Alaykum As Salaam," Killa sighed backed with the frustration of not having found his children as of yet, along with the sadness of having attended the loneliest funeral in the entire world.

Sincerity was sent off by the entire projects, as well as her cousins, aunts, and uncles. Once her funeral wrapped up, Killa had returned to the same funeral home to say his goodbyes to Yolo. She'd believed in there being only one God, but technically had no religion so he hadn't hired a preacher. Instead, he sat quietly and stared at her casket.

Once enough time had passed, she was taken to the same cemetery as Sincerity and buried right next to her. He felt it was only right since he loved them both equally. He had chosen one of them but now neither who ever know who. The world would never know, either.

"Have you seen Shyne and Sun?" Asad asked hopefully even though he could tell from the father's demeanor that he hadn't.

"Not yet, son. Don't worry, we'll find your fiancé," Killa said, trying to comfort him even though he himself was hurting inside as well. It hurt a little more upon seeing Asad drop his head in sorrow. He was too sad to ride his bike so he walked it back up the street and went home.

Christi perked up when the door open but her hopes were quickly dashed when Killa walked in alone. Her face was red and puffy from her constant crying. She was so distraught that she couldn't make it to the funeral. That meant getting dressed, which required standing up and that was more than she could bear to do.

"They'll turn up," he assured her confidently. He could feel them so he knew they were alive and well. For the time being, that is.

Chapter 42

"I want you to take Bruce Lee and the fire breathing girl to the Wrights' home in Parkchester," the lead social worker directed to an underling.

"But Miss Davis said..." she protested, but was cut short.

"Miss Davis is not in charge!" she shot back since the woman was on vacation. "Those bad ass kids have been here a month and haven't said a damn word!'

"Okay," the woman said, shrugged and called for security. No way was she dealing with those two on her own.

Sun and Shyne blinked in the bright sunshine as they left the building for the first time since entering it a month prior. They scanned the surroundings for danger, weapons, and escape routes. Sun looked left while Shyne's eyes went right. Finding nothing, they complied and got into the back of the car. Sun warned against moving in haste, which could make a bad situation worst.

"Where we going?" Shyne asked with her eyes. Sun shrugged 'I don't know' as they rode uptown. He discretely tried a door handle in hopes of making a break at the next red light but they were locked tight.

"Here we go," the social worker sighed in a tone that put the twins on high alert. The threat level went even higher when the stone-faced Wrights came outside to meet them.

He was a retired Marine who still rocked a close-cropped crew cut. It had greyed with age but he was still strong and stern. His wife was the same age and looked like she was either a bodybuilder or a man in her younger years.

Behind them, two teen thugs stepped out and snarled at the newcomers. They had both been kicked from home to home for their bad behavior until they'd arrived here. The Wrights' hands-on approach had broken them both. Now they wanted someone to break down themselves. Their eyes lit up when they locked on Sun.

Shyne's eyes lit up when she looked inside their garage. There, past the car, past the lawnmower, stood a shiny red gas can. They had both memorized the way they'd came and planned to leave first chance they got.

"Mr. and Mrs. Wright, this is....um...David and Dawn," the social worker said, finally giving the muted children names.

"They're kinda young for our program, aren't they?" Mr. Wright asked.

"And a girl?" Mrs. Wright asked of the anomaly. Still, she wanted to see if she could do some push-ups.

"It's only temporary. A week or so, tops," the social worker pleaded. She'd heard rumors of abuse about the couple but the system was so strained that they were overlooked.

"No problem. They'll have to share a room, though," the man of the house announced.

The worker gave the twins a sad sigh and got back into her car. Sun and Shyne scanned the area and tacitly agreed on an escape route.

"Well, come on inside. Get you some lunch," Mrs. Wright ordered.

The twins were hungry, so they complied and went in. The two teens blocked the door, forcing them to have to squeeze by. J.J thought it would be funny to see Sun fall so he stuck out his foot.

"Hey!" Sun protested and started to attack. The sixteen-year-old had at least fifty pounds on him but it wasn't enough. Sun would have hurt the boy if Shyne hadn't stopped him.

"Not yet," she said. stepping between them.

A fight now wouldn't help their cause. They needed a phone or internet service to get out of there.

****

"Is this...pork?" Shyne asked, turning her nose up at the pink meat between her slices of bread. Sun had already taken his out and bit into just the bread.

"As a matter of fact, it is! Do you have a problem with that? What, are y'all some Muslims? Harold, they done sent us some Muslims!" Mrs. Wright shouted.

"Muslims!" her husband demanded as he rushed in with J.J and Herb in tow. "Y'all two some Muslims?"

"No, we just don't eat pork," Sun replied.

"You do now!" Mrs. Wright huffed indignantly. "Uppity children wasting good food!"

"Eat it or I'll make J.J and Herb force feed it to you," Mr. Wright growled.

The two teens had been accused of both physical and sexual abuse at the other homes they'd been at. They snarled wickedly, ready to pounce.

Sun was ready to pounce as well, but once again, Shyne saved the day. She recalled the even Muslims were allowed to eat pork if it was all that was available or to save their lives. She took a bite of the pink meat and chewed it. Sun followed suit and saved the bloodshed for later.

****

A week of bullying and swine for breakfast, lunch and dinner later, and the twins still hadn't gotten access to a phone or the internet. Shyne had overheard a conversation and realized that the social worker wasn't coming back. Miss Davis had yet to return so she didn't know that they were gone. It was time to take matters into her own hands when the teens began to bully her brother.

"Sun! Sun! Get up!" Shyne demanded as she rushed back into the room they shared in the wee hours of the morning.

"You smell like...gas," was the first thing he noticed and said when he awoke. Then he felt the heat. "The house is on fire!"

"Duh!" Shyne mocked and pulled him out of the bed. She opened the window and led the way outside. It was the only way out since the rest of the house was now on fire.

"Are they still in there?" Sun asked as they walked briskly away from the burning house. He looked back and saw orange flames shooting out of every window.

"Yup," Shyne shot back quickly. She'd poured enough gas on and around their beds to make sure they were. Shyne had just killed four people at the age of nine. She was a late bloomer compared to both of her parents.

****

Sun and Shyne made it as far as the Cross Bronx Expressway before finally being caught. They refused to speak to police because anything they said could be used against them in a court of law. It got them taken right back to Child Protective Services.

The twins didn't even put up a fight. They just walked to their room in medical and closed the door behind them.

"Now what?" Sun asked, shaking his head.

"We have to find Daddy or Christi. Don't worry, we'll be okay," Shyne reassured her brother and gave him a hug.

"You smell like gas," he laughed and hugged her back.

They went to sleep and awoke to Miss Davis raising hell.

"You sent them where?" she screamed at her supervisor upon returning to work. She'd come back a day earlier when she'd seen the news about the Wrights' home being destroyed by fire.

"I had no choice! We couldn't just leave them in there!" she whined in defense of her bad decision.

"Well, I do!" she shot back and got on the phone. She had a friend who worked for Child Protective Services in Long Island so a few strings were pulled and she got them placed out there.

Sun and Shyne were almost home.

Chapter 43

Every day since the twins went missing was another day of agony for those who loved them most. Killa was unshaven and had lost weight from a lack of sleep and food. Christi had deep rings around her eyes from sleepless nights spent searching for her lost siblings. Poor Asad rode his bike to the house every day to check for his fiancé and best friend. To make matters worse, the news of a foster home fire that had claimed the lives of four people and left two more missing only served to add to their misery.

"Good morning, Christi, Mr. Forrest," Asad greeted hopefully as Christi let him in. He just hoped she would turn and call upstairs to let the kids know he was there, but there was no such luck.

"Good morning," Christi croaked, her voice was gruff since those were the first words she'd spoken since the day before. She noticed two twin gift wrapped items in Asad's hand and asked, "What's that?"

"They're for Shyne and Sun. It's their birthday," he replied and sat the presents on the coffee table. Muslims don't celebrate birthdays but his friends did, so he'd come bearing gifts.

"Oh my God! I forgot it's their birthday," Christi wailed and broke down once more.

Killa, of course, had remembered. He'd been present for all ten of their previous birthdays. Missing this one only fueled the rage burning inside of him. That meant that somebody, somewhere was about to get fucked up.

"How's school, Asad?" Killa asked to switch the direction of the conversation and lessen the gravity in the room.

"Great! I'm homeschooled now," he said with a smile of relief. Autism affects social interactions and the loud, rowdy kids made it impossible for Asad to focus. He knew as much karate as Sun and Shyne, but didn't have to use it.

"No one is picking on you, are they?" Killa asked, eager to go and retaliate on his behalf.

"No. They fight each other a lot, though. Fighting is bad."

"Well, sometimes you have to fight," Killa stated firmly, so it would stick. He knew Asad was a good person but the world was full of bad people. "Some people really need their asses kicked!"

"Amen to that!" Christi co-signed. She, too, had been forced to fight when she was in school. The group of mean girls who'd once taunted her hadn't amounted to a pile of shit. Christi, on the other hand. was in grad school while they were in traps, jails, delivery rooms and welfare lines. Funny how that worked out. They had been so concerned with turning up and now they'd turned up pregnant or infected.

"Okay," Asad nodded at the lesson. He let out a deep sigh and turned to leave.

"I'm out, too," Killa announced, and stood to leave as well.

"Where you going? Need me to come?" Christi asked, eager to help.

"I have to go down to Atlanta to see a preacher. I do believe a visit to Reverend Cash will be quite helpful," he replied over his shoulder as he left.

****

"Happy birthday, Sun," Shyne beamed and gave him her breakfast tray since it was the only thing she owned.

"Thanks," Sun said and accepted the extra food. Miss Davis made sure to throw them some extra food from time to time but there's no place like home.

"Aren't you forgetting something?" Shyne huffed, putting her hand where her hip would one day be and tapped her foot.

"Oh yeah! My bad. Happy birthday, Shyne," Sun said and gave her his breakfast tray.

Miss Davis popped in to check on the kids like she did every day. Every day, she brought a newspaper for Shyne and candy for Sun. Every day, she tried to get them to speak to no avail. Every day was just like every other day until it suddenly changed.

"Good morning!" Miss Davis cheered as she came into their room. Even Sun and Shyne perked up from her cheerful demeanor. "Great news! My friend on Long Island told me about a home that just came open! They have a pool, computers...,"

Sun and Shyne's mood toned down as she went on naming all the amenities that the couple had. All that sounded great, but there was no place like home. The twins listened until she finished knowing she meant well.

"Tie your shoe, David," she told Sun like she did every day. He shrugged his shoulders like he did every day, as if he didn't know how to tie his shoes. It worked just like every other day and she leaned in to tie it for him.

Shyne just shook her head at her brother as he peeked down the woman's shirt. The plump mounds of her breast meat always brought a smile to his face. He was indeed his father's son.

****

"Sup?" Killa asked when Christi took his call. Every day he called to check on his kids. He hoped for the best but so far, it hadn't come. Therefore, he also prepared himself for the worst.

"Hey. They're not home yet," Christi sighed. She frowned up at the background noise on the line. It sounded like someone speaking in tongues with a few curse words thrown in. "Who's that?"

"Reverend Cash," he replied as if that explained things. She'd just have to read about it like everyone else.

"Um...okay," she gave up. "I'll talk to you tomorrow. Love you, bye."

Meanwhile, Sun and Shyne had renewed hope as they rode back to Long Island. They recognized the names of all the towns as they passed by them on the expressway. It felt like they were going home until she passed their exit.

"Ah!" Sun grunted as the Wyandanch exit was sped past. Miss Davis swerved as she looked into the backseat. No more sounds came, so she continued to the town of Brentwood, New York. It was only three stops away on the Long Island Railroad.

Miss Davis followed the GPS while Sun and Shyne relied on their high IQs to remember the route. Sun checked the speed of the car and watched the clock while she memorized the turns and street names. Sun figured it was five miles from the train station when Miss Davis finally stopped.

"The Stevensons are a very nice couple," the social worker said hopefully.

She could only hope since she'd never met them or knew anything about them. She certainly didn't know the pedophiles had fled Kansas City before they could be arrested on all kinds of crimes against children. A new name in a new town granted them new kids to exploit. The couple was outside waiting when they pulled up.

"Look at what we have here!" a three hundred and fifty pound woman cheered and clapped her pudgy palms together as she rocked in glee and happiness. She loved kids like a fat kid loves cake. As a matter of fact, that's just what kids were to her; cake.

"Mm...hmm," the 5'2, two hundred and fifty pound Mr. Stevenson grunted when Shyne got out. He locked his beady little eyes on the little nubs on her chest before perusing her scrawny legs partially hidden under her shorts. When his eyes finally made it to her face, he saw her glaring back at him. She quickly crossed her arms over her chest to cover her little nubs that looked like a baby reindeer's first horns.

"Mr. and Mrs. Stevenson? This is David and Dawn, ages nine and ten," Miss Davis introduced. She had a bad feeling, but still hoped for the best. The spacious, well-kept home had to be better than being locked in a room on the medical floor of Child Protective Services.

"So tender at that age," Mr. Stevenson said as if Shyne were a cut of meat. A line of drool escaped his thin lips and got lost in the parade of stains on his shirt.

"Can we have them?" Mrs. Stevenson asked, barely able to conceal her lust.

"I guess..." Miss Davis answered warily after a moment of thought. In truth, the kids unnerved her at times. They never ever spoke, yet moved as one person. It was almost like they were communicating through mental telepathy. Sun and Shyne watched as she got back into her car and pulled off.

"Come on inside, guys. We'll show you to your rooms," Mrs. Stevenson urged.

"Once you guys get settled, you can take a dip in the pool," Mr. Stevenson said, eager to get the party started.

The twins looked at each other, took hands and followed them inside.

Mrs. Stevenson let out a grunt with every step as she climbed the stairs. Sun liked big butts and he could not lie, but the wide, flat butt in front of him made him turn his head. Shyne snickered at his dilemma under her breath.

"Whew!" she exclaimed when she conquered the flight of steps. She led them down the hall to two bedrooms opposite each other. "Pink is for girls and blue is for boys."

She wasn't talking about nothing as far as Shyne was concerned, so she followed Sun into his room. They sat on the bed until she intervened.

"Un uh, you have your own room," the woman stated and took Shyne by the hand. Shyne almost lost it when she felt the clammy hand on hers.

"Chill," Sun said with his eyes and she relaxed.

The woman led her across the hall and into her own room. She pasted a fake smile on her face and sat on the bed. Once the creaking stairs indicated she'd reached the bottom, Shyne got up and went back across the hall.

"What's the plan?" she asked as she took a seat next to Sun.

"Same as before, find Daddy so we can go home." he replied. "We better hurry, too, cuz that man is creepy. He's going to be a problem."

"No problem at all. Just get me some matches," Shyne giggled. She was definitely her mother's daughter.

Chapter 44

"You guys can go swimming before dinner!" Mr. Stevenson announced as if the kids had won some sort of sweepstakes. He extended swimsuits to the both of them. Shyne wanted to decline but saw her brother wanted to swim, so she gave in. The last couple of months had been hard and he needed some fun.

"Thank you, sir," they said as one and accepted the suits.

"Whoa! What's all this sir stuff! You guys can call me Father and the Mrs. Mother," he corrected.

"Motherfu-," Sun almost lost it but Shyne found it.

"Okay, Father," she smiled wickedly. Sometimes in life, you have to do things you don't want to do and this was one of them.

"Great! See you guys in a bit," he said happily and rushed away.

"Thanks," Sun said as Shyne left to go change. He knew she relented for his sake and appreciated it. She cracked a half smile as a 'you're welcome' and went to her room.

"A two piece!" She frowned upon seeing the swimsuit he'd given her to wear was a bikini. It was bad but got worse when she turned the bottom around. "Oh hell nah!"

"Hold up!" Sun protested as his sister barged in on him changing into his swim trunks. He quickly snatched them up since she still came on in anyway. "What?"

"This is what!" she snapped, showing him the little thong bikini.

Sun thought that was the funniest thing in the world. He doubled over with laughter while Shyne twisted her lips up at him. It took a few minutes for him to calm down. "You may as well wear it, you ain't got nothing!" Sun said and cracked up again. "Just swim in your shorts."

"Here they are!" Mr. Stevenson announced as Sun and Shyne stepped into the backyard. His face changed when he saw that Shyne hadn't. "Hey, where's your swimsuit?"

"That is not appropriate!" Shyne shot back indignantly.

Mrs. Stevenson gave her husband a look that said 'slow down.' They hadn't had any kids in a while and he was moving way too fast.

"You guys have fun. I'll start dinner," she sang and waddled back inside the house.

Sun ran to the pool and did a front flip into the water. Shyne did the same but added a twist to hers. The kids swam, laughed and squealed like the kids that they were. Their father had taught them how to swim, shoot and use a knife. They'd had fun while doing it but he knew that he was teaching them survival tactics. Dusk snuck up on them while they played.

"Dinner's ready, guys!" Mrs. Stevenson called from the door. She locked in on Sun as he climbed out of the pool. Her eyes lit up once he fully emerged from the water. Shyne snapped her head towards her brother to see what had the woman so happy.

"Sun! Your trunks!" she screamed, snatching her eyes away. The trunks were designed to become sheer when wet. They clung to his ten-year-old frame, showing off his ten-year-old package. The happy lady clapped happily. Sun covered his public privates and ran into the house with his sister's howling laughter ringing in his ears.

****

"That's not funny," Sun huffed when he met his sister in the hall to go to dinner.

"You right, it's hilarious!" she said and cracked up some more.

Ol' Sun could dish it out but couldn't take it when it was dished back. Shyne laughed all the way down the stairs but had her game face on when they reached the dining room.

"Dinner...is...served!" the fat lady sang as she sat the steaming bowls in front of the kids.

"What the he- What is this?" Sun wanted to know. He didn't recognize anything except the pieces of carrots.

"That's her famous beef tripe stew!" Mr. Stevenson said and pulled out a large piece of stomach meat and shoved it in his mouth.

Both kids retched but luckily for them, they had nothing in their stomachs to throw up.

"Eat up and you guys can get on the computer," Mrs. Stevenson said. They'd both noticed Mr. Stevenson sitting poolside on a laptop and had been plotting on how to get it. Now all that stood between them and the internet was a big, steamy bowl of cow's guts, or so they thought.

The twins looked at each other like they wanted to cry. They then shook their heads sadly and dug in. It would have been a lot easier if the tripe had been cut into pieces small enough to swallow but there was no such luck. Instead, they actually had to chew the tough meat enough to get it down their constricted throats.

"Good job!" Mrs. Stevenson cheered when the teary eyed children finished their food. "Would you guys like dessert?"

"Yes." "No," Sun and Shyne replied at the same time. His head nodded up and down while hers went left to right.

"Hog head cheese, coming up!" she squealed and served her husband and Sun.

Shyne fell out of her chair laughing. It took several minutes before he could get it down and it was finally computer time.

****

"Inbox Christi and Asad and tell them..." Sun said eagerly over Shyne's shoulder.

"Okay, okay. Oh no!" she whined and broke down. "There's no internet!"

"So we ate all that for nothing?" Sun said, feeling his stomach start to bubble. He took off like a rocket up the stairs and into the bathroom to throw it all up. Shyne just continued to stare at the screen for the next hour, plotting on Mrs. Stevenson laptop.

"Okay, guys, it's bath time!" Mr. Stevenson sang as he came in. He was so giddy, it put Shyne on high alert.

"Me first!" Sun shouted and rushed into the bathroom. Shyne knew he would be a while. He didn't use soap or the wash cloth as he played in the tub. Luckily for him, all the splashing rinsed the chlorine off of him. The water was ice cold when he finally got out.

Shyne made sure to lock the door when she entered the bathroom. She still felt like she was being watched as she came out of her clothes. She showered quickly and just as quickly got dressed again. Once she got into her room, she got into bed and took a nap.

Sun was sound asleep when Shyne crept back out of her room. She listened to the Stevensons having a snoring and farting contest for a minute and then made her move. She grabbed the laptop and tiptoed away.

"Come on! Come on!" Shyne urged as the computer slowly booted up and began beeping. "Shh!"

Shyne smiled when the laptop came on completely. Before she could click on the browser, two icons labeled David and Dawn caught her eye. Assuming it wasn't good, she clicked on her brother's first.

"Grrrr!" Shyne growled at the video of her brother swimming in the bathtub. She quickly deleted it and hers without looking at her own three minute shower.

She tried to click the browser again but was detoured by recent documents named David and Dawn. Clicking on them, she saw that they were ads listing two gently used ten-year-olds for sale. She was so repulsed that she closed the computer, tucked it under her arm and rushed across the hall.

"Sun, get up! Sun!" Shyne whispered harshly as she shook her brother awake. "Get dressed and let's go!"

Sun rolled out of bed and get dressed without question. He followed his sister down the stairs and out of the house. Shyne stopped and doubled back towards the garage.

"Where are you going?" Sun called after her.

"To find some gas! Nasty bastards was going to sell us!" she fumed.

"No time for that! Let's go home," he demanded. She kept marching so he grabbed her arm and pulled her away.

Shyne rattled turn left then turn right like a human GPS system as they hoofed it towards the train station. They didn't want a repeat of the last time they'd escaped, so they ducked and hid every time a car approached.

"It's locked," Sun announced when he tried the station's door.

"It doesn't open until 5:30. That's also when the next train leaves," Shyne said as she read from the terminal's schedule. A glance up at the clock showed it was now only two o'clock.

"Come on. We gotta stay outta sight until then," Sun reasoned. He led his sister away so they could find a place to hide out.

"Look! Phones!" Shyne cheered at the bank of pay phones on a wall. They both rushed over to the phones then paused, "How do they work?"

"Ion know. I thought you knew..."

****

"Shyne, wake up! Shyne, the train is coming!" Sun urged. He'd stayed awake and let her get some sleep. Droves of early morning commuters had filled the parking lots to begin their trek to work. They joined them on the crowded platform. The doors opened and they boarded.

"We need tickets," Shyne said into her brother's face when the conductor began collecting them.

"You need a toothbrush," he winced, referring to her tart morning breath before pulling her through the car. His plan was to move from car to car staying one step ahead of the conductor. It should work since it was standing room only and they only had a few stops to go.

"Uh oh, look!" Shyne said when she spotted another conductor working his way forward from the other end.

"In here," Sun said and pulled her into the bathroom. He then slid the lock to show that it was occupied. They had just pulled out of the Deer Park Station when the conductor reached them.

"Tickets!" the conductor called as he knocked on the locked bathroom door. It may have seemed like a good idea to the ten-year-olds but it was actually the oldest trick in the book.

"No speaky English!" Shyne called back and giggled at how clever she thought she was. She quickly shut up when the conductor began speaking fluent Spanish back to her.

"Open this door!" the conductor demanded after using his key to unlock it. The door opened inward and both twins held it closed with their feet. He put his grown man's weight against it from the other side.

"Get ready," Sun ordered when the train began to slow. Once it came to a stop, they stepped aside and the man fell inside. They scrambled over him and out of the train's doors.

Sun and Shyne marched up Straight Path Road towards home. They were both so anxious that neither said a word. Neither would relax until they made it into their house.

The twins passed by their school, but didn't even bother to turn their heads in its direction. The smell of the school's lunch wafted in the air, reminding them of how hungry they were and they put a little more pep in their step.

"Almost there," Sun announced when they turned on their street. Asad had just ridden out of their driveway after once again receiving his daily dose of bad news. Shyne saw her fiancé and took off running.

"Asad! Asad!" Shyne shouted and waved as she ran. Asad turned left and right upon hearing his name to see who was calling his name. Finally, he turned around and he saw her.

"Shyne!" he yelled and jumped off his bike. They ran full speed towards each other and knock each other down when they collided.

"Sorry," Asad offered and pulled her up. Shyne gave him their first kiss and hugged him tightly.

Sun finally caught up and made it a group hug.

They broke it off and ran to the house. Sun and Shyne had made it home.

Chapter 45

"Just told that child they're not back yet," Christi grumbled, assuming the knock on the door was Asad returning. It broke her heart to see how distraught he was every day when he got the same bad news. Then, later in the day, she had to again deliver bad news when their father called to check. She was at her wits' end and absolutely couldn't take another day of disappointment. Luckily, God doesn't place more on a person than they can handle. She let out a deep sigh and pulled the door open.

"Christi!" Sun and Shyne screamed as they ran in and tackled her.

"Oh my God! Thank you God!" Christi yelled as the twins brought her down. The siblings giggled as they hugged and kissed while Asad beamed happily. He picked up the laptop that had fallen once again. "Get up! We have to call your father!"

"Daddy! Daddy!" the twins chanted and bounced up and down while their sister dialed. Christi opened her mouth to speak, but Shyne snatched the phone out of her hand.

"Daddy?" the daddy's girl whimpered.

She braced herself to hear his baritone voice but it wasn't to be because Sun snatched the phone from her. The phone slid across the hardwood floor back towards Christi as the twins wrestled for it.

"Shyne?" Killa asked, hoping his ears hadn't played a cruel trick on him. That would have certainly put him in a bad mood, which meant somebody would certainly get fucked up.

"Hello!" Christi yelled into the phone causing Killa to wince. "They're home! They're here! Sun and Shyne are home!"

"I'm on my way!" Killa said and hung up. He turned back to Reverend Cash and said, "Goodbye."

Sun took it easy on his sister as they wrestled over the phone. He shouldn't have because Shyne kicked him right between his legs, causing Sun to go down in agony as she went for the phone.

"Hello?" she said out of breath. Winded or not, she still fixed her hair as if her father could see her. "Hello?"

"He's gone. He's in Atlanta, but he's on his way home now," Christi explained. The little girl's eyes welled with tears, breaking Christi's heart all over again.

"Cool laptop!" Asad announced, checking out the hardware. The little computer wiz began to rattle off its specs while Shyne came and took it away. She knew what it contained and didn't want to expose him to it. She was waiting to give it to her father.

"What's this?" Sun asked, seeing his and Shyne's birthday gifts still on the table where had left them.

"Oh, your presents," Asad cheered. He watched as he loaded the game disk into the system. Christi watched too, wondering what ordeals they may have encountered. She was glad they hadn't asked about their mother yet. She hoped Killa would be there when they did. Shyne went upstairs to change into her own clothes.

"Where'd you get this game from?" Sun demanded with a frown. The boy knew of every video game on the planet but had yet to see this one.

"I made it," he replied proudly. "Still gotta work the bugs out, though."

"Bugs in where?" Shyne asked when she returned. She may have been a black belt and excellent marksman but when it came to bugs, she was all girl.

"In the game I made," Asad replied then frowned at Shyne's shiny lips. "What's that?"

"Mango-strawberry-piña colada lip gloss. You like it?"

"Let me see..." Asad said moving closer. He took his palm and wiped her mouth clean. "Nope."

"You two are too cute!" Christi laughed. She thought it was adorable that they called themselves engaged instead of boyfriend and girlfriend. Yolo instilled in them both a high standard of character and morals. "Let me fix you guys some lunch."

"Okay!" the three of them agreed and got into the video game.

An hour later, Christi called them into the dining room.

"What is it?" Shyne asked, sniffing at her plate. Christi frowned in concern since she had fixed her favorite, salmon croquettes. A single tear escaped her eye but it was quickly followed by a flood. Soon after she was bawling out of control.

"It's okay, Shyne, you're home," Christi cooed softly as she wrapped her in her arms. "Don't worry, your father is on the way."

****

Killa made a sizeable donation to an Atlanta mega church on his way to the airport. It was a bit much but he was sure they would appreciate it. To his dismay, there were no direct flights to New York leaving anytime soon. He couldn't just sit idle in the airport for six hours so he bought a confusing array of connecting flights to Newark, New Jersey. In the end, he would arrive at the same time as if he waited for the direct flight.

He kept a car in Newark but didn't want to waste extra time going to retrieve it. Instead, he rented a car for the drive to Long Island.

"Easy, Killa..." Killa warned himself when he noticed how fast he was driving. He eased his foot from the gas pedal and slowed down.

The last thing he needed was to get pulled over by some cop. Usually that would lead to a gunfight but today he was totally unarmed. To ease his mind, he began to recite some of God's attributes to himself.

"Most Gracious, Most Merciful, Most Loving...," he said, feeling himself become at ease. It works every time because only in the remembrance of God do hearts find rest.

Killa pulled into the driveway and jumped out before putting the car in park. It rolled into the back of Christi's rental as he raced to the door. He stuck his key in the door but it was pulled open before he could turn it. Sun smiled up at his father then stepped aside so his sister could have him first.

"Daddy!" the girl squealed and jumped into his arms. She buried her face into him and broke down into sobs.

"I'm here, baby girl," the father assured his child. He held her and rocked until she got it all out. Once she regained her usual cool, he sat her down.

"Sup, yo," Sun said, offering his hand. He and his father exchanged pounds and man hugs the way men do. Christi was last to get a hug from her adopted stepdad. After an hour or so of small talk, she removed herself so the father could be with his children.

"Daddy...," Shyne began, then inserted a pause, indicating a serious question was to follow. "What happened to mommy?"

"Well..." Killa began with a pause of his own. He contemplated how much to tell them before he decided on whole story. Most of it, anyway, since they didn't need to know their mother killed his oldest son.

The story removed most of the air from the room along with all sounds as the children processed and reconciled what they'd just heard. The thought of their mother killing someone blew their little minds. If they only knew.

"So...we have brothers?" Sun finally asked of Rico and Xavier. Technically, Xavier was a step but where they do that? He was as much his as the ones he skeeted.

"I don't want no brothers!" Shyne huffed. Their mother killed her mother and she wanted nothing to do with them. Never mind that Yolo had killed their mother as well. The girl could be unreasonable at times. Killa wondered where she got that trait from.

"Well..." Killa said since that was all he could say. "I'll read you guys a bedtime story."

"We're ten years old, Pop!" Sun reeled, as if that was too old for bedtime stories. He wasn't too old for hugs, so he hugged his father's neck and kissed his cheek. "Night, Pops."

"Night, Sun," Killa chuckled in amusement. "What about you, you too old for bedtime stories too?"

"Actually, I have a story for you," Shyne said. She then turned on the laptop and told all that she knew about Mr. and Mrs. Stevenson.

Chapter 46

"Wow! Killa said to himself as he followed Shyne's turn-by-turn directions to the pedophiles' palace. The girl's details and descriptions were so vivid that they made him feel like he'd been there before.

Killa had no plans to harm the couple tonight. No, tonight he just wanted to see where they lived and scout out the area. That's why he hadn't brought his bag of tricks along. Besides a small 9mm, he was unarmed.

The only problem was that Killa grew angrier and angrier with each second that ticked away. His children had escaped harm but the laptop was filled with images of abuse of other children that made him sick to his stomach. They'd pulled him from the bed in the guestroom and into his car. Along with the porn, he'd also discovered a network of pedophiles. There were names and addresses of sick fucks of every race, religion and age group. Killa decided that he'd pay each and every one of them a visit. Sounds like a *Killa Season 3* to me.

"I'll just say hello," Killa convinced himself as he sat in front of the Stevensons'. To prove it, he left his pistol and got out the car. He made it up the walkway quickly in long, angry strides. He didn't even slow down when he reached the door. Instead, he just put his shoulder down and ran through it.

"Jared, someone's in here," Mrs. Stevenson whispered urgently to her sleeping husband.

"Just go back to sleep," the lazy man replied. Intruder or no intruder, he didn't feel like getting out of the bed. By then, even he'd heard someone rushing up the stairs.

He sat up just in time to see Killa enter their bedroom. The father was so mad that his face looked like one of those monsters in a Sci-fi movie. Killa threw a brutal right hook that broke the man's face into pieces. He then fell back onto his pillow, sound asleep.

"Help, hel-," Mrs. Stevenson shouted until Killa put her in a WWF wrestling hold.

She kicked her pudgy legs and clawed at his forearms when he cut off her air. The deep gouges drew blood as she fought to stay alive. She lost that fight when her brain went too long without oxygen.

"Your turn," Killa said to Mr. Stevenson as he dropped his wife to the floor.

He then pulled the man off the bed so that he'd have room to work. The jolt woke him up but that wouldn't last long. Killa took position over him and commenced to stomping him to death. Actually, he stomped him well past death because it got good to him.

When he snapped out of it, his pants were covered in blood and brains up to his knees. He noticed the scratches on his arms and knew his DNA was under the woman's fingernails. However, it didn't matter since Shyne had told him where a gas can was.

Killa quickly stripped out of his clothes and tossed them on top of the pile of dead pedophiles. He then entered the ensuite bathroom and rinsed the blood away from his body. Assuming that the couple wouldn't mind, he wrapped one of their bath sheets around his waist.

The can of gas was exactly where his daughter said it would be. Yolo was right, the child needed help. Now wasn't the time to think about it, though. He had a fire to start.

"It's gettin' hot in here..." Killa sang as he poured the gas on the couple. He had no say in who goes to hell or not, but the couple was going to burn tonight.

Most of the five gallons of gas went on the bodies, then he poured a thin trail down the hall and down the stairs. He ended the trail on the eye of the electric stove. A twist of the knob and he was on his way towards the door.

"Ten, nine, eight, seven, six..." he counted down as he sat in his car.

The eye lit the gas trail and fire followed it up the stairs. A bright orange flash in the window brought a smile to his face and was also his cue to leave, so he left.

Christi was sitting in the living room when he returned. She opened her mouth to speak then noticed that he wasn't wearing anything except a towel wrapped around his waist.

"Don't even ask," Killa said as he rushed by.

"I wasn't going to," she laughed to herself.

If living with Yolo had taught her anything, it was not to ask.

****

"Huh?" Christi asked when she saw Yolo's bedroom door ajar.

She hadn't so much as touched the doorknob since she came home. Even Killa slept in the guestroom to avoid the shrine. She cautiously approached and gasped when she saw Yolo sitting Indian-style on the bed. She then rubbed her eyes to make sure she'd seen what she thought she saw, but hadn't.

"I miss her," Shyne croaked. The entire front of her shirt was wet from her tears. "I miss my mommy."

"I miss her, too," Christi whimpered and walked inside. She sat on the bed and noticed the tiny book in Shyne's hands. "What's that?"

"A diary. My mom's diary," Shyne replied, flicking the open lock. She'd found it under her pillow right next to a fully loaded forty caliber pistol.

"Ha-have you read it?" Christi wondered.

"No. You think I should?" Shyne asked her older sister.

Christi looked upwards as if the answer was on the ceiling. "Yes," she replied after a moment of thought. "Just not yet. Not until you're older and can understand whatever might be in there."

It was a good answer, too, because the ten-year-old certainly wasn't ready for the contents of the book. It was full of secrets and dark stories that could only be called *Yolo 4: Diary of a Mad Woman*.

****

Killa changed clothes twice, checked his email three times and checked his hair one last time. He couldn't find anything else to stall with, so he finally gave up trying to. He let out a deep sigh and stepped from the guestroom. Christi was watching Asad and the twins playing video games when he arrived.

"Come on, guys," Killa said in a tone that excluded all, except the twins.

Christi picked up a book while Asad stood to leave. He and Shyne shared a quick hug before he left.

"Shotgun!" Sun called out when they reached the car. Little did he know, there really was a shotgun underneath the passenger's seat.

"So!" Shyne shrugged and got in the backseat. Her mother had always let her ride up front so she didn't mind letting him ride up next to their father.

"Where we going?" Shyne asked when Killa turned onto the expressway.

"To the city," he said as if that explained it. The last time they'd gone to the city, they'd lost their mother and it had taken months for them to get back home. Killa felt her and added, "I have some people I want you two to meet."

"Can I turn on the radio?" Sun asked as he turned the radio on.

"Sure, why not?" his sarcastic father quipped since he'd already turned it on.

"Ooh! That's my jam!" Shyne declared. The little girl raised her hands, closed her eyes and began winding her little bottom in the backseat. "Turn up! Turn up!"

"What the..." Killa shrieked and swerved when he saw her. "Hold the wheel."

"Wait, Daddy! I was just playing!" she swore, trying to scoot away from getting popped.

"I'm telling Asad," Sun vowed.

"So! Asad ain't my daddy! Daddy's my daddy!" Shyne spat, scrunched her face and moved her neck. "But don't tell him, okay? Okay?"

"That's better," Killa said as he flipped to the news station.

"President Donald Trump has just signed an executive order reinstating slavery. Last week he officially ordered women not to speak until spoken to..."

"Asshole," Shyne muttered from the backseat. Sun's eyes went wide knowing that if he'd heard her, their father had heard her as well.

Killa did hear her but she was right. Dude was an asshole so what else was there to say? The next story really caught his ear.

"The bodies of a Brentwood couple were found badly burned in a house fire. The couple was originally identified as a Mr. and Mrs. Stevenson, but were not. In fact, they were the Grubs and were wanted by the police in Kansas City for suspicion of several counts of child molestation."

Sun turned around and looked at Shyne. She looked at him and then they both turned their heads and looked at their father. Killa stared straight ahead and kept on driving. It was he who'd taught them that there was no such thing as coincidences in life. Everything that happened was written before it took place.

****

The playful mood turned somber the second they crossed the bridge into the Bronx. Two of the places they never wanted to go again in life were The Bronx Zoo and the projects. They both blew their breath loudly when Killa turned up the hill onto University towards the projects. Once again, Killa wrote his name on a piece of paper and stuck it in the window.

"Come on," he ordered when he got out and noticed that his children hadn't budged.

"Man," Shyne groaned and unbuckled her seatbelt to get out. Her daddy felt her pain and bit his tongue as he led them into the building.

Sun looked at his sister like 'you see this shit?' at the awe and respect that their father was shown. He came through like the Pope, nodding and waving. Killa once again led them into a pissy lobby and then into an even more pissy elevator. Once they got off, they walked halfway down a hall before stopping in front of an apartment's door.

Killa took the opportunity to warn and prepare his children for the grave danger ahead. "Here, put these in," he said, passing both Sun and Shyne each a mouth guard. "Now, bite down,"

"We about to fight?" Shyne asked. She wasn't scared, she just wanted to know.

"No, but brace yourselves," he advised as he unlocked the door with several keys.

As soon as they stepped inside, they were rushed.

"Oh my God! Look at these two!" Killa's grandma shouted and snatched her great grandkids into a deadly grandma's hug. All the air rushed from their little bodies while their little feet dangled in the air.

Killa smiled happily as Xavier and Rico emerged from a back room. They, however, weren't smiling, though. Both felt some kind of way about their grandmother hugging the next kids; especially since they were the kids whose mother had killed their mother.

"You guys look just like your father! Especially this one," she squealed, grabbing Sun's face. "X, Rico, come meet your...,"

Xavier and Rico turned their noses up and walked out of the apartment. Killa looked at his Grandma Diedra, who shrugged since she didn't know either. They both decided to let it go for now in hopes that it would all work itself out later.

Killa sat back and listened to his loved ones get acquainted. Of course, that led to Grandma wanting to cook for her babies.

"Can we go outside?" Shyne asked, so sweetly that neither knew she had something up her sleeve.

"Stay in the courtyard so I can see you from the window," Grandma Diedra replied.

"Okay," Sun and Shyne sang like twins do.

"Now you, Mister!" the grandmother said as she turned towards her grandson. He'd gladly accept the chewing out instead of one of her dangerous hugs. Luckily for him, a commotion from outside interrupted her. "Damn kids out there fighting again! All they do is fuss and fight."

Killa knew it was the truth since he'd grown up there. He'd also done a lot of fighting himself in that very same courtyard. Everyone loves a good fight so he stuck his head out the window to get a peek. He got a peek at his twins fighting his older sons.

"Damn it!" he growled and rushed from the apartment. The battle was in full swing by the time he reached the courtyard. Killa took a seat and watched like everyone else.

Xavier was fourteen and Rico was twelve to Sun and Shyne's ten. All had been trained by the legendary Karate Joe, so it was a good fight.

"Yo! They getting it in!" Little Villain said, passing his blunt to Killa.

"I got a yard on the little ones," Killa offered, but Grandma Diedra had made it down with her belt.

"Break it up! Get upstairs!" she fussed, popping and chasing her great grands around.

This was the start of a real sibling rivalry.

Chapter 47

"Where we going now?" Shyne fussed when their dad turned left instead of right towards Long Island.

"To say goodbye to your mother," Killa replied, killing all protest. The mood in the vehicle had become morbidly stoic as they rode to the North Bronx Cemetery.

Killa's feet felt like they were encased in cement as he walked through the tombstones. He'd personally filled enough of the graves to have his own wing in the cemetery. His heartbeat thundered in his ears as they reached the graves of the two women he loved.

"Go on," he said, pointing towards their mother's headstone.

Sun instinctively reached for his sister's hand as they inched forward.

"Hey, Mommy," Shyne offered with a weak smile. No tears came because her mother had prepared her for this day. Her smile widened as her mother's voice rang in her mind.

"Shyne, be a lady. Shyne, don't be a hoe. Shyne, take care of your brother. Shyne, know your worth. Shyne, Shyne, Shyne..."

Sun smiled too as his mother's admonishments reverberated in his thick skill as well.

"Sun, don't be no bitch! Sun, don't be no snitch! Sun, fuck friends! Sun, bitches ain't shit, so find you a lady. Sun, take care of your sister. Sun..."

Killa realized at that moment that he wasn't alone. Losing the two women that he loved at one time had been a major blow but he still had his children. He let out a sigh in hopes that they would one day all get along. Before parting, he pulled out his phone and took a picture of the twins as they stood at their mother's grave. That way, if anyone ever decided to write a book about them they could use it as the cover.

****

Two sets of children meant that Killa had to continue to maintain two separate households. Rico and Xavier lived in the Bronx with Grandma Diedra while Christi held the twins down in Long Island.

Killa is as Killa does, so he popped in regularly between making the world safer one murder at a time. He did his best to remove child molesters, crooked cops and other assorted scumbags from the planet.

Fifth and sixth grades flew by with minor issues. There was always someone who didn't believe that shit stunk until Sun or Shyne beat the shit out of them and made them smell it. Everything was pretty much the same until everything began to change.

****

"Good morning, Christi, Shyne," twelve-year-old Sun greeted as he came into the kitchen with his sisters.

"Morning, Sun," Christi replied while Shyne just rolled her eyes and sucked her teeth.

"I said, good morning, Shyne," Sun repeated and paid for it instantly.

"Why you all in my face? You stay in someone's business! You know if you spent half of the day staying out of my business and the other half of it minding your own business, you'd have a whole day to yourself! I just can't with you," Shyne fussed and stormed off.

"What...in the world just happened?" the confused boy asked.

"Your sister is now a woman," Christi replied.

It took Sun a full day to figure out what that meant. Shyne had reached puberty and he wasn't far behind.

****

"Coffee!" Sun demanded in his on again, off again deep voice. He would one day sound just like his father but for now, he sounded like a DJ cutting and scratching using a man and a boy's voice. Christi and Shyne paused their conversation to see what in the hell he was talking about.

"Um...anyway, so," Shyne said, and continued what they'd been talking about.

"Coffee, I said!" Sun repeated, giving the table a slap so they'd know that he was serious.

"Who are you?" Christi asked, squinting her eyes at him to bring him into focus. What she couldn't see was the lone pubic hair that made him a man. He had been waiting on that guy and would take it public if he had to.

"Sun Forrest, man of the house," he insisted. He would have said more but his sisters were laughing too hard to hear him. In the end, he settled for a juice box and went on his way.

****

"Daddy!" a fourteen-year-old Shyne squealed as her beloved father walked into the house. She was becoming more of a woman by the day, but was still a daddy's little girl whenever Killa came around.

"Hey, sweetheart," Killa said as he hugged his only daughter. "You guys ready?"

"Sup, Pops," Sun greeted as he came down the stairs. He wanted to yell 'Daddy' and jump in his arms too but he was way too cool for that.

"Yes, we ready," Shyne answered for the both of them. "I'll text Asad and tell him to come outside."

"Where y'all going?" Christi asked after getting her hug.

"To the range again," Killa replied. "Then the gym and then for some boxing."

"Why so much?" Christi wondered. All summer long, Killa had the twins and Asad in extra training.

"They're about to start high school. That's a whole different ball game," the father said with a timbre of concern evident in his voice.

"Yeah, and that school is rough! I don't know if Sun and Shyne are ready for that!"

"The real question is," Shyne interjected, "is that school ready for Sun and Shyne?"

The End